The Mystery of Miss Mason

The Lost Lords
Book Five

Chasity Bowlin

DRAGONBLADE PUBLISHING, INC.

Books from Dragonblade Publishing

Dangerous Lords Series by Maggi Andersen
The Baron's Betrothal
Seducing the Earl
The Viscount's Widowed Lady

Also from Maggi Andersen
The Marquess Meets His Match

Knights of Honor Series by Alexa Aston
Word of Honor
Marked by Honor
Code of Honor
Journey to Honor
Heart of Honor
Bold in Honor
Love and Honor
Gift of Honor
Path to Honor

Legends of Love Series by Avril Borthiry
The Wishing Well
Isolated Hearts
Sentinel

The Lost Lords Series by Chasity Bowlin
The Lost Lord of Castle Black
The Vanishing of Lord Vale
The Missing Marquess of Althorn
The Resurrection of Lady Ramsleigh
The Mystery of Miss Mason

By Elizabeth Ellen Carter
Captive of the Corsairs, *Heart of the Corsairs Series*
Revenge of the Corsairs, *Heart of the Corsairs Series*
Shadow of the Corsairs, *Heart of the Corsairs Series*
Dark Heart

Table of Contents

Abducted, held captive by unknown men for unknown reasons, Mary Mason had to use all of her resourcefulness to escape what would surely have been a terrible fate. But in the course of her escape, she encounters new dangers in the form of a mysterious man. Is he friend or foe? Can he be trusted or will she prove to be just a pawn in whatever game he is playing?

Alexander Carnahan, Lord Wolverton, is a pariah in society, a known murderer. But as he carries the unconscious Mary Mason back to his crumbling estate to care for her, he recognizes that she is far more than just the key to the mystery he's devoted himself to, the mystery of who murdered his late wife. She stirs something inside him he thought long dead... hope.

As Mary recovers from her ordeal in his home, the truth slowly emerges. Their pasts are intermingled, the intrigues and mysteries of their lives are connected and hide unspeakable horrors committed by common enemies. As they work together to reunite Mary with her brother and to prove Alex's innocence, their feelings for one another only grow more complex and more undeniable. But the course of true love never does run smooth, and there are more obstacles and dangers ahead of them than behind...

Prologue

Near Bath, 1820

FATIGUE WAS SETTING in for Lord Alexander Winston Carnahan, the Earl of Wolverton. He'd spent the better part of the night, as he had so many others, concealed in the shadows near the road—watching, waiting, hoping against hope that it would finally be the night when he discovered something useful. But it appeared his hopes had been futile. Dawn was approaching. Though still quite dark, the sky had begun to lighten, hinting at the morning to come.

If Harrelson had been out and about that night, committing whatever crimes and misdeeds it was that provided the man's astronomical income, he was certainly coming home much later than usual. Alex had made it a point to become an expert on the comings and goings of the man who'd ruined him. Given that most of Alex's own property now had been seized by the courts at the insistence of his late wife's family and subsequently "gifted" to Harrelson, it left Alex with little enough else to do.

There had been much more activity of late with disreputable-looking men, little more than hired ruffians really, traveling to Harrelson's estate in the dark of night. While he couldn't be entirely certain, Alex felt, or perhaps foolishly hoped, that one of the man's underhanded operations was on the verge of collapse. It would only take one chink in his armor to bring him down, of that he was certain.

A noise caught his attention, pulling him from his mildly self-pitying reverie and putting him instantly on alert. Sinking further into the shadows, Alex put one hand on the butt of the pistol he wore strapped to his thigh, and waited for whatever danger might be lurking nearby to make itself known. He was well prepared to face whatever or whoever it might be. Oddly enough, whoever it was, they were not overly concerned with being quiet. They thrashed through the brush, twigs snapping under their feet as they barreled through the woods.

Nothing could have shocked him more than the small, pale form of a girl emerging from the trees. *Woman*, he corrected his assessment. Her small stature had fooled him at first. But with a moment to observe her, he quickly realized his error. Dressed as she was, in only a torn and dirty shift, there was no mistaking her figure for anything other than that of a woman fully grown. Her breasts were full beneath the thin fabric and he could see the flare of her hips skimmed by the simple garment.

She continued toward the road, her movements frantic. There was something quite desperate about her, almost mad, he realized. As she neared the single road that bisected the heavy woods, she paused at the very last moment, hesitating as if sensing danger. In the distance, he could hear the sound of rumbling wheels. Harrelson's carriage approached. He thought to warn her, for whatever she feared and whatever she ran from, she would receive no aid from that source. But he need not have worried. Some instinct she possessed held her back. She ducked behind the thick cover of brush and stayed quiet. But he could see the wide-eyed fear, the sheer panic that raced through her.

Beyond the shadows of the trees, he heard the carriage braking, the horses' hoofbeats slowing on the hard-packed earth as the wheels creaked to a stop. "Why have we stopped?"

Alex recognized Harrelson's voice immediately, as well as the sharp tone he used on anyone he thought beneath him.

"I thought I saw somethin', my lord... runnin' alongside the road and into the trees!" The driver's response was surprising. Surely the man would know better than to think his employer would offer aid to anyone!

"It was a deer, most likely. Drive on!" Harrelson snapped.

"What if she's gotten out?"

Alex's eyes narrowed at that telling statement. Not just a simple servant, but an accomplice, he thought. The driver was involved, an active and knowing participant, in Harrelson's crimes. And so was the woman making her brave escape, albeit unwillingly.

Harrelson's dismissive snort of laughter echoed toward him. "No one ever has, Jones. Drive on."

The driver cracked a whip over the horses and they kicked up once more, the carriage lurching reluctantly into motion. All of his attention was focused on the woman. She'd held her breath the entire time, as if even an exhale might have been enough to give away her position. He saw her body sag as the air hissed out of her in a rush.

Emerging from the trees, just enough to let her see him, he asked the one question that had been burning in his mind since he'd watched her duck and hide from them. "How did you know?"

She peered toward him and he realized that given his shadowy position beneath the trees, he could see far more of her than she could see of him. He didn't want to frighten her, but his face was not unknown to the world. His infamy might prove to be his downfall if she recognized him. Keeping back into the shadows, he watched her carefully. He saw her shoulders stiffen and her chin come up defiantly.

"I won't go back. You may as well kill me now."

Her vow was uttered quietly with desperate bravado, but beneath that was a steely resolve that impressed him. Regardless of his grudging respect of her, he had to insist. She was the break he'd been looking for, after all. This woman, the daring escapee, was the link that would lead him to whatever despicable dealings Harrelson was involved with. He needed her to help him find the truth once and for all.

"You will go back," he said softly, but with complete conviction. He needed to know what they were doing, what part she had been expected to play in it, and how on earth Helena might have been involved.

He stepped closer, close enough that he could see the shadows of exhaustion beneath her eyes in the remnants of silvery moonlight giving way to dawn. "What is your name?"

"Mary Benedict."

It was a lie, of course. He couldn't keep a grin from spreading across his lips as he recognized it for a blatant untruth and admired her for it. Tiny as she was, there was something very fierce about her. That fierceness should have given him some clue as to her intentions. Alex reached for her but before his hand even closed on her wrist, she'd brought her knee up hard. He dodged the blow at the last second, managing to avoid a direct hit. The more vulnerable parts of his anatomy were still grazed enough by it to leave him gasping. He watched, stunned, as she fled once more into the woods.

Shaking his head to clear it, he resisted the urge to reassure himself that all parts of him were still there and functional. Alex wondered how such a slip of a girl had managed to very nearly unman him.

After a moment, when the fear of casting up his accounts from that particular agony had passed, he rose to his feet. Drawing several deep breaths to fortify himself, he loped after her in pursuit. Despite her exhaustion and her bare feet, she managed to go a greater distance than he would have given her credit for. She looked back at him over her shoulder, and then veered off the path into the denser trees.

He knew the woods like the back of his hand, and the area she'd stepped into was treacherous. The trees there had grown tangled over time, their heavy roots protruding from the ground like the twisted fingers of an aged crone, almost as if they meant to rise up against man. Alex opened his mouth to call out a warning, but it was too late. He saw her stumble over the gnarled roots of an alder tree and fall. She did not rise, but continued to lie there, her pale form completely still in the shadows as the forest grew eerily silent about them.

Rushing forward, he stared down her in horror. He could see a dark stain spreading over the dirty neckline of her shift, the thick and viscous liquid trickling over her pale flesh. Alex turned her gently, examining the wound just above her temple. There was blood, and quite a bit of it. But he knew that head wounds bled very easily. What worried him far more was how warm she felt. It wasn't the natural heat of exertion from her run. The girl was burning with fever. Cursing softly, he lifted her, carrying her in his arms to the edge of the woods where he'd left his horse tethered. He would return with her to Wolfhaven Hall and see her well, then he would find out precisely what she knew. He would have answers by fair means or foul. Too much was at stake for him to show more mercy than his circumstances would permit.

Chapter One

"**W**HO ARE YOU?"

Seated at the bedside of the woman he'd rescued, if one could call it that since she'd only been injured in fleeing from him, Alex had been staring at the faded carpet beneath his feet and contemplating just how far he'd fallen. At that soft whisper, he looked up. Her voice was hoarse, pained, and her speech somewhat slurred. Given that she'd been unconscious for nearly twenty-four hours, it was to be expected. He'd been correct in assuming her injury wasn't so severe, but the fever that raged within her was more than adequate cause for concern.

Dirty, her feet torn and bleeding, and with faint bruises at her wrist where she had been bound, it was apparent that whoever had held her captive had not been inclined to see to her comfort or her health. When he'd picked her up from the forest floor, her skin had been hot to the touch, feverish, in spite of the dampness of her inadequate clothing. It was likely that chill, coupled with whatever horrors she'd been through, that had resulted in her illness. The deep cough that occasionally wracked her frail form was worrisome, indeed, especially as it was increasing in both frequency and intensity.

He surveyed her carefully. In the dim glow of the firelight which provided the only illumination in the room, her blonde hair gleamed like burnished gold. Mrs. Epson, his housekeeper, had assisted him in bathing her though she'd done it under great protest. In the hours since, he'd remained at her bedside. Whether it was guilt, curiosity, or the strangely protective urges she stirred within him, he could not say.

But in that time, he'd had many hours to study the loveliness of her face, to memorize the gentle curve of her jaw, the stubborn jut of a chin that revealed far more of her personality and character than she likely wished, the slight upward tilt of her nose, and the perfect bow of her full lips. But it was the first time since their encounter in the woods when it had been far too dark to see much of anything that he'd had a chance to see her eyes. Framed by thick lashes, shades darker than her golden hair, their color was still a mystery to him. They were deep, either brown or a midnight blue, so dark that their true shade would likely only be discernible in the brightest light of day. They were also haunted and frightened, and he accepted no small amount of responsibility for that.

"Ambrose." The lie rolled easily off his tongue. It was simply the first name that had popped into his mind. It was the title of his trusted friend and while it lacked respectability, it wouldn't strike fear in her heart as his own name would. If he admitted to the terrified girl that he was Wolverton, she'd likely fall into a dead faint again or worse. She was in no condition to run from him and if she heard that name, she would. Exhausted, battered and bruised, no doubt terrified, the last thing she needed was confirmation that she was at the mercy of a known murderer. Of course, it wasn't entirely altruistic. He needed her trust. He needed her cooperation. It might make him a selfish bastard but, on a routine basis, he was accounted to be something far worse. *Murderer. Wife killer. Fiend.* He had been called all of those and so much more.

While his own ends certainly should take precedence, had to take precedence if he had any hope of salvaging his honor and his estates, he wasn't without sympathy for her. She looked lost for lack of a better word. Unable to stop himself, he reached out and gently touched her cheek, testing the softness of her skin even as he measured whether or not her fever had waned. Touching her was like touching the finest of silk. Gently bathing her brow with a damp cloth, he offered. "You struck your head. But I fear you've developed a lung ailment from the damp."

"In the woods," she paused, thinking back and then frowned, her eyes narrowing and a small line appearing between her brows as she tried to remember. "It was you."

"I didn't mean to frighten you," he said, and it was one of the few things in his life that he felt true remorse for. His single-mindedness had caused her injury. He'd thought only of his vow, of his obligation to the title and to all those who had passed before him, and not given a thought to the injured and terrified woman in front of him. It was no wonder she'd run. "It's my fault you were harmed."

Her frown deepened, her lips parted as if she meant to speak, and then she attempted to shake her head as if negating his statement, but she was too weak. A coughing spasm overcame her, so fierce that it lifted her upper body from the bed and left her gasping. When it passed, she collapsed back onto the bed so still and quiet he feared she had passed.

Terrified, he rose to his feet, pulled back the covers and watched the painfully shallow rise and fall of her chest. Relief washed through him, but he knew in that moment that it would take far more than simply rest in a warm room to see her well again. She needed medicine and the only man nearby who could provide it would never step foot in his home for any reason. "I have wronged you, Mary Benedict," he said in a gruff whisper. "Perhaps not so much as others have in your short life, but I mean to atone for it. I will find out who you were running from, who you were afraid of... and you will never have to fear them again." It was the least he could do.

The door opened behind him and his old, stooped housekeeper entered. She was the only one of the servants who remained aside from a groundskeeper and a stable master, one of the few who had not fled either because of his disgrace or his altered fortunes. Her age would have prevented her from getting work elsewhere. It wasn't loyalty that kept her at the Wolfhaven. It was fear of destitution. Her bitterness toward him over the death of Helena, the mistress she'd adored, was boundless. He tolerated her abuse daily because he frankly had no other choice, and perhaps because, in some perverse way, it reminded him of what everyone else thought of him. If he ever doubted that he needed to clear his name, even the briefest conversations with Mrs. Epson would remind him of why it was so urgent.

"It ain't right for you to be in here. The girl will be ruined—if she's not already. What kind of lady is out running about the woods anyway? Not a lady at all, to my mind! Likely some trollop with a pretty enough face to pass for genteel. Bringing her into my sweet mistress' house, putting her in nightclothes too fine for the likes of her!" The old crone finished her diatribe with a loud "harrumph."

"Mrs. Epson, I pay you to clean the four rooms of this house that are actually in use and to prepare food. I rarely quibble about the less than adequate job you do of both, or your impossible rudeness to me, but I will not tolerate that sort of mistreatment of Miss Benedict. To that end, I'll thank you to keep your opinions to yourself," he reminded her sharply.

The old woman squawked in indignation, set the tray of food she carried down with enough force that the lid of the soup tureen went careening off to the side. Had it not landed on the ancient and dust-ridden carpet, it would likely have shattered. She turned on her heel to shuffle back to the kitchens.

With her bent back and hooked nose, she looked like the witches from the stories his governess had told him as a child to frighten him away from the woods. Witches, he thought, as a memory stirred for him.

"Wait!" he called out. "Your sister is a healer, isn't she? And she lives nearby, does she not?"

The woman spat on the floor, an old gesture he'd seen farmers do over the years to ward away evil. "Aye, she does to my shame."

"She's skilled with herbs… the villagers and tenants go to her for remedies rather than the doctor." He vaguely remembered whispers of other, slightly darker tasks attributed to her, but as he was damned anyway, he had little care for such things. By most accounts, he was worse than any devil the crone might be in league with.

"She's dabbling with things good folks ought not!" The housekeeper turned once more toward the door. As she neared it, Miss Benedict coughed again, the fit so fierce it left her gasping. Mrs. Epson paused. "I don't suppose it matters much given how you found her. She's bound for hell anyway and so are you. She lives west of the ruined church at Burrow Mump. You ask any folks near there and they can tell you how to find her. But you'll not go at night. The girl will survive till morning or she's too far gone for help anyway! You can go after whatever wicked brew my sister concocts after the dawn breaks."

With that, the housekeeper stormed out, as much as a woman her age could storm anywhere. Still, the door slammed behind her with remarkable force.

On the bed, Miss Benedict stirred again, but did not waken. Leaving her for a moment, he crossed the room and ladled a bowl of the thick and unappetizing stew that had been prepared. It might have been mutton, or rabbit, or squirrel. With Mrs. Epson's culinary abilities, it hardly mattered. It would all be greasy and, if he were lucky, tasteless. Settling in before the fire, he contented himself to be near enough to offer aid should she need it.

There was something about her. She appeared so fragile and yet he knew her to be quite fierce. She had all but unmanned him in the woods, after all, with her precise and rather diabolical aim. Had it not been for his relatively quick reaction upon realizing her intent, the outcome might have been very different. She might have actually gotten away. But to what end? She would have still been burning with fever. Had she spent the night in the woods, damp and cold, she likely would have died. The very thought of it sickened him and so he put it from his mind. Instead, he focused on what he knew of her, aside from the fact that she'd lied about her name. She was an appealing package of contradictions—resourceful, strong, and determined, all while appearing so fragile with her stature and slender frame. Even in her current condition, Alex had to admit that he was drawn to her, attracted to her as he had not been to any woman for a very long time. Naught would come of it, of course. What woman in her right mind would want anything to do with him, after all?

He sat there for the longest time, not eating, simply holding the bowl in his hands and enjoying the warmth of it far more than he would ever enjoy whatever dubious nourishment it might provide. The weight of his burdens was pressing in on him. Debts, financial and moral, had to be paid. But until he managed to right the wrong that he'd inadvertently been a party to, to repair the damage he'd wrought in the lives of others, there was no hope of putting his own to rights. His gaze was drawn once more to the pale, wan figure of Mary Benedict lying in his bed, too ill to move. He didn't deserve to have his own life restored to its former glory, he thought bitterly. Why should he have a moment's peace when he'd condemned others to suffer so?

Miss Benedict stirred in her sleep, her dreams offering her no peace. Was it her captors who haunted her nightmares, or some strange man who had pursued her through the woods? He was still wreaking havoc on all those around him, whatever his good intentions might be. When she awoke, he'd find out where to send her to, to get her far away from him and whatever curse was on his head. She was a distraction and a temptation that he could ill afford.

Chapter Two

ALEX HAD NOT slept. He'd kept his vigil beside the girl's bed until the first rays of dawn had filtered into the room through the curtains. He'd gone outside, saddled his own horse and made the short ride to Burrow Mump. The house was easy enough to find. He'd passed two small children on the road, asked them where the healer lived and they'd given him the direction. Even as they'd done so, they'd made the sign to ward off the evil eye. One child even crossed himself but, as the boy most assuredly was not a Catholic, Alex had wisely kept to himself that genuflecting was likely not going to help him.

The small cottage was simple with a thatched roof, green shutters and various animals grazing in the yard as he approached. There were numerous plants, some flowering even in the cold, that surrounded the cottage. In all, it was bright and cheery and looked nothing like the sort of hovel one might expect to see a witch living in. But then he doubted very much that the woman was anything of the kind. He knew only too well how much rumor and gossip could color the perception of a person.

The door opened and an aged woman stepped out into the light. "My sister is too wretched to die, so I know that isn't why you've come."

As he had not identified himself to her, Alex was somewhat taken aback by her accurate ascertainment of his identity. "You know who I am?"

It might have been a smile that cracked the older woman's face or it could have been a grimace. Given the cragginess of her features and the deep wrinkles that bracketed her thin lips, one was indiscernible from the other. "Aye, I know who you are, m'lord." There was a certain amount of derision in the address. "They say you killed your wife. But you don't look much like a killer to me. If you were, then you'd have dispatched my vile wretch of a sister long before now!"

"If you mean Mrs. Epson, then I assure you she is quite well and as mean spirited as ever," Alex insisted.

"No one comes here without needing something, your lordship. What do you need of me?" she demanded, her tone as abrupt as her sister's.

"There is a woman, Miss Benedict, who is ill. She has a terrible fever and a fierce cough. I fear she will die," he admitted.

She eyed him steadily, her gaze piercing. It was as if she'd peeled back his skin and looked into the very heart of him. "And you think it will be your fault if she does?"

It would be his fault. That was an undeniable fact. "Yes," he admitted simply, not offering further explanation of how.

She eyed him for a few moments, staring at him as if she'd split him open and was looking deep inside of him. It was unnerving to say the least. Had he not been so desperate to get help for Mary, he would have simply left.

Finally, after a long tense moment, she commanded, "Tether your horse yon and come inside. I will give you what you need for her."

Alex did as he was bid. She had a manner about her that was similar to Mrs. Epson's, in that she was coarse and seemed to have just as little regard for his title. Though she clearly knew it, he reflected. But that was where the similarity ended. The bitterness that his housekeeper seemed to nurture like seeds in a garden was not present in her sister. Regardless, there was something rather terrifying about the woman. Otherworldly, even. But if she could provide the assistance he needed to save Miss Benedict, he would gladly forgo any rules of etiquette and ignore his own discomfort to curry favor with her.

Entering the cottage, he was greeted with rafters draped in dried herbs and shelves of jars full of things he could not identify. Some, he did not wish to identify. "You are a healer?" It had become more a question than a statement of fact.

"I am many things, a healer amongst them," she said, and pointed to a rather rickety chair of interwoven reeds. It was pushed up next to a rough-hewn table made of wide, scarred planks and littered with bowls and bottles and what he assumed were the tools of her peculiar trade. "I'll get the herbs you need to treat the cough and others to build up her blood. Don't let those idiot doctors bleed her unless you want her to die!" The last was uttered as a warning as she turned to one of the small shelves that lined the room and gathered an assortment of ingredients.

"There is only one doctor near us and he'd as soon step foot in hell itself as darken my door," Alex admitted. "And I've little enough faith in his abilities even if the situation were altered."

The woman nodded. "Just as well. They don't know anything when they think they know everything. They call themselves learned men. Fools, the lot of them."

Alex watched her as she used a pair of leather gloves to pinch leaves from a dried plant and place them in a mortar. With a pestle, she crushed them in a manner that was both practiced and efficient. It also belied her appearance. Stooped and weathered, he'd thought her old, but she did not move with the slow and stiff gait of an elderly person. When the chore was done, she then placed them in a small, leather pouch and retrieved a small vial of a dark liquid.

"Jimson weed," she said, holding up the pouch. "Some call it devil's trumpet, and if you misuse it, I imagine it's close enough to hell to warrant the name. It must not be ingested under any circumstances. To do so would induce terrible visions or even kill her outright. It must be burned and the smoke drawn into the lungs. Place it in a bowl and burn it near enough to her that she will be forced to inhale the fumes. The other is for the fever. Just a few drops in her tea or broth and it should help."

Carefully taking the herb and the elixir from her, he tucked them into the pocket of his coat while nodding his understanding. As Alex made to withdraw a few coins from a small purse, she placed a staying hand over his.

The old woman shook her head. "You'll not pay me with something as dirty as money. Not when you've kept my sister on in that house of yours rather than shuffling her off to me. The herbs are a gift... but I would have one thing from you, Lord Wolverton."

"And what is that?" he asked.

She held out her hand to him. "I would see your palm and know the nature of your character. I would know whether the tales of your wickedness are built on truth or lies."

It was superstitious nonsense but, given that she'd readily offered her aid, he didn't feel he could refuse. Removing his glove, he held out his hand to her, palm up. The old woman took it, her grip surprisingly firm as she traced each of the lines she found there. She contemplated the lines in silence for an uncomfortably long time, until the very air in the room crackled with tension. He moved to pull away, but she held him firmly, her strength surprising. More than surprising. Unnatural.

"You carry a heavy burden of guilt for an innocent man," she said. Her voice sounded distant, faraway, as if she were speaking from a great distance rather than sitting across the small scarred table from him. "The vengeance you seek, for your wife and now for this young woman who resides in your home—in your bed—they are the same. It was the same man who harmed them both. But you know that already, you simply do not yet know why... what the purposes of his schemes were. And your wife... she was no innocent. She's not with the dead, either. But she's somewhere in the in-between place." The old woman paused again, frowning at the strangeness of her own ramblings, it seemed. "The end is closer than you think. But beware you do not trade your future to avenge your past!"

A cold chill shivered through him. It wasn't even her words. He could feel power emanating from her, as if she were digging into the darkest recesses of his soul simply by looking at his palm. Abruptly, and with more force than necessary, he pulled it back, breaking free of her iron grip and rising to his feet. "I am well aware of Helena's faults, madam. I see no need to speak ill of her."

"I speak the truth, my lord, whether it is ill or not. As for your Miss Benedict... she lies. But her heart is pure. Remember that."

Alex had no response to that. He just nodded. "Thank you for your assistance, madam. I must be on my way. There is no time to lose for Miss Benedict's sake."

The old woman smiled toothlessly. "No. There is no time to lose. She came to you just when she should. Go, Lord Wolverton, and know that you will soon be free of your burdens."

Alex said nothing further and quickly made his exit. To say that he found her manner and her odd way of speaking unnerving was to put it mildly, indeed. He felt rather like he'd wandered onto the stage at Drury Lane without knowing his part. Taking up the reins once more, he mounted his horse and made for Wolfhaven at a speed that was irresponsible and bordered on reckless. He'd be lying if he said it was simply his rush to return to Miss Benedict with a remedy that he hoped would ease her suffering. It was also a burning need to get away from Mrs. Epson's sister and her strange prophecies. He didn't even know the woman's name, but she'd identified him clearly. Not only that, it very much felt as if she'd peered into his very soul. She'd unnerved him and that was a feat not many could lay claim to.

The ride helped to clear his head and to ease whatever irrational and superstitious fears that the old woman might have roused in him. He would not lend it any more credence than that. When he arrived at Wolfhaven, he found Mrs. Epson at the front door screeching. Dismounting, he tossed the reins to his stable master, another aged servant who'd stayed on simply because he had no place else to go. "What the devil are you wailing about?" he demanded.

"She's dying, my lord!" The woman sneered at him like she had the right to such insolence. "She's up there gasping and coughing and if she dies, it'll be on your head... again!"

Alex moved past her, taking the stairs two at a time. Miss Benedict was in the throes of a coughing fit so severe that he couldn't see how her slender body could possibly withstand it. Her back was bowed from it, the cough so deep and rasping that surely no one could survive such distress. Taking a small, silver cup from the tray by the fire, he placed a pinch of the herbs in the bottom of it and used one of the tapers from the mantel to light it. When the smoke began to billow from the cup, he crossed to the bed and held it close to her, forcing her to inhale the acrid and foul-smelling stuff.

Whatever it was, it worked. Within minutes, her coughing eased. The wheezing sound of her breathing began to lessen and, as she collapsed against the pillows once more, it seemed that for the first time since he'd found her in those woods, she truly rested. Placing the remainder of the herbs in a drawer beside the bed, he once again set himself to keeping watch over her.

It wasn't simply about responsibility, though he certainly felt that for her. There was something strange about Mary Benedict that drew him, that called to a part of him and tender feelings that he'd thought long dead. His late wife and the misery of their marriage, coupled with the destruction wrought by its aftermath, should have put him off women entirely save for those who could provide pleasure and require no commitment. And yet, Miss Benedict stirred him to long for more than that, for conversations over breakfast, for the hours after passion was spent when he could hold a woman in his arms. She had, it seemed, managed to resuscitate the romantic boy he'd once been from the bitter wreck of a man he now was.

MARY DREAMED, BY turns pleasant and horrific. Happy memories of her life in London with her brother and of her days at the school he'd worked so hard to send her to flitted through her mind. They were interspersed with nightmarish images of the viciousness of their childhood and of all that she'd endured in the last weeks. Occasionally, during the most horrific of those dreams, she heard a voice calling to her. Kind, gentle, concerned—it bore little similarity to all that she'd encountered as of late.

When she finally managed to open her eyes again, bright sunlight was filtering through the rather faded curtains of the bed. Struggling a bit, she managed to sit up. Her head ached, but it wasn't the same sort of splitting headache that had erupted upon her last waking. Her heart was thumping in her chest. Fear. It was an emotion she was all too familiar with. She had no notion of where she was or who it was that had brought her there. The vague memories from the woods provided little insight. Ambrose, he'd said earlier when she asked for his name. But he'd hesitated. Why would he lie unless he was also a villain who meant her harm? Other memories aside from those fleeting ones of her dreams stirred—memories of him holding a burning bowl to her mouth and forcing her to inhale the fumes from it, of weak tea and broth being spooned into her mouth. She'd seen him, opened her eyes enough in those moments of near consciousness to look at him fully. It had been he who had cared for her, and with more tenderness than she might have expected.

Silent, not even daring to breathe, she surveyed her surroundings. The room was worn from time, in desperate need of a good cleaning. But it was easy to see that, at one point, it had been exquisite. Intricately-carved wood furnishings, gilt-trimmed moldings, and once-luxurious fabrics that were now moth-eaten, faded, and dusty hinted at some terrible reversal of fortune. Where in heaven's name was she?

As if in answer to her question, a door concealed in the paneled wall opened and a man stepped inside. His dark brown hair was damp and brushed back from a broad, strong forehead. Cleanly shaven, he wore only shirtsleeves and breeches and was in the process of donning his waistcoat. He paused mid-stride and met her gaze with a rather surprised expression crossing his rather rugged features. Immediately, he schooled his expression into one of cool unaffectedness.

"Good afternoon," he said.

"Afternoon?" Mary repeated the word with a feeling of dread. "How long have I been unconscious?"

"For nigh on two days," he answered. "You struck your head, if you recall. But it was the fever and the lung ailment that nearly saw an end to you. I thought many times through yesterday and even into the night that you would breathe your last. But you have rallied and I am remarkably glad for it."

The bruised feeling in her ribs told the truth of it. It was not the first time in her life that she'd been wracked with such horrible coughing. The last time the doctor had given her an elixir of laudanum and other herbs. It had curbed the cough but at a high cost. Still, whatever he had done, she felt better. The tight feeling in her chest was far less severe that it normally was after such illnesses. "You fetched a doctor, then? And explained my presence in your home to him?"

"No, I did not fetch the doctor and you should be glad enough of it. He'd have set the leeches to you and then wiped his hands of the entire situation. Worthless man," he said.

"But what were those herbs you were burning?" she asked. "How did you know the proper way to treat my ailment without the aid of a physician?"

"I sought the aid of a natural healer, what the tenant farmers would refer to as a wise woman, who lives in this area. She provided some herbs that seem to have done wonders for you," he explained. "Your fever burned and subsided by equal measure through the night, but I think it has broken for good this morning. I have to say, Miss Benedict, that you gave us all quite a fright."

His assertion that she'd lain senseless and entirely at his mercy for days was troubling on numerous levels. She had no real inkling as to his true character, despite whatever dreamlike memories she thought she had of his ministrations. The one thing she was entirely certain she did know of him was that he was a liar. But then she was, as well, so reviling him for that would have made her the worst sort of hypocrite.

But you are weaker, at a disadvantage, and you have no one to protect you. Those words allowed her to stifle her conscience and to question him further without guilt. "You said your name was Ambrose."

"I did," he said, inclining his head as he buttoned the last button on the waistcoat that fit his lean waist and broad shoulders to perfection. He moved deeper into the room and settled himself on a chair before the hearth. Retrieving the boots that were warming before the fire, he tugged them on.

Mary looked away but then immediately forced herself to look back. She would not allow her discomfort to make her look weak or fearful. It wasn't as if he was unclothed, after all. She had seen men in their shirtsleeves often enough. *But not in a bedchamber.* Not while she was wearing so very little herself. It seemed terribly intimate at the same time to be lying in a bed, in his presence, wearing only a borrowed nightrail and watching him dress. To ease her discomfort and, perhaps, to feel somewhat empowered in a situation in which she was distinctly aware of her vulnerability, Mary said, "What is your name, really? Because I know it isn't Ambrose."

With one boot on and the other still held in what appeared to be strong and very capable hands, he arched one eyebrow at her. "How, precisely, did you reach such a conclusion, Miss *Benedict?*" He put a healthy emphasis on the last name she'd provided, like he knew it was false. He'd suspected as much already, and Mrs. Epson's peculiar sister had all but confirmed it.

"You hesitated," she replied, calling on all the bravado she possessed as she attempted to ferret out what manner of man whose company she was in. She could not yet be certain if he was her savior or captor. Caring for her while she was ill did not offer any certainty that his motives would be pure when she was well. "When you told me your name, you had to search for it first… highly unlikely if it were truly yours."

"Are you so adept at identifying untruths?" His query was accompanied by a mocking expression and a cocked brow.

"Quite so. My brother is an excellent card player and while I do not share his love of gaming, he felt that it was quite important that I should learn how to read people as if I were sitting across from them at a card table." She paused then, allowing that information to sink in while she observed him carefully. "You were dishonest, but you have been kind to me and taken care of me when I was ill. I do not think you a bad man—quite the contrary. But there must be a reason!"

"For my kindness or for my lie?" he asked.

"Both," she answered without hesitation. "Kindness is rarely ever meted out without expectation of reward and dishonesty is typically used to avoid a negative consequence for oneself or to create a negative consequence for others. I would know the truth of it, sir."

"Are you always so direct, Miss Benedict?"

A guilty flush, in part because of her rudeness and in part because of her own subterfuge, pinkened her cheeks. "I try to be. I find that, barring a few exceptional circumstances, honesty is usually the best course of action. I pose no threat to you, but the same cannot be said of our situations in reverse. I have many reasons to fear you. That you feel the need to conceal your true identity is one of them."

He sat back in the chair, his wrists draped over heavily-muscled thighs encased in tight doeskin breeches. "My name would offer you little comfort. I do mean you no harm, Miss Benedict. I can attest to that! But there are scandals attached to my name that would make you question that statement, and that is why I concealed my identity. Given your injury and illness, I did not wish to overset you further."

"I am capable of judging for myself, I think," she said firmly and insistently.

"Very well," he relented. "If you insist, then you must know that I am Lord Alexander Carnahan, Earl of Wolverton... I daresay the knowledge has not increased your feelings of safety and security in my presence."

Mary went entirely still. She said nothing and dared not even breathe. Of course, she knew the name. Recalling the scandal sheets she'd pored over and that Benedict had teased her unmercifully about, she knew the story of The Murderous Earl, as the papers had dubbed him. The man had killed his wife in a mindless, jealous rage and lost everything for it. It was the scandal of the century. Nearly all of his holdings, or at least any that were not entailed, had been stripped from him by the courts. As an added punishment, the Lord High Steward had then granted those properties and all of the money to Wolverton's late wife's family.

It was an unheard of ruling and sentencing, one that had shocked all of London, perhaps all of England. It was a rare thing for the nobility to react so forcefully to the misdeeds of one of their own, but the nature of the murder had warranted it. The manner of death had been particularly violent and gruesome. The woman had been bludgeoned to death, the newspapers had said, so much so that she had only been recognizable by her very distinctive wedding ring and the dark hair she'd been known for. The strangest of all was that he had not claimed privilege of peerage when it was within his rights to do so, and had instead taken the punishment. Most had seen that as an admission of guilt on his part and as, perhaps, his penance for his sins.

"And we are at your family seat, I presume? In Somerset?" Mary asked. The question revealed much to him about her foreknowledge of his scandalous name, just as she had intended.

His lips quirked upward at one corner in sardonic amusement. "I see you are well informed, Miss Benedict."

"How is that you were found guilty but did not hang?" she asked. Perhaps it was rude to put it so bluntly, but she needed to know and her memory on that score was failing her terribly.

"I am a peer of the realm. It does come with some privileges. My assets were stripped from me in civil proceedings. But in the criminal case, my peers refused to convict me for lack of evidence. So I am labeled a murderer but have never been convicted as one, despite my current impoverishment for just that crime." He paused. "Now, it is time for you to answer one of my questions… who were the men holding you captive in the woods near my land?"

"How do you know I was a captive?" she challenged, wondering if, perhaps, he'd been involved from the start. Perhaps, she thought rather fearfully, he was not her savior at all.

"Because I have seen the marks on your wrists and your ankles to know that very recently you have been bound. Because you were running as if you feared for your life and you refused—rather adamantly and with remarkably good aim—to go back from whence you'd come. So who was holding you against your will, Miss Benedict, and what was it you feared from them?"

His reasonable assessment left her with no option but to answer. "I wish I had an answer for that... but I don't know them. The man who held me there was not the same one who abducted me from the street. And I strongly doubt that either one of them was the mastermind of anything. They were lackeys at best." It was the truth, but she didn't mention where she'd been abducted from or that she'd been investigating what she believed to be her adopted brother's true identity when she was taken. She had no notion as of yet whether Lord Wolverton could be trusted. While all the gossip and rumors she'd heard during the scandalous trial would point to the contrary, the man before her hardly seemed a cold-blooded killer. "What is your interest in these men? You have surely discharged any Christian duty you might have to an injured person. More to the point, what were you doing lurking in the woods in the dark of night?"

He surveyed her intently, his gaze hard and his expression inscrutable. After a moment that grew uncomfortably taut, he finally said, "I believe that these men, or others like them in the employ of the same villain, are the ones truly responsible for the death of my wife... and the subsequent loss of everything that I owned of any value. In short, Miss Benedict, I seek them because they have aided in my ruination. I have spent every night since watching those woods, looking for anything out of the ordinary that might lead me to the proof I require to finally clear my family's honored name of this very dark stain."

Mary's eyebrows arched up in shock as a disbelieving laugh escaped her lips. "You deny that you killed your wife? The courts found you guilty! In a world where aristocrats and nobleman are rarely ever made to endure the very bitter justice of our society, you were found guilty of a heinous crime! And I should believe you, why?"

He shrugged, but it wasn't a careless gesture. As he lifted his broad shoulders and let them fall, it seemed to her as if the very weight of the world rested upon them.

"The courts can be manipulated, Miss Benedict. Wealth, power, prestige—all those things can be utilized to influence the outcome to one's own liking," he offered dispassionately. "My name was a well-respected one, but my fortune was never such that I could hold sway in such exalted halls. I'll remind you that I was found not guilty of murder by my peers. I understand your concern and because you find yourself here at my mercy, I am inclined to offer you the assurances I have never offered to anyone else who dared question me... I did not kill my wife. I did not employ anyone else to do so in my stead. While we were not a love match and, in truth, the union was entirely miserable, I was content to get my heir and allow my wife to live as she pleased with the understanding that I would do the same."

"You would turn a blind eye to affairs?"

A sardonic smile curves his lips, but his eyes were completely cold when he replied, "I had been turning a blind eye to her affairs from the moment we wed. Three years in, it hardly warranted acknowledgement anymore."

For better or worse, she believed him. It wasn't so much what he said or even the manner in which he offered it. It was the weariness she sensed in him, the bone-deep exhaustion of a man too tired to defend himself against sharp, well-aimed, and vicious gossip. The world believed the worst of him and he'd stopped trying to fight them. But for the benefit of her peace of mind, he once more took up the gauntlet. Thinking of the many young women she'd attended her very special school with, whose fathers ran the gamut from wrongly maligned to the truly wicked, and how those poor girls had been tainted by their fathers' reputations, she knew it could be quite unfair. "I am very sorry then that you have been wrongly convicted both in court and in public opinion, Lord Wolverton. I understand how painful gossip can be and what it does to a person over time."

"Thank you for that, Miss Benedict," he said as he finished tugging on his second boot. "I must go for a bit. I have to meet someone who may have information about the men I suspect are responsible for your abduction. I will be going to the inn in the village and will return with food that is more palatable than whatever putrid refuse my housekeeper will plop onto a tray."

Her stomach growled. But, thankfully, the noise was either too low for him to hear or he was enough of a gentleman to pretend it had not occurred. "Thank you. I am quite famished. If I may ask, Lord Wolverton, how far are we from Bath?" If she could get to Bath and reclaim her things at Mrs. Simms' house, or beg the woman to send word to Benedict, she could return to London and put the horror of the last week behind her.

"Nearly thirty miles, Miss Benedict. Is Bath where you reside?" The question was pointed, as he was clearly trying to discern more about her.

Mary started to shake her head, but abruptly discontinued the gesture. Even that slight movement reminded her that she had struck her head rather hard. "I was visiting Bath when I was abducted from the streets." The distance he'd named surprised her. She hadn't thought they had traveled so far, but she'd been heavily drugged. The news was also disheartening. It was too far to travel on foot and certainly too far for her to travel in any manner given her current condition. For the time being, she was well and truly stuck.

He arched one eyebrow, his expression clearly indicating his suspicions. "Without a chaperone?"

It would seem strange to most, she supposed. Her speech was that of a lady thanks to her time spent at the Darrow School for Young Ladies. Having begun her education there much later than many of the girls, Miss Euphemia Darrow had taken her under her wing and tutored her personally so that her manners, speech, and understanding of the rules of society would allow her to function in it as if she had truly been a gently-bred young miss. It was a far cry from what would normally be expected for a foundling child raised by people little better than vicious animals. Benedict was responsible for her current confusing status. He'd done everything he could to ensure she had a future that was far different from the manner in which they'd been raised, but there was no place in the world for a girl like her. She spoke like a lady but wasn't one. She carried herself like a debutante but would never be permitted in society. And now, any chance of a respectable match had been thoroughly ruined by her abduction. No man would believe her chaste after what she'd been through, regardless of whether it was true or not.

Realizing that she had been silent for too long, Mary blushed again. Perhaps it was the fact that he was rather handsome. Perhaps it was the fact that he stood before her fully clothed while she had only a thin nightrail and the bedclothes she currently clutched to her to shield her modesty. Either way, she was acutely aware of him and of the impropriety of their current situation. His question also raised her awareness of her own vulnerability. She was very much alone with him, in a bedchamber with only a deaf, old woman in the house to hear her scream, and no one knew where she was.

Pulling herself together, she stated imperiously, "I am of a class where such things are not of such great concern, my lord. My education elevated my speech to a point that I might be employable as a governess in fine households, but I have not yet obtained a position. I was visiting a friend in Bath, Mrs. Simms." It was the same lie she'd told her brother. At a distance of thirty miles, she could only hope he would not take it upon himself to check. Mrs. Simms had been little more than a stranger to her, after all, as the only transactions which had transpired between them had been related directly to her room for let.

"And was Mrs. Simms helping you to find a position then?"

"She was providing guidance that I needed in my quest," she answered vaguely. It was true enough. The woman had often provided directions to the various locations about Bath that she'd scoured the papers to see if Lady Vale frequented.

He nodded, clearly unimpressed with her vague answer. "I see. When I return, if you are feeling well enough, I would like very much to discuss the details of your abduction as you recall it."

"Certainly. I will be happy to tell you what I can remember." So long as it had nothing to do with her reasons for being outside

Madame Zula's home, then there was no reason to keep it a secret. She would not jeopardize Benedict's future by playing that hand too soon.

ALEXANDER MADE HIS way down the stairs and out the front door of the house. She was lying. What about, he could not yet be sure, but he was certain that Miss Mary Benedict, if that was in fact her name, was hiding something. The only facts he could trust were that she had been abducted, held against her will, and that at some point in her life, someone had taken it upon themselves to see her educated in such a manner that she could speak well and comport herself in society. Beyond that, she was quite a mystery.

Stepping outside, he was greeted by his stable master. Again, the servant had stayed because he was too old to obtain work elsewhere, but at least Tom took pride in his work and did his job as well as his advanced age and stooped back permitted. The few horses that remained and his carriage were in tip-top shape. It was the one area of his life where things seemed to be going remarkably well.

"The girl is recovering, my lord?" Tom asked.

"She's still weak and far too frail to travel yet. But yes, she is on the mend," Alex answered, taking the reins and hoisting himself into the saddle. "I shall be certain to tell her you asked after her."

"Oh, no. She wouldn't care a bit to think of servants like me gossiping about her. Still, when I saw you bringing her home, she's a little bit of a thing. Reminds me of my own daughters that way! Grown and married now, the lot of them, but they were all wee, pretty things."

"I see. I doubt Miss Benedict would be affronted by your concern. She strikes me as a very reasonable and not high in the instep sort of girl at all," Alex offered. But she wasn't a girl. And that was very much part of the problem. Miss Benedict was most assuredly a woman grown, even if her diminutive stature might have led some to believe otherwise. For himself, based solely on her composure and the manner in which she appeared to be taking her current situation in stride, he knew that she had passed girlhood some time ago. It only complicated the situation. "I'm heading for the Bell and Whistle to get food that is actually edible. I fear what might become of poor Miss Benedict if she must subsist on Mrs. Epson's cooking while recovering."

Tom gave a snort of laughter. "Dry as dust when it ought to be moist, and swimming in grease when it ought to be dry! I do believe she does it apurpose, my lord. No woman can cook that poorly without making an effort at it. And given my late wife's abilities, I ought to know." The stable master was still chortling as he ambled away.

Wheeling his mount, Alex galloped down the drive and onto the road beyond. He needed to clear his head, and he needed to put some distance between himself and Miss Benedict, or whatever her actual name was. She was too appealing for his peace of mind and regardless of her appeal, he could not allow himself to lose sight of his ultimate goal. The trip to the inn was as much to gather information as it was to obtain a decent meal for them. The man he'd had positioned in Bath was to meet him there with news. The message had arrived earlier that morning.

The short ride helped to clear his head and to ease some of the tension in him. Dismounting, he tossed the reins to the ostler and ducked his head as he entered through the low-hanging door frame. The interior was dark and smoky. It was hardly a respectable inn and its patronage reflected that. Thieves, highwaymen, murderers, and men in disgrace, as he was, gathered there. He spotted the man he'd hired lurking in the back corner near the hearth. Stepping deeper into the room, he was aware of people watching him. Even the lowest of the low knew his name and his face, thanks to the numerous sketches and newssheets that had been passed around during the more lurid aspects of his trial.

Alex ignored them and, instead, simply took a seat near the hearth and signaled the serving girl for a tankard of ale. When it arrived, he looked at the man he was there to meet and asked, "You have news?"

"It was Harrelson," he said in a low whisper. "I followed the man you seen the night of the murder. He got into a carriage and it took him to Harrelson's estate."

It was not new information. Given what he'd heard the night he'd discovered Miss Benedict, it was just as he'd suspected. Still, the very name made his blood boil. Harrelson's perversions and his wickedness were boundless. It had been Harrelson who had provided the "evidence" against him that had permitted the courts to levy such a judgement against him and award all of his non-entailed holdings to the family of his late wife. "Lord Wendell Harrelson? You're certain of it? You did not mistake his identity?" It wasn't the sort of definitive proof that he needed, however. Just talking to the man wasn't enough to prove collusion in relation to Helena's death.

"Certain as anyone can be... but there's more. I saw the man, the one you'd caught your late wife with as you pointed him out to me in Bath. He's come and gone countless times in the city, but that was the first time I ever seen him go to the estate. He was brought by two other men and wore a hood. So whatever their business was, it was clear to me Harrelson didn't trust the man."

Alexander pondered that thought carefully. "What else? You said this was urgent and all of that could easily have been relayed in a letter."

The man pitched his voice lower, "Harrelson is dead. Poisoned by the psychic. She killed him and then offed herself the same way. Poison is an ugly way to die, I think. Much rather have a knife blade in my ribs to end it quick like, than to lay there gasping for breath and knowing the end was coming."

Or a pistol ball directly to the brain. That had been the method he had considered when at his lowest and then immediately discounted. It was a mortal sin, after all. But more than that, it would have been an admission of guilt. He had no intention of allowing the world to continue believing him a murderer, regardless of whatever fate had befallen one of the men who'd orchestrated his downfall. "When did this happen?"

"Only just this morning, my lord. In the wee hours before dawn it was, so I heard. Saw the magistrate's lackeys carting the bodies out myself, I did! Rode here straightaway to tell you."

Alex considered the implications of that very carefully. "What was his connection to the psychic?"

The man leaned in. "All them missing girls from Bath… they went missing from her establishment. Taken right out in front of it, right in the streets they were."

"What missing girls? I haven't been to Bath in ages and haven't read a news sheet in months." Because even after a year, they still randomly published fantastical articles about him, the reclusive wife killer.

"Several girls—all young, all pretty, and most fairly genteel—have gone missing from Bath in the last few weeks. And at least three of them had gone to see the mystic, Madame Zula, the very one who was found dead with Lord Harrelson!"

Alex felt his heart pounding. Young, pretty, and genteel could not have been a better description for Miss Benedict, unless one also included remarkably cagey. "Their names?"

"Mary Mason was one. I only remember it cause her brother caught me outside the psychic's house one day and asked me if I'd seen her, showed me a tiny portrait of her, and she was right pretty, she was. I think she was the last one taken, as well, missing for just over a week now… the others I don't know for sure."

It was no coincidence. Of that he was certain. Mary was a common enough name but, given the rather extraordinary circumstances, he had no choice but to believe Miss Mary Benedict who was currently occupying his bedroom at Wolfhaven could be no other than Miss Mary Mason. He'd known she was lying, but it was curious to him. Her identity wasn't so exalted that she'd need to hide it. Why the lie? What else was the girl hiding? He'd have the answers soon enough.

"What color was her hair?"

The man frowned, as if it were a silly question. "Blonde, my lord. Like the angels I've seen painted in the church."

It was all the confirmation he required. He'd confront her with it when he returned, Alex decided. To his soon to be unemployed spy, he directed, "Get into Harrelson's study by whatever means necessary. Look for any letters or any journal entries that connect Harrelson to Albert Hamilton or Freddy Hamilton… and, more importantly, anything that would connect the Hamiltons to this Madame Zula."

"I'm no housebreaker!" the man protested, looking as scandalized as any society matron.

Alex rolled his eyes. For a criminal, his new employee certainly seemed to have a great deal of very inconvenient ethics. "Fine, I'll do it. But for now, you get back to Bath, locate the brother of Miss Mary Mason and keep your eye on him. I want to know how all of this is connected, and if or how the Hamiltons are involved with it." There was little doubt in his mind that if Harrelson was involved, Albert was right there with him. The pair of them had been thick as thieves from the outset. Albert had been, in the eyes of the law at least, her half-brother. Born two years into the marriage between her mother and Albert's father, it had been an open secret that Helena was not the elder Hamilton's child. In fact, none of the children born from that cursed union had been his. Helena's morals and sense of fidelity had clearly been inherited from her mother.

Recalling the early days of his rather disappointing courtship of Helena, Alex frowned. He had met her while she'd been attending a social function at Harrelson's estate. While he'd never been overly fond of Harrelson and his somewhat questionable behavior, they were neighbors and so he'd attended. The nature of the kinship between Helena and Lord Harrelson had given him pause, as she was the man's niece, after all, at least by marriage. But with the very generous marriage contract and Helena's assurances that she truly wished to marry him—something he'd learned early on after their wedding was a lie—he'd been swayed. The fortune she'd brought to the marriage should have been enough to restore his estates to their proper glory. But now, all of that was gone.

Bigger questions remained, however. Primarily, who in the devil was Mary Mason and how, precisely, was she involved?

Chapter Three

MARY HAD MADE such a nuisance of herself to the housekeeper that the old woman had finally located a wrapper for her. It was miles too long, and likely had belonged to Lord Wolverton's late wife. Any misgivings she had at wearing garments that belonged to a murdered woman were superseded by the idea of facing off with Lord Wolverton once more while wearing only a thin shift. Her battered dignity would simply not allow for it, though she did hope it would not stir unwanted feelings or antagonize him to see it.

Her cough had returned, but milder than before. The tightness in her chest had eased significantly and she was feeling much stronger than she had when she'd faced him upon waking. She'd even managed to get out of bed and was now seated in the very chair he'd occupied earlier, enjoying the warmth of the fire on her bare toes. The cursory inspection of her feet had revealed just how much damage her barefoot race through the woods had inflicted. It would be days before she could walk without limping, and longer still before she could go any distance beyond the confines of the bedchamber.

The soft knock on the door was her only warning. He did not wait to be bade entrance, but simply opened the door and stepped inside. She might have taken umbrage but for the hamper of food he carried. She could smell the freshly-baked bread inside it. Her stomach rumbled in response as she clutched the wrapper more tightly about her.

He paused in the doorway, glancing at the empty bed and then toward the fire. If the wrapper and its previous owner crossed his mind, his expression gave no indication. Instead, he stepped deeper inside, placed the basket on the floor and then stepped through the same hidden panel he'd utilized earlier. A moment later, he returned with a second chair which he placed near hers before tugging a small table over.

"I thought we'd dine together," he said, as he began unloading items from the hamper. "It appears you are feeling much stronger and we have a great deal to discuss, Miss Benedict... or should I call you Miss Mason?"

Mary paused in the act of unfolding one of the serviettes that had been placed on the top of the hamper. It was panic, pure and simple, as she met his knowing gaze. How on earth would she explain it?

Her mouth dropped open and she blinked rapidly. How had he discovered the truth so quickly? "I'm not sure I understand," she said finally, a feeble attempt to brazen it out.

"Your name is not Mary Benedict. It is Mary Mason, and you were reported missing from Bath more than a week ago. Why did you lie?" His tone was firm, but he did not appear to be angry. Still, there was little doubt that any continued dishonesty on that front would not be tolerated.

Mary sighed. "I did not wish to disclose my name because my reasons for being in Bath pertain to my brother and might create difficulty for him. I cannot and will not tell you what those reasons are, because they have no bearing whatsoever on all of this. I firmly believe that my abduction was a mere coincidence. The more important question is, how did you discover this information?"

He removed several cloth-wrapped packages from the hamper. There was ham, cheese, fresh baked bread, and a crock of something that smelled utterly delicious. "Roasted chicken with root vegetables," he said, as if reading her mind. "As to your question, I have a man in Bath who has been keeping an eye on things related to my enemies for me. He reported to me today that there have been a number of women who have gone missing from the city. And one of them was named Mary Mason."

"I see… and the other women? Do you know what has become of them?"

He was silent for a moment, but she could see the ticking of a muscle in his jaw. It was all the answer she required. Those women, for all intents and purposes, were lost.

"Perhaps we should speak of something less distressing?" she suggested. "The food does smell delicious. Thank you for bringing it."

Lord Wolverton inclined his head in acknowledgment of the thanks. "I would advise eating lightly to start. You've been so long without food, eating too much will see you casting up your accounts."

She shuddered delicately. "I've suffered enough humiliations already. I will heed your warning. Some of the chicken, perhaps?"

"A good choice," he said, and dished some out onto one of the plates that had been tucked into the hamper. "Tell me what you recall of your abduction, Miss Mason. And I need all of the details, where you were when it happened, and anything you might recall about your abductors."

Mary considered what she could safely say. She had not been dissuaded in her belief that Benedict was the lost heir to the Vale title. Would exposing that suspicion cause any sort of harm? Could she conceal it from a man who, despite what she'd believed upon their first meeting, had been all that was honorable? She couldn't risk it, she decided. Try as she might, and wish as she might, there was no reasonable way to provide the information he asked without at least exposing some of her theory. And she would not give him the name of the woman she believed to be Benedict's mother. If she was wrong, it would be too damaging.

"I was visiting a mystic, Madame Zula."

He gave her an arched look. "I find it difficult to believe that you would fall prey to such nonsense. You strike me as a very pragmatic sort, Miss Mason."

"I have no illusions about Madame Zula's ability to commune with the spirit world, Lord Wolverton," Mary replied. It was difficult to provide a vague enough description of the horror that was their childhood and the ever-changing stories they'd gotten from their adoptive mother about their true origins. While the vile creature they'd been forced to call mother would never have admitted it to Benedict, she'd told Mary once, her tone smug and superior, that Benedict was the son of a fine lord and lady. She'd savored revealing that as he'd mucked out stalls when he was far too young to be able to do such strenuous work alone. That and a chance encounter with Lady Vale on Bond Street had given birth to her theory. "My brother and I were both adopted as very young children. But I had reason to believe that the woman I had identified as possibly being my brother's true mother was a client of Madame Zula's. I had hoped that by also becoming a client, I might gain some insight as to her reasons for visiting."

"Why would you think that?"

Mary drew a deep and shuddering breath. "We were adopted at different times, you see? From what I can gather, Benedict would have been about four or five at the time he came to live with our parents. I arrived two years later, possibly around the age of three or so. We really don't know how old we are, where we were born, or who our actual parents were. And our adoptive mother said things during the years that led me to believe—" She broke off abruptly, searching for a way to confess it without revealing the true cruelty of those who had adopted them. Finally, and rather lamely, she continued, "We also cannot be certain that our true parents gave us willingly into the care of the couple who raised us."

"You believe you were abducted as children and given into the care of your adoptive parents?"

"I think my brother was, due to some things our adoptive mother said to me... but for myself, I do not know."

"They were unkind to you and your brother, then?"

Unkind was not a fit description for the people who had adopted them. "I would rather not speak of that, Lord Wolverton, and it hardly has any bearing on our current situation." Her tone was firm and she lifted her chin in an unconscious challenge.

After a moment of tense silence, he nodded in agreement and didn't press her further for details about their childhood, a fact for which she was grateful. Instead, he focused his attentions on her time in Bath. "Did you learn anything useful from this Madame Zula? About your brother's identity or the woman you believe to be his mother?"

Mary took a bite of the chicken, as much to ease her hunger as to provide a moment in which to gather her thoughts and offer up what was pertinent without revealing too much. "The woman I believe to be Benedict's actual mother—I will not reveal her identity because I'm not sure it's relevant and I've no wish to stir idle gossip that might harm either her or my brother—"

"And to whom would I gossip?" he demanded pointedly. "In case you were unaware, Miss Mason, the only person, aside from my less than hardworking handful of servants, that I have spoken to in weeks, is you."

She said nothing to that, only graced him with an arched look and continued, "I did not. But I did see something much more concerning, something that made me believe that Madame Zula might actually be involved in something far more nefarious than simply swindling those who seek her aid."

"Given the numerous missing girls, Miss Mason, and the fact that your investigation led you directly to the center of a kidnapping scheme, I'd say your instincts for finding the truth are very good. A pity they are not more capable of identifying danger," he said. "But do go on. I'd like to know how you reached this conclusion."

"While observing this woman, I saw her companion enter Madame Zula's home where she conducted her readings. There was a man following her and he appeared to be rather unsavory. After the companion left, I saw Madame Zula's manservant come outside and speak to him. They appeared to be very familiar with one another. I encountered the companion again at the Pump Room and, as I left, noted that very same man loitering outside. I was suspicious of him and his motives and thought that the best way to uncover what they might be about was to become a client of Madame Zula's myself."

Lord Wolverton leaned forward, resting his elbows on his knees. "What did this man look like?"

"He was roughly dressed, tall and lean but not thin. He wore dark clothes and a wide-brimmed hat. He did not have a beard but always appeared to be in need of shaving. Dark hair, small eyes... and a scar on his chin," Mary said. She noted Lord Wolverton's response to that description, the tension that settled over him and the ticking of a muscle in his jaw. "Do you know this man?"

"I do not know him. But I saw him—moments before I discovered my wife, bleeding and near dead," he said, his words sharp and hard. After taking a deep breath, he continued, "And how did you think this might have anything to do with your brother?"

Mary knew that he had no wish to revisit such painful memories and was content to turn the conversation back to Benedict and how she'd come to be abducted. "Well, I assumed that the companion was visiting Madame Zula on behalf of her employer... that perhaps her employer thought to retain Madame Zula and her suspect skills in ascertaining the location of her missing son."

He frowned then. "And?"

"That's really all there is to tell. I made an appointment, went to it, and as I was leaving was set upon by a trio of men who scooped me up, tossed me into the back of a wagon with a cloth over my head and took me to some dirty and dingy warehouse within the city. It wasn't until the next night that they came and hauled me away again... only this time I must have been in that wagon for a terribly long time. When I awoke, I was in an underground room, rather like a cell. There were no windows, only a dirt floor, and a single servant to bring food and water to me." Mary shivered at the memory of that cold, damp room and the unending fear that had been her only companion there. "What they wanted with me, I cannot say."

"They did not harm you?" he asked.

The question had been phrased delicately, but Mary was not so innocent of the workings of the world that she did not understand his meaning. "Other than to bind me and transport me from one place to another, no one touched me," she confirmed. "I am not unaware of the dangers that women face from unscrupulous men. I can only imagine that their reward would be greater if I were to be delivered to my final destination unscathed, as it were."

THEIR CONVERSATION HAD confirmed two things for Alex. The first was that Miss Mason was incredibly lucky to have escaped the fate that awaited her. Abducting girls and even young boys from the streets had been a very profitable business for unscrupulous souls for ages. There were more than enough houses of ill repute in London that didn't really care if their staffs were employed willingly or not. Likely, that had been the fate in store for her. A gently-bred young woman or, at the very least, one who spoke as and possessed the demeanor of a lady, especially with Miss Mason's delicate beauty, would fetch a high price. The second thing that he became rather uncomfortably aware of was that Miss Mason was rather worldly. She understood perfectly what he'd meant when asking if she was unharmed. He now could not help but speculate on just how knowledgeable she was. It was hardly an appropriate train of thought for him, given that she was still quite ill and they were alone in his bedchamber. For her sake, as well as his, he needed to maintain a suitable distance between them.

"And was the man you saw stalking this companion of your brother's potential mother the same man who abducted you?" Alex asked, noting that the entire thing was incredibly convoluted. It would be easier if she would simply identify the woman to him, but she clearly had her reasons for wishing to keep that information a secret.

"I believe so. It was very dark and difficult to see, then my head was covered entirely, but I caught a glimpse of him that night. Enough to think that it was the same man," she answered.

Alex leaned back in his chair, contemplating the answer as Mrs. Epson banged on the door and then entered carrying a tea tray. He could trust her to prepare little more than that. Even she could not make a muck of boiling water.

"We're out of milk," she groused.

"Then we shall have our tea without it," he said firmly, the dismissal apparent in his voice.

Mrs. Epson continued on, "Farmer Hayes hasn't brought any this week."

"I'll go and get some tomorrow," Alex replied. "You may go, Mrs. Epson."

The housekeeper set the tray down with a thump before the hearth. She made a loud grunting sound that might have been either disapproval or agreement. Her temperament was such that the two were indistinguishable regardless. "Don't seem right. Pays little to no rent. Don't bring the things he's supposed to. Got plenty of money to spend in the village though, he does! Ain't right. Nothing in the godforsaken place is right though!"

"That will be all, Mrs. Epson. It's hardly fitting to air our business in front of Miss Mason."

The old woman narrowed her eyes. "Thought her name was Benedict?"

"I misspoke," he replied easily. "Her name is Miss Mary Mason. Benedict is her brother's given name."

The old woman eyed her steadily for a moment, her mouth twisted into a disapproving grimace. "Seems this house is full of lies and liars these days."

"That will be all, Mrs. Epson!" Alex repeated, and his voice thundered loudly enough that both women jumped. The housekeeper did at least shuffle toward the door though nothing halted the grumbling under her breath or the daggers she glared at the both of them as she left.

"Your servants do appear to be remarkably cavalier about the permanency of their employment, Lord Wolverton. I am sorry my presence here has made things more difficult for you than they already were," Miss Mason remarked.

"They are aware, as am I, that I'd be unlikely to find anyone willing to replace them," he admitted. "After all, very few people are willing to overlook the fact that I am known to be both a murderer and quite poor. I find that the former is infinitely more forgivable for most than the latter. Much can be ignored or forgiven when payment is assured."

His admission of his financial straits seemed to make her uncomfortable as there was no proper way to respond to it, so Alex changed the subject. "If I were to return you to the area where I first found you, do you think you could lead me to the place where you were held? When you are well enough, of course. I would not risk further injury or a relapse for you. I have suspicions about where it might have been, but I don't wish to color your memories or judgement by voicing them."

"I cannot say," she stated evenly, though he could see that the idea of it unnerved her. "I never really saw it. My head was covered when they took me there, and it was still dark when I fled. Once I was out, I didn't bother to look back. I just ran."

"You paused at the roadside," he said, "when you saw the approaching carriage. How did you know that they meant you ill?"

"I just had a feeling, is all. I can't really explain it beyond that. I thought to flag them down and beg for assistance but then wondered why they were traveling such a desolate stretch of road at night anyway... and wondered if, perhaps, they were not involved."

"Does the name Harrelson mean anything to you?" he asked. "Or Hamilton?"

"I've never heard either."

Alex nodded. "Just as well. Finish your supper and then back to bed. You'll need to inhale more of that foul herbal smoke when you've finished your meal."

Her eyes flashed brightly. "I'm not a child, Lord Wolverton."

No, she was not. He was acutely aware of that fact as he'd been the one to strip her ruined garments from her and place her in the borrowed nightrail that did not conceal nearly enough of her charms.

That vision of her haunted his dreams and infringed far more regularly on his waking hours than was good for either of them. "Miss Mason, you are alone in a bedchamber with me. The only servant in this house is an old woman who sometimes fails to hear a shout when it happens right next to her ear! It would be far better for us both if I could view you as such."

He didn't wait for her to reply. He simply rose and stalked from the room. Away from her, he could think. Free of her presence, he did not have to feel the weight of his scandal-ridden name and all that it precluded him from. But there was another part of him, the wicked part, that reminded him she was not a lady of quality and the same rules did not apply. He could make her his mistress, if she were willing. But he recoiled from that. He would not, despite whatever temptation was placed in his path, become the very thing that people had accused him of.

The sad truth of his situation was that she was everything he'd ever desired in a woman. Clearly, she was brave and resourceful, and fiercely loyal to and protective of those she loved. She was also remarkably intelligent, that was obvious from their conversations. All of that coupled with her beauty and the warmth that seemed to radiate from her had left him smitten with her when there was no possibility of a future for them. Whatever the circumstances of her birth, there was no denying that Mary Mason had the bearing and manners of a lady, and to treat her as anything less would be to sacrifice his own honor. So he would continue to desire her, continue to be haunted by the possibilities of what might have been if he'd been in a position to pursue her as a gentleman ought to.

Chapter Four

B ENEDICT MASON, THE newly acknowledged, at least by the family, Benedict Middlethorp, Lord Vale, studied the small cell. It was their second trip to Lord Harrelson's estate and the place where it appeared his sister had been held. The small room hewn out of the walls of the abandoned salt mine were rough and damp. The dirt floor was cold to the touch. It was as silent as a tomb and yielded nothing in the way of new information.

"You are tormenting yourself, Benedict. You must stop this. Mary is not here. If there were any sign of her in this place, you would have discovered it by now!"

He looked up at his betrothed and noted the worried frown that curved her pretty lips downward. They would wed on the morrow in a simple ceremony at a small church in Bath. They had decided to marry by common license rather than have the banns posted and wait additional weeks. It bothered him that he was moving ahead in such a fashion without his sister present, but he also knew that they could not afford to wait. On the off chance that Elizabeth carried his child, it was imperative that they wed as soon as possible. "I cannot help but feel I've missed something, Elizabeth. That there must be some clue here to Mary's whereabouts. She cannot have simply have vanished into thin air."

"I do not believe there is a clue here, Benedict. I think Mary fled this place and, perhaps, she was injured in her escape. But I cannot help thinking that she has been rescued by some well-meaning person. Even now, she could be in a coach making for London, thinking to return there to you! If your sister managed to escape this cell, overpowering a guard who was stronger and larger than she could ever hope to be, you must have a little faith in her ability to fend for herself."

Even after all she'd been through and the evil they had been forced to confront, Elizabeth had hope for the world. He did not. It was just as likely, if not more so, that Mary had not been rescued at all but that she'd been re-apprehended and handed over to the very people Harrelson had sold her to. If that were the case, they might never find her. But saying that to Elizabeth on the eve of their wedding would only rob her of joy. He sighed. "I pray you are right. If you are not, I've engaged an artist to make a drawing based on the miniature of Mary. It will be given to a printer and distributed in every town and village in this county. If someone found her or saw her, they will come forward and claim the offered reward... I hope."

Elizabeth frowned as she stepped closer to him. She placed one hand tenderly on his face, "What is it that you really fear, my love?"

He should have known he wouldn't be able to hide anything from her. She saw right through him and had from the very moment of their first meeting. "That Harrelson found her. That when she fled this dungeon, she made her way straight into his clutches... and now he is dead and we may never know what fate he sent her to," Benedict admitted. It was the first time he'd voiced that terrible fear aloud but, with it out, he could not take it back. "I promised her that I would always keep her safe and I have failed her miserably."

"Mary is a grown woman, Benedict. Take it from me when I tell you that women don't always need to be sheltered or protected. She figured out who you were before anyone else did. Mary knew that you were Lord Vale! If she was intelligent enough to piece all of that together, to escape this place by duping her guard, then I cannot imagine she would be so easily recaptured. You give her far too little credit," Elizabeth chided.

"I am her brother—"

"And she lied to you about where she was going and what she was doing because she was driven by the same need to protect her sibling that you feel now. Trust that she is resourceful enough to have rescued herself, Benedict. Otherwise you will drive yourself mad."

He rose to his feet. "You are correct. I know that you are. But what I feel isn't rational, Elizabeth. For so long, all we had was one another. I need to know she is safe!"

"Then we will postpone our wedding and you will be able to devote the time you need to solving this mystery and locating your sister," she offered.

"I don't want to do that. We cannot afford to do that. It is scandalous enough that a lost heir who's been running a gaming hell will now lay claim to a title and marry his mother's companion! If you are with child and that child is born even a week sooner than anticipated—"

"Then we will get to rejoice in the birth of our child a week sooner than anticipated," she interrupted. "Neither of us is free from scandal. If Freddy tells everyone about my past then it will not matter what we do. All of society will slam their doors in our faces, and I'm not even certain that I care. Let us focus on the important things here! Let us find your sister and when she is returned to you, she can attend our wedding and celebrate our happiness with us."

He pulled her close, kissed her tenderly, and whispered, "I do not deserve you, but I mean to keep you all the same."

"I will remind you of that when you receive the bill for my trousseau," she teased. "Now, let's retrace our steps to the road and the point where you found that scrap of her clothing. We may yet find something new to lead us in the right direction."

He nodded in agreement and they left the small cell, making their way out of the darkened tunnels of the mine with the light of a single lantern. Once they emerged into the brilliant sunlight of the afternoon, Benedict aided Elizabeth to mount her horse. His hand strayed momentarily beneath the hem of her riding habit, tracing the curve of a shapely calf until she smacked his hand. "Behave."

"That would be a very unlikely turn of events," he replied with a grin, more like his old self than when in the awful cell that had been

Mary's. "I've never been very good at it."

"Try to be better," she said. "Or at the very least, restrict your misbehavior to more private times."

Neither of them had noted the small, thin man who followed them. He skulked behind trees, hid behind rocks, and made himself invisible to them as he observed them. He was following his instructions and keeping a close watch on Benedict Middlethorp, the newly recognized Lord Vale, just as Lord Wolverton had asked. When the couple rode away, he allowed the distance between them to grow. He did not need to follow them as he knew precisely where they were going. What he did need to do was find out if what he'd heard was actually true. Was Miss Mason's brother the long lost Viscount Vale? The answers would be found in Bath. There was a pretty housemaid there that often fed him tidbits of information. No doubt, she'd be able to get what he needed from one of the servants in Lord Vale's house.

ALEX DID NOT go far after leaving Miss Mason's room—and he forced himself to think of her thusly. To fall into the habit of thinking of her so familiarly that he should call her by her given name was a disaster waiting to happen. Already, she consumed too much of his time and his thoughts. Enough proprieties had already been sacrificed in his care of her without him taking additional liberties, even if they were only in his mind. She was not the type of woman to be a man's mistress, and he was not a man in position to offer anything else. Alex cursed. He couldn't even afford a mistress, after all, much less a wife. In all of Wolfhaven Hall, there were a grand total of four rooms, kitchen and servants quarters aside, that remained habitable. Everything else had been closed up, draped in Holland cloths and ignored. He'd even given up the master suite as it was too far removed from the great hall and the kitchens. With only the uncooperative Mrs. Epson to serve him, he'd have starved to death at such a distance. But even though the rooms were closed off and rarely used, they were still accessible and he found himself heading in the direction of one room in particular. He needed to ground himself, to remind himself of what was at stake.

The poor state of his home should have been enough to deter him from thinking of Miss Mason as anything other than an unexpected guest. Of course, it wasn't simply his finances that precluded any relationship between them beyond that of temporary caregiver. It wasn't even the scandal and his own honor. Everything about her indicated to him that she would make a very lucky man a most excellent wife. To give in to his own baser urges, to act on his attraction for her with the full knowledge that he could never offer her permanency, would be to ruin her chances of making a good match elsewhere. He wasn't the murderer that society gossip purported him to be, but he wasn't innocent either. A healthy share of misdeeds could be laid upon his head. He would not add the seduction of an innocent, if she was, to the list. Even if she was not entirely innocent, it was clear that she'd been in a very traumatic situation. He would not be the villain others painted him to be by taking advantage of her while she was clearly vulnerable. He would not destroy her future for his own selfish whims.

With all the reasons he should remain as aloof from her as possible whirling through his mind like the spokes on a wheel, he did something that he knew would only strengthen his resolve. Making his way down the dark and dusty corridor, he opened the heavy and intricately carved doors that led to the portrait gallery. He'd managed, only just, to avoid having to sell off the likenesses of his forebears, though they would hardly have brought much revenue. Bypassing the older portraits, all of them still shrouded with Holland covers to protect them from dust, he made his way unerringly to the lone portrait that hung near the end. It had been a wedding gift from his bride's father-in-name-only.

Removing the cover from it, he stared at the lovely face of his late wife. It wasn't grief that brought him there. She was a stranger to him, a woman he'd married but never truly known. He'd bedded her, and she hadn't denied him, but neither of them had found any joy or pleasure in the act. It had been perfunctory at best and infrequent. Every attempt at seduction, at bringing her any sort of pleasure, every attempt to make their marriage something more than a hollow sham, had been met with coldness from her. He'd prayed for her to become with child so they could halt their physical intimacy once and for all. He was certain that if Helena prayed, she had asked for the same. But his wife had not been a very devout woman. Outside of their wedding, he'd never known her to step foot in church. And yet her body had been found only yards away from the ancient, ruined chapel on his property.

Neither given to long walks in nature, nor any particular interest in religious antiquities or architecture, the location had been as much a mystery to him as the true identity of her killer. It had made no sense. Nothing about her death had. She had been unrecognizable, her face battered and the bones beneath so fractured she'd no longer looked human, much less like the renowned beauty he had wed. The magistrate had asked him to identify any marks on her person and he'd been forced to admit, much to his humiliation, that he was ignorant of them. Their brief and very businesslike couplings had been accomplished in darkness. She'd refused light and any semblance of foreplay, urging him instead to simply get it over with.

Even with his need for an heir, he'd been utterly disgusted by it all and had not sought his husbandly rights in months prior to the murder. Which begged one final and haunting question... whose child, tiny and perfectly formed, had been expelled from the body of his wife at the moment of her death? Because there was not a chance in hell it had been his.

As it always did, visiting Helena's portrait gave him a renewed sense of purpose, a renewed drive to find her killer and to clear his name once and for all. But as he turned to leave the portrait gallery, it wasn't Helena who occupied his thoughts. It was the pale, lovely beauty who had taken over his own chamber. Mary Mason was a problem, and he hadn't a clue what to do about her.

He would have to face her soon enough. She would need to inhale the herb smoke once more before retiring for the night but, for now, he needed a reprieve. So he sought out the one thing that always cleared his head—a bruising ride through the countryside would do him a world of good. If he were lucky, the bracing air would cure him of any wayward or heated thoughts.

MARY WATCHED THE rather ill-tempered housekeeper as she moved about the room and did the poorest job of tidying up that had ever been achieved. The dust was simply disturbed and left to settle again. "This is a lovely room," Mary offered. "Are all the guest accommodations here furnished with such lovely antiques?"

"Guest accommodations!" the old woman snorted. "More like only accommodation. Don't have money to keep body and soul together, much less heat this whole house! What a sight that would be! Might as well burn bank notes!" Under her breath she added, "If he had any."

Mary frowned, uncertain as to the housekeeper's meaning. It surely couldn't be the only room! "Are you saying that this is the only habitable room at... I'm sorry, I forget the name of this estate."

"Wolfhaven! Ain't much of a haven though, now is it? Poor as church mice! And yes, it's the only habitable chamber, less I give up my own. I'll not be doing that for the likes of you, missy!" The old woman wagged a finger at her in warning. "I seen the way he looks at you. Don't go thinking to trap yourself a lord! You'll regret it if you do! A pauper with a title more like... and a temper. You could ask my poor mistress about that, if you could manage to get yourself to the churchyard where she's buried!"

Realization dawned on her. A slow, sinking feeling settled in the pit of her stomach as she considered the ramifications. "This is Lord Wolverton's chamber?"

"Aye! Where'd you think you were? Carlton Place?" Mrs. Epson cackled at her own jest, prompting the tea cups and plates to rattle on the tray she carried as she exited the room.

She hadn't just been alone in a bedchamber with him. She'd been alone in *his* bedchamber with him. Somehow, that made it far, far worse. Intimate. Scandalous. And if she were entirely honest, thrilling. What on earth did it say about the nature of her character that she was so drawn to a man who was reputed to be a killer? Perhaps she was more like her adoptive mother than she thought, attracted to men who were dangerous and unpredictable.

Thoughts racing to and fro, Mary seized on one thing. If it was his chamber, his things were there. *Papers. A journal or diary perhaps.* She might be able to suss out the truth about him and about the death of his wife. At the very least, she might get some inkling about what sort of man he truly was and whether or not she could trust him. Her own judgement was clouded by how handsome he was, by her own foolish romanticism. Benedict had often warned her against reading the ridiculous novels, as he called them, of Mrs. Radcliffe.

Getting out of bed, Mary crossed the room to the same panel she'd seen him come through earlier. Each step was an agony, but she had to know. Initially, she'd assumed it was a passage that connected rooms. But now, armed with more knowledge and a clearer picture of her surroundings, she understood that it was, in fact, his dressing room. Surely, if evidence was to be found, it would be uncovered there.

It wasn't her finest moment, Mary reasoned, as she flipped the small latch that would open the panel in the wall that led to what she assumed was his dressing room. No sooner had the thought crossed her mind than she dismissed any notion of guilt. She was entitled to know more about him. It was paramount to her own safety and wellbeing to ascertain the truth of his character while she was so completely vulnerable to him. *And she was a dirty, little snoop.*

Stepping into the small room, she was immediately assailed by the scent of pine and sandalwood. Following her nose, she found a bit of shaving soap on the washstand. He had no valet, so he'd stood there in that very spot, scraping the whiskers from his strong and chiseled jaw.

What had he been wearing? Had he stood there in his shirtsleeves, or had he completed the task bare chested? Or, heaven forbid, entirely nude?

Feeling warmer than was likely good for her given the tentative nature of her recovery, Mary moved away from the washstand and her own wayward thoughts. She could not allow herself to be distracted or swayed by how handsome he was or by the deep sadness she sensed within him. She focused instead on the heavy and intricately carved chest in the far corner. Comprised of a mixture of drawers and cabinets, it was a treasure trove of hiding spots. She meant to search every last one.

Easing the first drawer open, she found only cravats and neck-cloths. She couldn't imagine that Mrs. Epson had folded them so carefully. Who took care of such simple and mundane tasks for him? It was too farfetched to believe a gentleman, even one in such dire financial straits as Wolverton likely was, would stoop to doing such chores. Was there a woman who tended to him then? A lover, perhaps? The thought filled her with unnatural and unwelcome jealousy.

After going through them one by one and finding nothing but shockingly clean and elegantly starched neckcloths, she replaced them carefully. The next drawer was filled with smallclothes. Mary quickly shut that one back. She wouldn't search every drawer, after all. It was too impossibly intimate. Her cheeks flamed at the thought of it.

Opening one of the cabinets, she found a small box that contained cravat pins and watch fobs. They were simple and few in number, most of them gold or silver, and hardly any containing jewels at all. He must have sold the rest of them off, she realized. Replacing that box, she moved it aside and behind it found a small, leather pouch. It was surprisingly heavy as she lifted it.

"That contains my mother's pearls."

Mary screamed, nearly dropped the pouch and caught it at the last second before it tumbled to the floor. Turning, red-faced and equally red-handed, she met the mildly amused face of the very man she'd been spying on. "You must think me terribly impertinent."

He stepped into the room, retrieved the pouch from her hand, and rather than replacing it in the cabinet, opened it and showed her strands of perfectly matched pearls in a lovely shade of cream. "Only pearls. There are a few other pieces of her jewelry left, under lock and key in the home of a trusted friend. The debt collectors could take a lot of things, but I drew the line at these and some of her other more prized possessions."

"I'm terribly sorry," Mary stammered. "I shouldn't have been snooping—"

"Why ever not? I am a stranger to you, a man reported by all accounts to be guilty of murder. If you didn't snoop when given the opportunity, I would, quite frankly, be forced to question your intelligence," he said.

"Then you aren't angry?"

His lips firmed. "I am not angry at you, Miss Mason. I am angry at a situation that makes you feel as if you must search through my things in order to ascertain your own safety. I am assuming it was that and not simply idle curiosity that lured you from your sickbed?"

Mary frowned. "You are the strangest of men."

He smiled in a self-deprecating manner, not at all arguing the point. "What were you looking for?"

"Nothing, really!"

"Tell me, Mary Mason, what were you looking for?" He was insistent, his voice firm, but not angry. It wasn't a request, but a command. She heard it in his voice.

"Fine," she acquiesced. "I was looking for a journal or diary. I thought if I found such, I would have better insight into your character and my own safety while residing under your roof."

"And whether or not I murdered my wife," he added.

Mary said nothing, simply ducked her head as a blush stained her cheeks. She felt like such a terrible woman in that moment. He wasn't angry, but he was offended. And yet, he reacted to it the same as she had reacted to beatings as a child, as if they were commonplace. Every

day of his life, he was insulted and maligned, and she had just partici-
pated in it, albeit unwittingly.

He moved past her, reached into the very bottom drawer of the
chest and retrieved two slim, leather-bound volumes. "This one," he
held up the first, "was from my adolescence. Unless you have an
unquenchable thirst for reading terrible poetry written at great length
about my obsession with the baker's daughter, I'd advise skipping it
altogether or skimming only briefly."

Mary shook her head. "I was wrong to do this. I was wrong to go
through your things. You have been all that is kind and gracious to me,
my lord, and I must beg your forgiveness."

"This," he held up the second book and continued as if she hadn't
spoken, "is from the few months leading up to my marriage and it
stops short of the month when Helena was found murdered only yards
from here. You're welcome to read it at your leisure. But it will not
answer your question. I told you once, I did not kill her. I can say it
again, but—"

"I believe you," she said in a rush. "I believe that you didn't kill
her. And I don't think I'm in any danger here. Not from you."

Somehow, in the course of imploring him to stop, to halt acting as
if he were some sort of criminal who had to justify everything about
himself, she'd stepped closer to him. They were so close, in fact, that
she could smell the same spicy scent of shaving soap on him that she'd
noted earlier upon entering the dressing room. But it was different:
warmed by his skin and mingled with his natural scent, it became far
more heady and, if she were to admit it, far more tempting.

Mary's breath caught as he moved closer still. Anticipation bubbled within her as she waited with bated breath for his lips to touch
hers. But he made no move to kiss her. They stood there for the
longest time, an indecipherable tension building between them. The
only sound in the small room was that of their mingled breaths,
naturally in sync with one another's. When at last he moved, Mary
thought that it would happen—a kiss. The touch of his lips on hers
seemed so inevitable. Instead, he simply reached past her, placed the

items back in the open drawer of the wardrobe and then stepped back from her. Mary frowned, as confused by his actions as she was by the severity of her own disappointment.

"Since you are well enough to be up and about, we'll see about getting something more appropriate for you to wear. I'll go now and speak to Mrs. Epson about locating and airing out some of Helena's dresses that are surely still here," he said as he pushed the drawer closed, and abruptly turned on his heel and left.

She felt strangely bereft when he was gone. The room had been dwarfed by his presence and, now, alone in that dressing chamber, the space felt hollow and empty. It echoed her own feelings too closely for comfort. Mary started to leave but, as an afterthought, reached back and withdrew the two journals from the drawer. She would read them. She would read them—not because she required peace of mind about whether or not he was the killer others claimed him to be, but because she selfishly wished to know him.

Chapter Five

ALEX HAD SPOKEN with Mrs. Epson. The housekeeper had protested at first, refusing to do anything more for Miss Mason than she already had, which by his estimation was, in fact, very little. But after he'd insisted that it was comply or seek her sister's mercy, the woman had relented. Very shortly, Miss Mason would be properly clothed and, he hoped, sufficiently less tempting. That aching moment in his dressing chamber, when he'd come so dangerously close to giving in and kissing her delectable lips, had been a narrowly averted disaster. Mary Mason was too lovely for his peace of mind and far too innocent for his very carnal inclinations toward her. Her character, by turns emboldened and then painfully shy, was intriguing to him, as was her independent nature. Had he ever known a woman who would take off on her own to investigate her brother's identity or origins? No, he certainly had not. She'd defied convention and risked everything for someone she cared for. He'd hardly ever encountered such bravery in his life.

It was unfair to compare Mary to Helena. Helena would never compare favorably, after all. Cold, avaricious and, despite what he'd been led to believe prior to their marriage, not an innocent. The rumors of her affair with Albert Hamilton had been confirmed, and her continued coldness toward him had confirmed something else— she would only ever love the man that the world believed to be her half-brother. He'd overheard a conversation once between Helena and her maid about her having ended a pregnancy. When he'd questioned Helena about it, furiously thinking that it was his own child she'd so callously discarded, she'd waved her hand, dismissing it entirely. A youthful foible, she'd said, years ago. Her lack of feeling for the child had shocked him, so much so that he'd asked her how she could be so cold. It was a mistake he had never repeated. Her reply had left him utterly disgusted.

"I'm glad the little bastard has died. So much easier than lying about her age forever. Thankfully, my figure returned to normal and no one was the wiser."

There had been no hint of grief for the child, no hint of remorse for what she'd done to the child or to him. Her only concern had been for what her concerns always were centered upon—herself.

Their relationship, never very good, had disintegrated into nothing at that point. She'd gone to Bath rather than London, likely because it kept her closer to Hamilton and the nest of vipers she called family. He'd been happy to see the back of her. She'd never returned to Wolfhaven as far as he'd known, not until the day he'd discovered her body. He would not have even recognized her, badly beaten as she was, had it not been for the distinctive ring he'd placed on her finger upon their doomed betrothal.

He'd not grieved for Helena. It had saddened him, of course, that someone so young and beautiful should die so cruelly and that the beauty she had so cherished had been taken from her in death. Her life had been wasted it seemed, and their marriage, in the end, had been naught but a sham.

Unable to seek the solitude he usually found within his chambers, he retreated instead to his study. It, his bedchamber, the dining room and the great hall were the only fully opened and functional rooms in the house. He could foresee spending a great deal of time in his study in the near future, at least until Miss Mason was fully recovered and returned to the bosom of her family. He should write to her brother, but he wasn't quite ready to let her go just yet. He needed her to lead him to wherever it was she'd been running from that night. He needed to know if it was the same horrible place Helena had whispered of in her final moments.

In some ways, he thought, he was little better than her abductors. He had an agenda and Miss Mason was very much a part of it, unwitting and unwilling as she may be. But if he did not clear his name, if he did not find some way of proving his innocence and appealing to the court to overturn the fines levied against him, he'd live in penury forever. It would be the end of his family line, for no woman would ever consent to be married to a man both scandalous and poor. The weight of responsibility—to the title, to provide justice for Helena by seeing her true killer punished, to whatever other victims Harrelson might have, to Mary Mason and whatever torment she'd suffered at the hands of villains he'd failed to stop—pressed in on him.

To combat that as well as his unfortunate desire for a girl he could never and should never possess, and also to ease his own misery, Alex reached for the decanter of brandy that sat on his desk. It wasn't good brandy, but it would suffice. He needed to take the edge off before he saw her again, and before he played housebreaker in the dark of night. He needed to get in there before Harrelson's heirs began descending on the estate and picking it clean of any incriminating documents. If he could just trace Harrelson's illegal dealings back to Hamilton, Albert or Freddy, it wouldn't prove his innocence, but it would certainly raise questions and, perhaps, warrant a second look by the powers that be. Helena's closeness with her pseudo-brother had often been remarked upon and it was not without reason that his enemies had used Helena to exact their revenge. If nothing else, it would, perhaps, open doors for him socially once more that would allow him to further his business interests and see to the replenishing of the family coffers.

Savoring the slow burn of the liquid with each small sip, he contemplated what he knew thus far. Helena's dying words had painted a picture he couldn't quite fathom. She'd spoken insensibly, her words garbled and difficult to understand. But she had talked of other girls, locked in tiny cells and crying in fear and desperation. It had only been minutes from the time he'd found her while out for a morning ride until she'd breathed her last in his arms. She had never managed to identify the "man" in question. Now, he'd discovered Miss Mason, fleeing for her very life, in the woods not very far from where he'd found Helena's battered and bruised body.

Albert Hamilton had arrived before her body was even cold, proof that he'd been nearby. Despite their strange relationship, his reaction had been a rather puzzling non-reaction, as he and Helena had always been remarkably close. Of course, rumor had reared its ugly head then about the nature of their relationship. It had been hotly denied by Albert. Alex no longer wondered if it was true. He knew it. And given how quick Freddy had been to lay the blame for her death at Alex's door, he knew it, too. Freddy and Albert had been the favored nephews of Harrelson and had often spent time at Harrelson's estate, which neighbored Wolfhaven. At one time, he'd pondered whether or not Harrelson had also been Helena's lover. There were more questions at every turn than answers. It seemed for the past year and a half he'd been digging in the sand, trying and failing to adequately unearth the truth.

Harrelson's estates were no more profitable than his own. Yet, Harrelson had a steady stream of income that could not otherwise be accounted for. A well-placed bribe and numerous potent beverages had made Harrelson's man of affairs quite talkative. Even he had no notion of where the steady stream of cash came from. It stood to reason then that it was from nefarious activities. Blackmail, of a certain variety, was a gentleman's crime and certainly not outside the realm of possibility. But given Helena's dying words, Miss Mason's abduction and reappearance on Harrelson's estate, it seemed only likely that the man was peddling unwilling flesh instead of simply secrets. Had both Freddy and Albert Hamilton been a part of it? For that matter, had Helena? He could not say with any conviction that she would have had any moral compunction about it. Even her deathbed confession might not have been altruistic in nature, but rather hedging her bets on the Almighty's forgiveness.

Fortified by second-rate brandy, Alex placed his glass on the desktop then turned to exit the room. He would see Miss Mason medicated once more and then it would be full dark and time to engage in his own criminal activity. His window of opportunity to explore Harrelson's study at leisure was limited. It would only be a matter of days before the heirs descended to pick the place clean like so many crows.

Climbing the stairs, he felt very much like he was climbing the gallows. Every moment he spent in her company reminded him of just how far he had fallen and how far he would have to go in order to be free of his current burdens. But she made him long for that freedom as nothing else had. Miss Mary Mason, with her golden hair and dark, soulful eyes made him long for things best forgotten.

He needed an ally. From above, Mrs. Epson's wailing reached him and a heavy sigh passed his lips. He needed one night where he did not feel plagued by women—living, dead, or currently precariously employed by him.

3rd of November, 1819

Wolverton,

We are neighbors, but more than that, I feel that we are friends in spite of vastly different lifestyles. It is because of that friendship and our long acquaintance that I am writing this letter to you. It is not an easy thing for me to do and undertaking it involved a significant degree of consideration. Upon reflection, I have reached the conclusion that my silence will do more harm than good and, to that end, I am informing you that you must call your wife back to Wolfhaven Hall immediately. Due to my own ill health, I have quit London for Bath and in so doing, have become aware of very ugly tales spreading throughout polite society.

These last weeks in town, your wife has been at the center of very scandalous and damaging rumors. If I thought these rumors were unfounded, I would likely have said nothing. But sadly, there appears to be truth to them. Normally, I have little care for how married ladies carry on, as that is their husbands' prerogative to deal with and not my own. But the nature of her behavior could have disastrous consequences for you, my friend, and any heirs born of your union.

Prior to the marriage, we had discussed the lady's relationship with her elder half-brother who is, in fact, only her stepbrother. The scurrilous gossip was discounted by assurances from the lady's family that they were naught but lies created by social rivals. But those rumors have resurfaced along with the additional conjecture about the lack of actual kinship between the siblings. That was recently confirmed to me by your wife's own mother. I digress. The rumors that abounded prior to your marriage, that Helena's relationship with her brother (by law at any rate), Albert Hamilton, are true, my friend. She has been caught out with him in a manner that is nothing short of ruinous. They are trying desperately to cover it up and say that it was only a familial embrace, and not the passionate clutch that is being reported by mean-spirited gossips. But I know the person who laid eyes on them in that position, Lord Wolverton, and I must tell you that it is true. There was talk of charging Hamilton with incest, but Harrelson, the uncle, has managed to sweep that under the carpets.

You had best call your bride home, my friend, and do it soon. I cannot think how this will go for you if you do not. She is on the verge of calamity and will take you with her if you do not get her in hand.

Lord A.

It was an informal note, dated only weeks before Lady Wolverton had been murdered. Mary knew that Lord Wolverton considered Lord Ambrose to be a friend, so much so that he had "borrowed" the man's identity at the outset of their acquaintance. The letter, tucked into the journal she had taken from his dressing room, proved that the man was, indeed, a true friend. A notorious rake and libertine in his own rights, it seemed that he was not lacking honor in that regard, at least.

It was, unfortunately, a damning bit of correspondence, for it established a motive for Lady Wolverton's murder that pointed very solidly at her own husband. Why would he have given her access to the books if he knew they would not clear him of suspicion? It was a conundrum and one that Mary had no answer for.

A loud knock sounded upon the door and startled Mary like a guilty child sneaking sweets or forbidden books to her bed. Closing the book and tucking it beneath the pillow, she tried to pass for at least slightly innocent as Mrs. Epson entered the room.

The woman carried an armful of gowns and the necessary under-things to go with them. She deposited the lot of them on the trunk at the foot of the bed. "His lordship," the words were uttered with a sneer, "insisted that I bring you some of the mistress' things so that you might be properly dressed. Tis a crime and a shame that such things would be wasted on the likes of you. Sadly, she was too fashionable a lady to have garments in her wardrobe such as you'd deserve."

"Mrs. Epson, the gowns will only be borrowed until I can return to Bath and retrieve things of my own," Mary vowed, as she rose from the bed and picked up one of the simple gowns. Unless, of course, Mrs. Simms had sold them to cover lack of payment on her room. That was an unfortunate and very real possibility.

Holding the gown up in front of her, she saw immediately that there would be a problem. Apparently, the late Lady Wolverton had been significantly taller than she was. "I will need to take these up, I fear!"

"I won't have it!" the old woman shouted. "An upstart trollop like you wearing my mistress' things is bad enough! I won't have you cutting them to shreds for it!"

The housekeeper was going to be impossibly difficult, but then, Mrs. Epson seemed to thrive on being difficult. Mary eyed the pool of fabric at her feet and was tempted to simply make do, but it was impossible. It was miles too long for her and her considerable lack of natural grace was already compromised by her heavily-bandaged feet. Her height, or lack thereof, had been the bane of her existence for as long as she could remember. It was the lot in life for any very short girl destined for hand-me-downs, as she had always been.

"If you could bring me a sewing basket, I can take up the hem—"

"I will not!" The housekeeper was shrieking, her voice rising to the rafters. "He said you could wear the mistress' clothes. He never said you could have them remade to suit you! You'll wear them as they are or run naked through the halls for all I care! You're not fit to touch those garments; you're not!"

"I only mean to raise the hem, Mrs. Epson. I won't even remove the excess fabric, just tuck it in a bit—"

"I won't have it," the housekeeper shouted again. "I see what you are, missy! Dirty, thieving, grasping... finagling your way into this house thinking to trap yourself a fine lord! More the fool you for he hasn't two pence to rub together! My dear sweet mistress, Lady Wolverton, was too good for the likes of him from the outset... and what did it get her but murdered by his hand! I ought to be hoping you do manage to ensnare him. Then he could rid the world of you and they'd hang him for certain this time!"

Mary didn't bother offering another protest. In many ways, Mrs. Epson was just like her adoptive mother had been. Hateful, with a mood that could shift from simply sour, to vicious and biting within seconds—there was simply no reasoning with her. Offering further protests or assurances would only invite more abuse and accusations. Better to simply let the women vent her spleen and then move on. She'd ask Lord Wolverton to find the sewing box for her or have him instruct Mrs. Epson to do so when next she saw him.

As if her thoughts had summoned him, there was a knock upon the chamber door. It opened inward and his dark countenance appeared, glowering at the recalcitrant housekeeper. "What are you squawking about, Mrs. Epson?"

The housekeeper whirled on him, her movements deceptively spry for one so ancient and bent. "This high and mighty miss thinks she can just go cutting up her ladyship's gowns—"

"Her ladyship hardly has need of them now, does she, Mrs. Epson?"

The statement was expressed so coldly, and with such complete lack of emotion that Mary was taken aback. She'd been entirely convinced earlier in the dressing room that he was not guilty. But now, having read the letter from Lord Ambrose and seeing this coldness in him, she was forced to wonder once more if he was truly her savior, or if he was just another villain.

He continued, looking pointedly at the gowns and then at her, but speaking to the housekeeper. "Lady Wolverton was at least five inches taller and a stone heavier than Miss Mason. I daresay the gowns could use some cutting up if she's to have any use of them," he said simply.

The housekeeper's lips firmed into a mutinous line. "It ain't right! Gutter trash like her wearing the gowns of a fine lady like—"

"Enough!"

His voice thundered through the room, echoing off the stone walls with such force that Mary couldn't help but flinch. It was clear that he had a fierce temper when pressed and Mrs. Epson had clearly taken it upon herself to press him beyond reason. How often did the woman push him to such displays of anger?

"Mrs. Epson," he began, his tone even and belying the angry outburst that had just erupted from him. "When I brought Helena, Lady Wolverton, to this house, you referred to her as a high-flyer, fast, loose, and every other insult that you could hurl at a lady of quality short of calling her a whore. It is only in death that she has suddenly become eligible for sainthood! Now, here you are hurling similar insults at Miss Mason with little to no provocation. You may heap your abuse upon me at will, but you will not abuse those who are partaking of hospitality beneath this roof."

"You don't know a thing about her! She could be some doxy straight from the wharf or a camp follower—"

The earl held up his hand and Mrs. Epson fell silent immediately. "I've had enough. More than enough, Mrs. Epson. If you wish to remain here, you will remember your place and not speak to or about guests in anything less than a respectful manner."

"And where would I go?" the housekeeper challenged.

"I neither know nor care. Your sister has made it clear you would not be welcomed by her, likely because you've been as foul to her as to everyone else you've encountered. But I will toss you out without a thought and without a reference, though given my state, that could be a stroke of luck for you. Either hush or leave. Those are your only choices. Do you understand, Mrs. Epson?"

The old woman glared for a second longer and then abruptly cut her eyes to the side, glaring in Mary's direction. "Aye, my lord. I understand perfectly."

"Then you will retrieve whatever items Miss Mason requires in order to make the gowns more functional for her and not another word will be said about it."

Mrs. Epson didn't speak, just nodded and abruptly left, pushing past Lord Wolverton and into the hall. Alone with him once more, Mary wasn't quite sure where to even begin. She could only think of that tense moment in the dressing chamber earlier. She was sure he'd meant to kiss her and she was even more sure that she'd wanted him to. Now, it seemed as if that moment was impossibly distant and this cold, angry man before her was a complete stranger. Humiliated by the interaction with Mrs. Epson and all the atrocious things the woman had said about her in front of him, her face flamed.

"I apologize," he said stiffly. "It's not enough that the accommodations I offer you are so meager and that my staff is beyond ill-trained—"

Mary, after a gasp at his skewed version of events, interrupted him while shaking her head furiously. "You have nothing to apologize for, Lord Wolverton. You saved me, after all. You've provided shelter, clothing, medical care, and all without any recompense... I have invaded your life, your home, and brought nothing but upheaval with my presence. It is I who should apologize to you," she said.

He stared at her for the longest moment, his expression inscrutable. At last, he ducked his head and cleared his throat. "I must go out for a bit. Can you use the medicinal herbs on your own or do you require my assistance?"

"I can strike a match to tinder as well as anyone, my lord. I'll be fine. You should attend to whatever it is you need to do without any further worry for me," she offered as reassuringly as possible.

"Then I will leave you to your sewing. I am glad that you will be able to make use of the gowns, Miss Mason. It's far better than having them moldering in a trunk," he said.

Mary watched him turn to leave. She wasn't quite sure what prompted it, but impulsively she blurted out, "Be careful, my lord!"

"Excuse me?"

"I just have a feeling that whatever errand it is that you're leaving for... well, I fear that it might be dangerous and I—well, I would prefer to have you return in one piece," she admitted lamely.

He didn't make a jest at her expense or make light of her concerns. He simply regarded her in that very serious way he had before nodding once. "I shall endeavor to be careful, Miss Mason. And I will see you on the morrow."

Mary watched him leave and, once more, seated herself on the chair before the fire. After a few moments, Mrs. Epson came in and brought the sewing basket, departing immediately. She didn't grumble under her breath, but she was certainly no friendlier than she had been before. When the housekeeper had come and gone, Mary took the gown she'd first picked up and set to work. She was no seamstress, but even she could manage to hem a skirt. At the very least, she'd have something to wear the next time she saw him that wasn't a nightrail. It would put them on slightly more even footing, she hoped, and make her feel like less of a gauche fool.

Chapter Six

ALEX KEPT TO the trees. He'd avoided the road altogether and had, instead, taken his mount through the woods. The estate was quiet. Many of the servants were taking advantage of having no master for the interim and had made their way into the village. They were drinking at the inn, leaving the estate largely unmanned. Those few that remained were cozied up with whatever willing partner they could find for the night or had likely made free with Harrelson's wine cellar and would be of no trouble to him. He'd elected to watch the kitchens as a means of gauging whether or not it was safe to enter. As the last of the lights were extinguished and the house went fully dark, he knew he'd made the right choice.

Moving stealthily along the perimeter of the house, he made his way to the double glass doors on the terrace that would provide entrance to Harrelson's study. Removing the small leather packet from his pocket, he opened it to reveal the small collection of lock picking tools he'd procured. It wasn't as easy as his new employee had led him to believe. It took several minutes before the lock finally gave. With a soft snick, it released and door opened inward.

After pausing for a moment to make sure no one sounded the alarm, Alex let himself into the room. It was quiet and dark, the hearth cold and Harrelson's papers still spread across the desk. No one had touched anything in their employer's absence. Closing the door behind him, he drew the curtains tight. Using the small throw that had been draped over the chair before the fire, he stuffed it against the door to the hall so that the light wouldn't be seen. Satisfied that his snooping would be free of discovery and interruption, he lit the taper on the desk and began examining all the paperwork that was readily visible. Bills of sale, bills from his tailor and wine merchant – there was nothing of any significant importance, but it did appear that the man had left in a hurry. The room, aside from the desk, was tidy, but not in the way of having been cleaned by a servant. The brandy decanter was placed neatly on the tray. The small crystal dish with the remnants of a cheroot in it was free from any ash or dust around it. Yet, the book-shelves were slightly dusty, almost as if servants were forbidden free entrance to the room. Why would he limit their access to the room if not to hide whatever misdeeds he was about?

Alex reached for the top desk drawer, but he found it locked. That was promising, he thought. Anything Harrelson needed to keep locked away was likely just was he was in search of. Resorting to his trusty lock picks once more, the drawer lock proved much more stubborn than that of the exterior door. Finally, after numerous attempts and several quiet curses, the lock sprang free. Any keen observer would be able to see that the lock had been tampered with, but he could only hope no one would be examining it too closely. Inside the drawer were bundled letters and several slim, leather-bound volumes. Those he would examine at his leisure after returning home. Each of the subsequent drawers yielded some amount of evidence that would require continued and careful perusal. But in the very bottom drawer, he found something that made his heart race. It was a simple locket that he'd given to Helena on the eve of their wedding. Lifting it out, he examined it closely, including the inscription. *With affection, Wolverton, 7th of May, 1818.* The bride gift he'd presented her with was inscribed in such an impersonal way it offered proof enough that the marriage had been a disastrous mistake.

The presence of the locket implicated Harrelson as nothing else could. To that end, Alex carefully replaced it in the small wooden box it had been stored in. It would remain there and if he had a remarkable turn of luck, there it would stay until he could use the remainder of the evidence gathered to convince the Lord High Steward to consider his appeal.

Using the same tools as before, he relocked the drawer and had just gathered up his finds when he heard a noise outside the door. Cursing, he extinguished the taper, stuffed the lot of it inside his coat and then quickly exited through the terrace doors he'd used to gain entrance. He would have to wait until he could get back to the safety and relative seclusion of Wolfhaven Hall before he could inspect any of it.

Outside, he pressed himself flat against the building and waited. It didn't take long. A footman opened the terrace doors, peered outside and, seeing no one, stepped back inside, locking the door tightly behind him. When he heard the door close softly and the lock click into place, he breathed a heartfelt sigh at having not been discovered. After a heartbeat had passed, and he could be sure that he wasn't being observed, Alex dashed for the trees and his waiting mount.

Through the woods, from Harrelson's manor house to his own, was only a five mile ride. Making that ride while constantly waiting for the hounds to be released by Harrelson's lackeys to fall in behind him in full pursuit made it seem infinitely longer. When he'd finally reached the shelter of Wolfhaven, only then did Alex begin to relax. By nature, he was not a rule breaker, nor one given to bouts of criminal activity. He hadn't the heart or the stomach for it, he feared.

Entering the house, it was quiet. Mrs. Epson would long be abed and he could only hope for the sake of what little of his sanity remained that Miss Mason would be abed as well. Another charged encounter with her, and he was not entirely certain he could maintain what little claim he had to the title of gentleman. He'd come perilously close to breaking his own rules that afternoon. Finding her in his dressing room, pilfering through his belongings, hadn't angered him. Rather, he'd been impressed by her resourcefulness, by her determination to take control in her current weakened state, instead of simply trusting that total strangers had her best interests at heart. Her sense of self-preservation and her will were both formidable and quite awe inspiring. Life had become of very little value to him and he realized it was in large part because he hadn't been focused on living it. Instead, he'd become mired in the misery of his situation and the driving need to right the wrongs visited upon him. It had robbed him of enjoyment of even the most simple of pleasures.

In short, Miss Mason was a distraction and try as he might, he was having a very difficult time bringing himself to mind. It was a very dangerous thing to find himself longing for her company, wondering what she might have to say on any given topic or, in general, feeling compelled to simply look upon her remarkably lovely countenance.

She would be well enough soon to lead him to where she had been held, if she could locate it. Then he would see her returned to her brother and put her from his mind forever. If he should find himself missing her or longing for her company, he need only remind himself of how disastrous any connection to him would be for a respectable or gently-bred young woman.

Forcing himself to attend to his present task and push any thoughts of Miss Mason aside, he lit several tapers on his desk and then stoked the banked fire in the hearth. Once the blaze had roared to life once more, he retreated to his desk and began examining the items he'd managed to abscond with. The small packet of letters he set aside. Those, he'd pore through carefully and one at a time. It was the small, leather-bound volumes that intrigued him. They had the look of ledgers: whether they tracked the illegal activities themselves, or simply the ensuing income from them, remained to be seen.

Opening the first, he found a series of columns. There were dates, abbreviations and numbers as well as locations, typically by city, but sometimes by neighborhood or street. Next to each one was a sum of money. He was pages deep in the journal before a single notation made him stop, aghast at what he read. The line, scrawled carelessly in the margin, stated, *The youngest and only boy died of fever. The receiving family thusly paid half.*

Alex read it again, several times, just to be certain he had not misinterpreted it. Someone had paid for children. To what end, he did not know, but that much was irrefutable. Flipping through page after page with growing horror, Alex figured they numbered well into the hundreds if not the thousands. Did each of those notations represent someone to whom Harrelson had plied his trade? Had each of those transactions recorded in that book represented the sale of one human being to another?

Based on that single notation, he could only believe it did. It was the only indication in the entire book of what the source of the payments was. Given what he'd seen of Mary Mason, and what his employee had discovered in Bath about missing girls, it wasn't simply unwanted children being sold to families. It appeared Harrelson had made a fortune for himself or, based on the numbers he'd seen, several fortunes, by fulfilling whatever desires people had. If they wanted children to complete their family, he provided them. If they wanted young women, or even young boys and girls to do with as they pleased, that was provided as well.

Sickened, filled with a kind of dread that he hadn't felt since the day he'd discovered Helena, Alex closed the book. Even expecting to find such crimes had not prepared him for the scale of them. The sheer quantity of people that Harrelson had enslaved and bartered was mind-boggling. And there, but for the grace of God and her own remarkable ingenuity, Mary Mason would have been counted amongst their number. She had managed to escape when hundreds of others had not. If that was not a testament to just how unique and industrious she was, nothing else could be.

With what he considered to be irrefutable proof of Harrelson's crimes, there were three burning questions left to answer. Was Hamilton involved? What had Helena discovered or done that had prompted them to end her so brutally? Had she been involved? It wasn't out of the question, he thought. The very coldness of her nature had often left him confused and uncomfortable in her presence. He simply didn't know how to speak to her when she was demanding that he raise rents on tenants who were barely able to feed and clothe their children. Self-serving and without any compassion for others, if it had benefited Helena in some way, she would not have balked at it.

Alex leaned back in his chair and scrubbed his hands over his face. What on earth had his late wife gotten herself involved in?

IT WAS RESTLESSNESS, and if she were entirely honest, there was also a healthy dose of insatiable curiosity that had prompted her to leave the relative safety of the chamber she'd been given. She wanted to see the rest of the house, or as much of it as was open. There was a part of her that hoped seeing it would provide more insight into the very enigmatic man who had rescued her. But as Mary crept silently down the stairs, she realized she'd greatly overestimated the degree of her recovery. Every step was a misery. Her poor feet were beyond abused. Even bandaged as they were, the hard stone beneath them seemed to inflame every scrape, cut and bruise she'd amassed during her escape. She was too far from her chamber to turn back. Unaided, she would likely wind up in a crying heap on the floor of the hall, if she even managed to get that far. The ground floor and the promise of a chair or settee she might rest her poor feet upon were too great to ignore. Besides, the indignity of plopping her bottom on the stairs and waiting to be rescued, yet again, was mortifying.

Clinging to the banister, she limped the last few steps down and whimpered as her feet touched the colder marble of the foyer floor. There were no chairs to be had in the foyer but, earlier, Mrs. Epson had indicated that the library was still a room in use. And if Lord Wolverton was still out for whatever late night assignation it was that had taken him from the safety of his home, perhaps she could regroup in there enough that she might, once more, be able to face traversing the stairs. She might very well have to crawl back to her chamber. *His chamber.*

Easing her way across the hall, in a pathetic shuffling sort of limp, she managed to open the door. With several pained steps, she entered the room and closed the door behind her. Leaning heavily against it, she took a fortifying breath and closed her eyes as she considered what to do next.

"It's a bit late for an evening stroll, Miss Mason... and you're hardly in any condition for it."

She squeaked more than screamed at the gently-voiced admonishment. Clutching her throat, her eyes traveled the room until they came to rest upon him. He was seated in a chair near the hearth, half-hidden from view. She glared at the half of his face that was visible to her. His profile was too perfect, too appealing, and it only intensified her dislike of him in that moment. The man had the ability to discomfit her in so many ways, she didn't know if she was coming or going.

"I thought you'd gone out," she finally managed.

"Did you feel the need to snoop through my desk as well as my dressing chamber?" he demanded, though there was more amusement than censure in his tone.

Mary blushed and prayed the room was dim enough to camouflage it. "I only wanted to move about. I've been cramped in the same room for days and thought I might take a bit of air... I hadn't realized how much my feet would hurt from such a short distance. I came in here to rest before attempting the trek back to my—to your—to the bedchamber," she finished lamely. It seemed imprudent to continuously remind either of them that she was currently occupying his bed, regardless of the innocuous circumstances for it.

He said nothing for the longest time, but she felt his very serious regard of her. The weight of his gaze upon her was an almost tangible thing. The silence stretched between them, taut but not uncomfortable. Expectant might have been a better description, she thought. Every moment she spent in his presence made her feel as if something unknown and foreign were about to happen, as if, perhaps, it should. Perhaps, it was only wishful thinking on her part, the belief that there was more to their interactions, some deeper meaning in the long looks that passed between them.

Abruptly, he rose from the chair and approached her. Mary didn't shrink back. She had no fear of him. Despite her earlier misgivings and doubts, and even what she'd read in the letter from Lord Ambrose and in his journal, when she was in his presence, it was impossible to believe that he was capable of what he'd been accused of. Whatever he was about, she had absolutely no question that she was in no danger from him. Regardless of her suspicion during their strange meeting in the woods, she felt very certain that Lord Wolverton meant her no harm whatsoever.

Mary hadn't expected that he would simply sweep one arm behind her shoulders and the other beneath her knees and lift her to him. Cradled against his chest, her lips parted on a sharp exhale of shock. "What are you doing?" she demanded. "You must put me down, Lord Wolverton!"

"I fully intend to, Miss Mason," he replied, his tone reasonable and even somewhat amused at her scandalized tone. "On that settee... right over there. You should not have walked so far. No doubt, some of the more serious cuts have reopened and will require further bandaging. I'll see to it before carrying you back to *your* bedchamber."

A blush stained her cheeks and she was thankful for the dim lighting of the room that would, hopefully, conceal it. For that flush could not be laid at the door of embarrassment. Rather, it was her awareness of him, of how firm his chest felt against her, how very strong his arms were as he carried her, of how tenderly he held her. Would every touch from him be as tender? It was wicked of her, but there was a part of her, the same part that had stayed awake until all hours of the night consuming every novel by Mrs. Radcliffe, that hoped he would simply ravish her. She wanted him to kiss her as if he had no control over himself, as if he were starved for it. Rather than implore him to do just that, Mary lowered her gaze from the hard, firm line of his jaw and confessed something far more innocent, "I am sorry to be such a burden, Lord Wolverton. I truly did not think my feet were so gravely injured still after so many days."

"They were terribly bruised," he said. "And bleeding. I don't know how you ran as far and as fast as you did that night. I am rather in awe of you, Miss Mason. You have no idea how remarkable you truly are."

"Do not be awed by me, my lord. Fear is a great motivator."

He placed her gently on the settee in a reclining position. Then he knelt beside it to examine her bandages. "Tell me what you feared, Miss Mason. What did you know or, at the very least, suspect, about the fate that awaited you at the hands of your captors."

It was a test. She was certain of it. Looking down, noting how the firelight danced over the planes and angles of his handsome face, she could see from his expression that he was gauging her response, but for what reason she did not know. "I may be innocent, Lord Wolverton—and whatever you may think of me, I am—my brother has moved heaven and earth to protect me in a world where innocence is all too often sacrificed... but I am not naïve. I know those men intended to sell me. Likely to a man who had paid them to procure someone who met specific standards. If not that, then to an abbess."

His expression went from shock to resignation very quickly. "No, Miss Mason, it would appear you are not naïve. How is it that your brother has allowed you to gain such knowledge while retaining your innocence? Who is this man you are so devoted to?"

"Benedict Mason... he owns a gaming hell in London. That is where I have lived with him for the past five years, since I completed school. I wanted to work as a governess. It's what I trained to do, after all. But, he would not have it. He insisted that I simply remain with him and run his house, as it is."

"He permitted you to live in a gaming hell?"

There was censure in his voice then, she heard it clear as a bell. But it was not for her so much as it was for Benedict. She would tolerate many things, but never someone to demean her brother in such a manner. "He's a very good brother, Lord Wolverton," she insisted, firmly and with great conviction. "I cannot tell you how much he has sacrificed and how very hard he has worked that we would be able to escape the poverty and the abuse we suffered from our adoptive parents. You've no notion of the cruelty we suffered at their hands and how, all too often, Benedict would spark their ire and take a beating from them just so that I might avoid one. He has always taken care of me. Perhaps it was foolish of me, but I thought that if I could find his true family for him, I might be able to repay him for all that he has given me!" She paused, took a deep breath, and then continued much more calmly, but with just as much certainty, "Yes, I live in an apartment above a gaming hell, and during the hours of operation there are numerous guards posted there so that no one should ever breach the sanctity of our home. It may be unorthodox, but we've only ever had one another. And I'd rather flaunt tradition and convention than to abandon someone who has only ever cared for me. Can you not understand that?"

"I cannot," he admitted, his voice rather strained and his expression was impossible for her to decipher. "For I've never had anyone so devoted to me. Not since my mother died, at any rate, Miss Mason. I find on that score, I am rather envious of what you and your brother have."

Mary frowned. Had he been so deprived then? Had even his wife not shown him that sort of devotion? "How old were you when you lost your mother?"

"A boy, eight years old. She had been sick for most of my childhood. I think she had always been of frail health and, though it was cautioned against, she was determined to give my father more children. Alas, she did not succeed and her efforts cost her life."

"I am very sorry for your loss, Lord Wolverton. It is hard to imagine, having only my brother, what I would do if he were gone. No person should be fully devoid of loved ones in their life."

"It appears we have both had our share of misfortune, Miss Mason, but we have both been blessed to know people in our lives who have loved us unconditionally." He fell silent, staring at her intently.

Mary felt the weight of his gaze. It was almost a tangible thing, as if he had touched her, though he had not but to carry her to the settee. She fervently wished that he would, that he might wrap his arms around her and hold her. Why she longed for such a thing from someone she barely knew she could not fathom. But it seemed from the instant of her waking, there had been a connection between them, an attraction that she could not deny, even when she knew that she should.

Finally, he looked away, his gaze drifting to the fire that burned low in the hearth. "I must ask you very difficult questions now, and I pray you will answer them to the best of your ability without being too overset by them. It pertains to your time in captivity."

Mary drew a shuddering breath. She hated to think of it, but it was very important to him or he would not have asked. That, she was certain of. "I will answer any question that I can as honestly I can, Lord Wolverton. For much of the earlier days of it, I was heavily-drugged, I believe. I remember, at various times, they would hold a foul smelling cloth over my mouth... usually before moving me from one location to the next. My memory of the entire ordeal is somewhat indistinct at best, or utterly absent at its worst."

"Were there other women, children, anyone else where you were held?"

Mary frowned. "Not that I'm aware. If there were others, I certainly never saw them. How I hate to think I might have run off and left them behind! But I was so terribly frightened then that I never even thought to look." She paused, shaking her head to clear it of the troubling thought that she might have abandoned others to the same fate that had awaited her. Scrambling for any inkling of memory that might offer ease, the one thing that offered her some small amount of peace had been the tomb-like quiet of the place she had been held. Surely, she would have heard something if there had been others!

"It is possible you were alone there," he said, as if sensing her distress.

"I heard nothing while I was held in that cave that would have led me to believe I was not alone in there... no voices or comings and goings of the single guard except for when he approached my cell, for lack of a better word. I would have heard something, don't you think? Heaven knows, it was certainly a circumstance to inspire weeping and there is no other sound that carries so keenly."

His eyes narrowed at her description. One of his hands moved, hovering over hers for a moment as if he meant to offer comfort. At the last moment, he withdrew it out of an abundance of caution and, perhaps, in concession to the fact that they had already crossed enough of the boundaries of propriety without sliding further down that very slippery slope. "It was a cave? You're certain of that?"

"The walls were very rough stone and quite damp, the floor dirt and rock. There were tunnels surrounding it, so I would imagine it is a series of caves," Mary replied, recalling the small, dungeon-like space.

"Or perhaps a mine?" The question was posed thoughtfully, as if he had already discovered the answer and was simply awaiting confirmation.

Mary's eyes widened. "I hadn't considered it, but that seems a more likely description. There was a heavy, wooden door over the small chamber where I was held. It was kept locked at all times... I managed, through some degree of trickery, to lure the guard inside. There had been a loose stone on the floor and I used that to bash him about the head and flee. I feel terrible if I've left anyone behind there."

"I think I know the place where you were kept, Miss Mason... and if you would accompany me on the morrow, we will investigate it further and determine whether or not I am correct. We will also be certain that no one has been left behind in your courageous escape."

It filled her with dread but, under the circumstances, she could not refuse. "Why do you think there were others, Lord Wolverton?"

"I have reason to believe that a gentleman by the name Lord Wendell Harrelson was behind your abduction. The mine I spoke of is on his property."

"Surely, you have greater reason than the location of the mine itself to think he is involved!"

"He was an unscrupulous man, Miss Mason, and has lived the entirety of his life taking advantage of others. I fear he is guilty of a great number of crimes—blackmail, I know for certain. Abduction and the selling of poor, unfortunate women and children into slavery now very much appears to be another of his heinous actions. He was the uncle of my late wife, and may have supported her in certain ill-advised affairs that surely led to her death. In effect, he was a murder-er, even if the killing blows were never struck by his hand."

"Was?" she asked. "Am I to assume that this man is no longer of this world?"

Lord Wolverton rose then and moved away from her, crossing to the fireplace. "Lord Harrelson has died, whether by his own hand or Madame Zula's, or if, perhaps, they were both murdered by another unknown person, remains to be seen. He was found in her home and the both of them had succumbed to poison."

Mary gasped at that, a little stunned and terribly frightened. "I must warn the lady I think is Benedict's mother. If Lord Harrelson and Madame Zula were murdered by some unknown person instead of it being a case of murder and suicide, she could be in danger."

"About your brother, Miss Mason... I cannot say for certain if he is still in Bath, but he was some days ago. I had hired a man to watch Lord Harrelson and, in so doing, he found himself near Madame Zula's home. Your brother was canvasing the area with a miniature of you, looking for anyone who might know where you were. At the time, my employee did not know you had been rescued and brought here. We have no direction for your brother in Bath, but I wonder if, perhaps, he has not already gone back to London hoping you would turn up there."

Mary shook her head. "No, I don't think he would have. I think Benedict is likely still turning the city of Bath upside down in his attempts to find me. How far into the distant past do Lord Harrelson's crimes extend, my lord?"

"I'm not yet sure, Miss Mason," he admitted. "I have not had an opportunity to examine all of the evidence yet."

Mary frowned. "You have proof, then? It isn't simply conjecture that he's committed these acts?"

Lord Wolverton nodded. "I found notations and records in a ledg-er I retrieved from his home tonight that indicated to me that he may have made it his business to procure individuals for others."

"He sold them to houses of ill repute, didn't he?" Part of her wanted to think that was the only source of profit for the vile man. But Mary was a realist and she knew that the likelihood of encountering not one but two kidnappers in her short life was limited, indeed. It was far more likely, especially if Lord Harrelson had been engaging in those activities for some time, that he was responsible for placing her and Benedict with the Masons at the outset of their respective stories.

"Amongst other things," he said sadly. "Miss Mason, it is my belief that he also made a habit of procuring children for those individuals who were incapable of having their own, or for those who had an unnatural affection for children. You stated that you weren't entirely certain that your adoptive parents had been entrusted with your care willingly. You came to Bath to investigate what you thought might be your brother's true identity because you believed he had been taken from his true family. Is it possible that Lord Harrelson's activities extend back so far that he might have been involved not in just your current situation, but also that which brought you and your brother together to start?"

Mary's heart began to pound. She'd researched and read every account of the abduction of Lord Vale, even including the descriptions of his abductors. The man she'd encountered outside of Madame Zula's house could very well have been one of them, but she had not made the connection at that time. How could she, after all? Now, however, all of the pieces were falling into place and painting a picture that was rife with scandal and wickedness on a scale she could not begin to fathom. "It is possible, Lord Wolverton, though I confess that it never occurred to me to consider the possibility until now. I need to see that book... I must."

"I will share it with you. But not tonight, I think. We are both exhausted and you are overwrought. It is clear to me that you are not yet well enough to have heard what I imparted to you tonight, nor were you well enough to discuss the details of your captivity. Your voice is hoarse and your breathing has become much more labored. You will need more of those herbs before sleeping. It was unforgivable of me to make you revisit such painful and traumatic events so soon."

"I am not fragile, my lord. Despite my recent illness and in spite of my rather small stature which often makes people, specifically men, underestimate me, I am not weak, fragile, broken, or in need of being coddled!"

He looked at her oddly for a moment, the silence drawing taut between them. "I know that you are not weak or fragile. But I also know that you did very nearly die, and that alone bears consideration, Miss Mason. I will not have a relapse of your illness on my conscience. Indeed, I lack the room to bear the weight of responsibility for yet another woman's death."

Mary had nothing to say to that. He'd denied killing his wife, and she believed with all her heart that he was innocent of the crime. Yet it was clear from his words that he still blamed himself for her death.

"I am very tired, Lord Wolverton," she said finally. It was as close to a concession as she was willing to make.

"Let me return you to your room," he said, his voice gruff with concern. "I daresay your wounded feet are still far too painful to attempt the stairs alone."

Mary had no warning. He simply swept her once more into his arms and left the library. His long strides carried them up the staircase and toward the bedchamber with ease. Indeed, the exertion of it seemed not to have even winded him. Once more inside the bedchamber, he set her on her feet near the fireplace.

"I trust you will be able to navigate this smaller space without doing injury to yourself." His tone wasn't amused or teasing. It was tight, gruff, and there was something in it that made her want him to hold her just a bit longer.

"I will be fine, Lord Wolverton," Mary insisted. "But it isn't right that I've denied you your own room. I'm sure there is a more suitable space in the house that I could occupy so that you would not be put out—"

"I won't hear of it," he insisted. "You will remain here."

"And you will remain in your dressing room?" Mary asked. "It isn't right, my lord."

His eyes narrowed and the expression that etched his face could only be described as feral. "I will not remain in my dressing room. I may be a gentleman, Miss Mason, but I am still only a man... I am as prone to temptation as any. Would you truly have me just on the other side of that door while you are asleep and at your most vulnerable? Do you trust so easily, even after your ordeal?"

"I trust you," she stated firmly. And she did, so long as he was near her and her own overactive imagination was not given leave to run amok.

He stepped closer to her, so close that she could feel his breath stirring her hair and that the heat of his body seeped through the borrowed gown she wore to warm her skin beneath. "You should not, Miss Mason."

Mary didn't step back or squeak in fear. She knew that he expected her to do both. But curiosity was a dangerous and heady thing. The need to know what his kiss would feel like had plagued her from that tense moment in his dressing room earlier. With the answer nigh, she would not have faltered for her life. Instead, she leaned in, allowed her eyes to flutter closed while lifting her lips to him. When his breath fanned over her lips, she sighed in anticipation.

It was not at all what she'd expected. There was no crushing of his mouth upon hers, no fierce and passionate embrace. It was the gentlest of touches, feather light but no less potent. Only his lips touched hers, nothing more. She was giddy with it regardless. The way his lips moved upon hers, gentle and insistent like the slow and languorous savoring of a sweet, thrilled her.

In all, it lasted only seconds. There was no abrupt departure. After a brief moment, the pressure lessened and then was gone. When her eyes opened again, he had stepped back, putting enough distance between them that she had to wonder if it had happened at all. Had it not been for the thrumming of her pulse and the very faint taste of brandy, she might have thought it had been the product of her own wild imaginings.

"Have you ever been kissed, Miss Mason?"

The question had been voiced gently, his tone soft and yet there was tension in his voice, an ache that she could not identify. "Not until now," she admitted.

He said nothing for the longest time, simply regarded her in that familiar intense and quiet way that she was becoming accustomed to from him. Finally, he said, "I bid you good night, Miss Mason—Mary."

The desire to call him back, to ask him to kiss her once more, was insistent, but somehow she quelled it. She would not press her luck any further than she already had. Instead, she would go to bed and allow the memory of it to cloud her dreams with visions of passion and romance. Her foolishness did not go so far that she imagined any sort of future for them. He was a peer, after all, and she'd grown up on an impoverished farm. Even with the fortune her brother had amassed, she would never be of such an elevated station that he might see her as anything more than a flirtation, and an unwise one, at that.

Retreating to the bed, Mary slid between the cool sheets and wondered if his dreams would feature her as singularly as hers were sure to feature him. Unwise as it was, she hoped so. The idea that she would be so affected by him while he was immune was too mortifying to bear.

Tucking her hand beneath the pillow, she encountered the journals she'd hidden there earlier. As sleep would likely be a long time in coming, Mary retrieved one of them and lit the candle on the bedside table. It would be difficult reading with such poor lighting, but if it offered her even a hint of insight into the strange and compelling man who had just kissed her, it would be well worth it.

HEADING DOWN THE stairs with the echoing slam of his chamber door behind him, Alex bit back a curse. It didn't take the promise of a sleepless night ahead to make him regret kissing her. He'd regretted it the moment his lips touched hers. There was nothing so bitter as being granted a small taste of what you desired most only to know the whole of it would ever be denied you. From the sweetly expectant visage of her upturned face as she waited for his kiss, to the pliant and silken texture of her full lips, he'd known the truth of her innocence. Any doubts he'd had about whether or not her knowledge of the world was such that he could indulge his desire for her without risking what was left of his soul had been summarily shattered. To take more than that sweet and hopelessly chaste kiss would be to rob her of any chance for a respectable future. He would not be that sort of black-guard regardless of what the world thought him.

Rather than tempt fate and his own restraint, Alex returned to the library. The settee there was too short for him but, as the sweet taste of Miss Mason's lips would deny him any rest regardless, it hardly mattered.

For her sake and for his own, he would return her to her brother at the first possible opportunity. If he was to maintain any sort of honor, that was the only option.

Chapter Seven

THE RIGHT HONORABLE Mr. Albert Hamilton entered the house at Number 27 Royal Crescent and was unsurprised to find the lower floors dark. With only a handful of servants on staff, it was frequently so. But that was a necessity. The best way to maintain a secret was to ensure that as few people as possible knew it. Servants gossiped. It was a fact of life for the aristocracy but, in this case, gossip could very well ruin everything. All that they had worked for would be for naught. It might anyway, he thought bitterly.

He slammed the door behind him, much harder than necessary. A small painting, a hunting scene he'd never much cared for anyway, fell from the wall and crashed to the floor. The frame separated at the corner, bits of the elaborately carved trim splintering over the marble tiles, and he gave a satisfied smirk. Cold fury was pushing him, pressing in on him in ways that he had never experienced before. While he lacked the ability to lay claim to any sort of righteousness, his current mood could only be described as righteously indignant.

All that he'd worked for, all that he'd suffered while tolerating Harrelson's pettiness and insults was now gone—ripped from him by that charlatan, Madame Zula. In one fell stroke, she'd destroyed all of them and had shuffled off the mortal coil herself in the process to avoid any punishment for her own crimes and misdeeds. And now, he would have to face *her*. While he adored every licentious and wicked beat of her cold heart, he had little doubt that she'd take more than a pound of flesh from him in the process.

Climbing the stairs, he entered the master bedchamber and surveyed the chaos within. She was growing restless being locked away, but it would not be for much longer.

"Helena," he said. It was all he had opportunity to say for she turned then, whirling, and flew into his embrace, kissing his face wildly and enthusiastically.

"My darling," she breathed. "Oh, how I've missed you! I've been so terribly lonely here! And that butler... I want him fired, Albie! He's horrid. An atrocious man. Always skulking about and spying on me!"

Hamilton sighed. It wasn't the first time she'd made such an accusation. Sometimes, he wondered if Helena wasn't half-mad. Even as a girl, she'd been all but convinced that people were plotting against her for various reasons. "My dear, he is not spying on you. He is spying for you. It's his job to be certain that no one from outside can come inside. It would spoil everything! Don't you see?"

"I want to go outside!" she shouted, stamping her feet much like a child. "I want to shop and take the waters and gossip. I want to ride down Milsom Street in a fast carriage and watch the old biddies gasp with horror at the sight! I would never have agreed to this ridiculous plan if I'd known I'd be a prisoner for more than a year! You said it would be over quickly! You and Harrelson both said they'd hang him and then it wouldn't matter!" She was in a full tantrum now, dudgeon high, and every object within reach was hurled at him.

Hamilton sighed wearily. He didn't even bother ducking as Helena's aim was notoriously poor. He simply allowed her to smash all of her pretty things and waited for her to tire. They'd had this same argument before, far too many times to count if the truth of it were told. Of late, they were having it much more frequently. He did not remind her of one very important fact as to do so would ensure that things would go very poorly for him, indeed. All of this, the ruse of her death, going into hiding with the belief that eventually Wolverton would either be hanged for the crime, or be so downtrodden with the gossip and ensuing poverty that he would do what any other nobleman would in his shoes and end his miserable life – it had all been her idea. "We had no way of knowing that two of the gentlemen Harrelson had blackmailed would die before the trial! With the loss of our majority we simply had to take what we could get! Isn't it enough that he's as poor as a church mouse?"

"Then he should have found something to blackmail them with! That's what all of this was, after all! He'd sell them a girl or a boy or a grown woman and then use that very sale as a means of controlling them forever! Half the exalted men of the *ton* obtained their unwilling mistresses and paramours from him! He's ruined everything! It's all been for naught!"

Hoping to defuse her temper, he said softly, "I didn't come here to argue with you about this, Helena. I have news."

"What is it?" she snapped. "Has my honorable, upstanding and deadly bore of a husband remarried, then, and gone about the business of finally producing an heir? An heir to what? A worthless title and a shambles of a rotting house is all he has left!"

"No, he has not married. And likely will not. We all know that your husband's rather firm grasp of honor would not allow such a thing. It's the only reason he hasn't put a pistol ball in his brain," Hamilton replied dismissively. "No. This is news on another front. I fear it is not good news, my dear."

She turned then, eyes flashing. "What is it then? What has occurred?"

Taking a fortifying breath, he summoned all of his courage and confessed in a rush, "Harrelson is dead. Poisoned by one of his compatriots."

She gasped, her eyes widening with terror. "I was right. It has all been for naught!" she cried. Falling to her knees on the floor, she began tearing at her hair in the same manner she had as a child. "This is all falling apart! Without Harrelson, I won't be able to produce an appropriately aged heir apparent once Alex is dead! If he'd only gone to the gallows or taken his own life instead of being so ridiculously moral about everything!"

"But darling, our plan was solely so that Harrelson would be able to get his hands on Alex's entailed estate. Now that Harrelson has gone, we can abandon it altogether. We must only think of how to come out of this in the best way for ourselves! And I have a plan," he offered with a cool smile.

Helena glared at her lover, a man the world thought to be her half-brother. He'd been a young boy when her mother married his father and then cuckolded him with half the men in society. None of the four children produced during that marriage shared a father and not a single one of them had been sired by her mother's husband. There was not an ounce of blood shared between them and yet, in so many ways, they were alike. Albie understood her as no one else ever had. And the world judged them for it, calling them all manner of things. *Unnatural. Incestuous. Scandalous.* The whispers had been endless, until marrying her prig of a husband had been the only way to salvage anything. Even then, it had failed, because try as she might, staying away from Albie had been impossible for her. She craved him as others craved opium. "What is your plan then?"

"It may sound mad, but you must hear me out, dearest. What if you were to return to your husband?"

She laughed bitterly. "Return to him? You're an absolute fool! The entire world believes me dead and most of them think he's the very culprit who did me in! I cannot return to him. Besides, all of this was so that you and I could be together!" Suddenly, her face crumpled and she looked much like a child denied a treat. "Have you grown tired of me, then? Do you wish to be rid of me, Albie? After all that we've endured to be together, would you send me away so cruelly?"

It was their only option. He knew that and had to find some way to make her see it. Harrelson had left them all but penniless, all his promises of wealth and prestige going to the grave with him. Approaching her cautiously, he knelt before her until they were eye to eye. "I will never tire of you. I will never not desire you. We are the same, you and I. Wicked to our very souls and better for it together."

"How on earth can we be together when you want to send me back to Wolverton? He despises you and he's utterly repulsed by me!"

"We will be together, my darling, just not immediately. I don't intend that you should have a happy and longstanding reunion with him, my sweet Helena. Only that you return for now. We'll find some excuse for your absence and have the court reverse its decision and return all of Wolverton's significant wealth to him! After a suitable period of time has passed, Alex can succumb to an unfortunate fever. There are numerous poisons that will produce just such a death!"

"After all this, after all that we did so that I would never again have to endure his touch," Helena sobbed. "You would send me back to him. You don't love me anymore. You no longer desire me for your own!"

"I do, my dearest," he said, taking her into his arms and soothing her. "But this is the only way. We have no money. Harrelson took everything. I bribed the clerk that works in his solicitor's office and he's left everything to that toad, Freddy. All the money. Even this house will be given to my blasted brother!" Even thinking of it infuriated him. Oh, Freddy had toadied to Harrelson just as he had, but when it had come time to do the really dirty work, it had been he who had risked the bitter end of the gallows for their schemes.

"Freddy! Oh, I hate him so! And how dare Harrelson do this to us! It was all to come to you! He said so!" Helena protested.

"And Harrelson was a liar and a criminal. It's hardly surprising that he's broken faith with us… but we are not without hope. If you return, alive and with some reasonable excuse for having been gone so long that your husband was tried for your murder, then perhaps the conviction and sentence will be overthrown. It is the only way, my love!" he finished imploringly.

She threw her hands up in the air, pacing the room in a fury-driven haste. "And when we kill him and I have no child in my belly—what then, Albie? Because all of that lovely money you are so very concerned about will go to someone else altogether!"

"There could be a child in your belly, Helena. And if we postpone your return just long enough, it could be mine," he urged. "All you have to do is stop taking that little herbal potion I get from that vile creature at Burrow Mump."

She pouted. "I'll grow fat and hideous and you won't love me anymore. You'll abandon me to rusticate there at that hovel of an estate of his!"

"You will never be hideous, my darling... but we must all make sacrifices if we are to have the kind of life we desire. Harrelson was too tightfisted when he was alive for us to amass the wealth we needed from assisting him. He kept the lion's share and forced us to live in near poverty. That was likely his plan all along, to keep us leashed to him like poorly behaved pets," he mused. "But never again. Never again. You will bear my child and raise it as the heir to the Wolverton Earldom. It's the perfect revenge, don't you think?"

"Against Alex? It isn't vengeance, Albie. He's too much of a gentleman to have ever done anything warranting vengeance! If we're to do this, let us at least be honest about our motives. We hate him because he's a bore, and because I was forced to marry him by Freddy and Harrelson so they could get their hands on his money and his lands! And you, too. You were right there with them insisting it was the only way!"

"And it was, my darling. We had to bury the gossip about us because you behaved imprudently, Helena. Let us not forget that! No one would have ever suspected that our relationship was anything more than familial had you not made such a scene when I proposed to that horrid Landers girl!"

"She was ugly. I won't be thrown over for an ugly woman!"

"You weren't being thrown over! I was going to marry her, get her fortune, and then see her dead before the year was out! But you cannot control that vile temper of yours! Between your temper and Harrelson's greed, I'm still living on the pitiful allowance my father threatens to cut off every time I displease him! Which appears to be with every other breath! And now with Freddy getting Harrelson's wealth and lands... what else are we to do, Helena?"

She eyed him suspiciously. "Are you certain it was the psychic who got rid of him, after all? Given that he was your friend and your partner, you don't seem overly heartbroken at his demise!"

"There is only one person who will ever have a place in my heart... that is you," he cooed at her. "Now, we must come up with a reasonable story for why you have been gone for so long."

"Why not use Harrelson? Maybe he's kept me prisoner in his house for these past two years... abusing me horribly for his own perverse pleasure?" Even as she asked the question, she was disrobing, allowing her already sheer dressing gown to fall to the floor, baring the matching confection of lace and silk beneath.

Hamilton smiled. "My sly, little fox... what a criminal mastermind you are!"

"If I'm to submit myself once more to Alexander's touch, then tonight, my love, I would know yours," she said. "Take me, Albie, as a man should!"

His heart beat faster in anticipation. Helena would never be content with a man who would simply make love to her. She could only find release in violence, in domination. Her greatest satisfaction came in the form of pain and degradation. That their desires so closely aligned, his need to inflict pain and her ability to receive absolute pleasure from it, had been the basis of their relationship to start. But it had been her utter lack of morals, and her willingness to involve herself fully in the flesh peddling enterprise that he and Harrelson had used to shore up the flagging finances of their estates, that had truly made him worship her. Never in his life had he had the pleasure of being with someone so completely avaricious. If he'd believed in such a thing as soul mates, he might have thought she was his.

"Kneel on the bed and present your lovely arse for a spanking, Helena. You'll need to be adequately punished for your wickedness," he said.

She shivered, her nipples pebbling beneath the satin of her gown, but she quickly moved to do his bidding. Crossing the room, he opened the wardrobe and removed the item that always elicited the most excitement from her. A single cane, the ends of it wrapped in soft leather so it would not cut her skin, hung from a hook inside it.

"Tell me how naughty you've been, Helena," he urged.

"I yelled at the servants. And I shouted at you," she admitted, her voice quavering slightly. "I've challenged your authority shamelessly."

"Is there more?"

She looked up at him through lowered lashes in a position of mock submission. It was belied by the fire of passion that burned so brightly in her eyes. "So very much more."

"We'll start with that for now… and then see if you require further discipline."

"As you wish, my lord," she replied meekly.

She was a harlot with the manners of a lady, and he adored her for it, he thought. Raising the cane, he brought it down hard on the soft, supple flesh of her bottom. She cried out, but not from pain or fear. It was excitement and they both knew it.

Hamilton smiled as he raised his arm to deliver the next blow. She was maddening, difficult, often obstinate, childish and unabashedly selfish. But for him, she was perfect.

Chapter Eight

MARY HAD NOT slept at all. She'd burned the single candle by her bedside until it was down to the barest nub as she consumed the pages of his journals. The first one, from his youth, had prompted smiles and even a bit of laughter. He had not exaggerated when he'd told her of his painful attempts at poetry. They were utterly atrocious, but sweet because they'd been completely heartfelt. At dawn, she'd risen and moved to the window, and used the sun to continue her exploration of his musings and memories.

There was one passage in particular that she had read and reread. She found herself returning to it over and over again. With a guilty flush, she flipped back to that page once more. It was dated just a few days after Lord Ambrose's letter and dealt with what he had learned from his friend regarding his wife's alleged infidelity.

> *I had no romantic inclinations at the prospect of marrying Helena. I was charmed by her beauty, as was any man who met her. But I was not swept away by her and, perhaps, if I had been wiser, I would have refused for that reason. One should be swept away with a passion for the woman he marries. It's a foolish notion, a romantic one that I can ill afford and yet, I think now, that I would rather have married by standards some would deem poor, meaning that there were no financial gains from the union and have, if not happiness, then at least contentment.*
>
> *We have been wed for two years. There are no children from this union and given the disappointment that is our marriage bed, I cannot see that altering in the foreseeable future.*

Wolfhaven is colder and lonelier than ever. Looking back at my parents, at their arranged marriage and how wonderfully it had turned out for the both of them, at least until my mother's death and my father's unending grief at her loss, my belief that such an arrangement for myself and Helena might also give way to romantic feelings and devotion was foolhardy and rather naïvely optimistic. I think that, perhaps, Helena does not wish to be happy. Her mood shifts like the wind, always capricious. Her good humor is the most precarious thing I have ever beheld. Perhaps it is my fault, for whenever she has wished to go to London or Bath, or even her family's estates, I confess that I am happy to see her go, happy to have a moment's peace without tempers and tantrums and tears. And yet all of that is followed on her return by stony silence and an iciness that makes me question whether I ever witnessed an outburst from her at all.

There are whispers now, sly and sidelong looks, and the occasional laughter when I go into the village. I know why, of course. The time she has spent at Harrelson's estate, under the guise of visiting with her uncle, was nothing more than a ruse to allow for her infidelity. Her misbehavior in London and now in Bath has reached far and wide it seems. The rumor of her unnatural relationship with her brother, Albert, has once more reared its ugly head. The only thing saving her from total ruin is that everyone knows she and Albert do not actually share any parentage. Her mother, his stepmother's infidelity, is legendary.

I regret that I married her. I regret that she will never be happy with me nor I with her. I regret that we have both sentenced ourselves to eternal dissatisfaction with one another until one of us manages to shuffle off the mortal coil.

It did not absolve him of guilt in the crime of murder. In fact, for those who did not know him, or did not know the circumstances she was now aware of regarding Lord Harrelson and his possible involvement in unspeakable crimes, it would have made him appear quite guilty. But that wasn't what she took from it. What she saw in it was the hopes he'd had for his marriage, and the ultimate disappointment he came to feel. It saddened her that he had suffered such bitter unhappiness when all he had done was to behave honorably.

Mary closed the book and retreated to the bed once more to tuck it beneath the pillows. She made the bed up herself, not wanting Mrs. Epson to find her treasure trove of his secrets and brand her a thief and a liar, again. After, Mary washed with the cold water from the ewer and then fashioned her hair once more into a simple braid, tied with a length of ribbon she'd found in the sewing box. The green walking dress she'd been provided the day before had been taken up with the use of some very strategically placed gathers along the side. It would, in the long run, do the least amount of damage to the fabric and had required the least amount of sewing.

After she'd dressed, she sat once more beside the window and waited for Lord Wolverton to come for her. It was sad and telling that she was so eager for his company even when she dreaded the purpose of their excursion. She was drawn to him, far too much for her own security and peace of mind. It would be very easy to cast caution to the wind for a man such as him—one haunted by a painful past and yet with such goodness in his heart. Mary knew that the greatest danger she now faced was falling in love with a man she could never possibly be with.

ALEX ROSE EARLY, if one could call what he'd experienced the night before sleep at all. After spending hours with his tall frame draped over the much shorter settee, every part of him hurt. His neck and shoulders ached and his back was near broken from it. But the option of lying on the small cot in his dressing room, with only a single door between himself and Miss Mary Mason was far worse. It would have created its own kind of agony.

The chaste kiss they had shared, one that, upon its completion, he knew to be her very first, had stirred a raging fire in him. Sweet, untutored, unspoiled, and given freely—it was a heady thing for him.

The truth was that marriage to Helena had nearly broken him. She'd despised his touch and he'd visited her bed so infrequently, he'd all but turned into a monk during their short union. Regardless of how much he desired Miss Mason, he was not so without honor that he would give in to it or indulge it further. His place in hell was secured already without need of further misdeeds. The only things he could afford to think about, to focus on, were proving his innocence in Helena's death and, possibly, if such a thing could even be achieved, having the settlements he'd paid returned to him. Mary Mason with her dark, soulful eyes and softly sweet lips would need to be banished from his thoughts. The easiest way to achieve that was to banish her from his home.

Stretching to ease the kinks in his neck, Alex left the library and climbed the stairs to the bedchamber. He could hear Mrs. Epson inside, haranguing Miss Mason for being a lazy slugabed who ought to be fetching her own breakfast instead of being waited on by a servant as if it were her right. Muttering a curse beneath his breath that would surely have sent both the women into fits, he knocked sharply upon the door and let himself in.

Miss Mason was most certainly not a slugabed. She was up, seated before the fireplace, wearing a recently hemmed walking dress in a dark shade of green. Her hair had been combed back and braids that she'd managed to twist into a simple chignon were secured with a length of ribbon. Where it had come from he could not guess, for it was with complete certainty he could say Mrs. Epson had not provided something she would deem so frivolous.

"You are looking well this morning, Miss Mason. That's a pretty bit of ribbon," he commented on the sapphire silk that wound through the tight braids.

"Thank you, Lord Wolverton. I found it in the sewing box and as I had no hair pins... I hope you do not think me too forward for borrowing it," she finished weakly, a blush stealing over her cheeks.

Alex noted that she did not make eye contact with him, but instead kept her head down and her gaze averted. He knew why, of course. It was not the ribbon to which she referred at all, but to their midnight kiss. A smile twisted his lips and he offered her his assurances. "I would never think you forward, Miss Mason. I will always think you are exactly what a lady ought to be. If you are feeling well enough, I thought we might go exploring a bit today. I'd prefer to do our searching of Harrelson's properties before his heirs descend. The lot of them is rather distasteful."

"I am feeling much improved, my lord. I had thought we might visit the area of the woods where you found me. That is why I am up and about so early... and if all goes well, perhaps, that is, I wondered—" She broke off, took a deep, settling breath. "I cannot stay here with you, Lord Wolverton, not now that I am well again. If you'd be so kind, you might see me on to Bath tomorrow. I can seek the assistance of Mrs. Simms and write to my brother. If I send word to his establishment in London, surely they will know how to reach him in Bath."

She had it all figured out. It was perverse of him, but knowing that she wanted to leave inspired him to wish to keep her there longer. He tamped down the urge. What she'd asked was perfectly in line with what he'd decided on only moments before. But it was much easier to think of sending her away when he wasn't looking at her, when he wasn't tempted by the lush curves he knew were concealed by her gown or by the sunlight from the window falling on the curve of one rounded cheek that he knew felt like silk beneath his palm.

Instead, he said the only thing that he could, "We are of an accord, Miss Mason. I was going to suggest the very thing myself. Let us see how you fare on our outing this morning before we decide further."

There was a flash of something in her eyes—a single second where he could see something that looked either like disappointment or hurt. It only strengthened his resolve. For him to desire Miss Mason was only natural. She was a beautiful woman and it had been a considerable length of time since he'd had the good fortune to indulge in any sort of carnal activities. But she was untouched, innocent—and, for her, it would not be about the physical intimacy, but about the involvement of her heart and more tender feelings. To take that from her, to allow any continued intimacy between them knowing it would come to naught, would be a kind of cruelty that he'd never indulged in before. Whatever the world believed of him, he would not be that sort of man.

"I will require your assistance, I fear. The slippers that were brought down are much too large. Even with the bandages on my feet, they will not fit. I will not be able to walk, but I can ride," she said. "If there is a mount available?"

His lips quirked in a vague approximation of a smile. "I am not so poor that I have had to sacrifice all of the horseflesh in my stable. I think I can find one from the handful that remains that will suffice. You are certain you can ride for thirty miles?"

"I can. I must. It is impossible for me to continue imposing upon your goodwill and hospitality," she said. "And Mrs. Epson's, of course."

He laughed then. "My dear Miss Mason, that you exist at all, and that I do, are each an imposition upon her goodwill. I will change and see that the horses are ready, and then return for you. Excuse me."

Alex left her then, moving toward the dressing room. The walls were thin and if Mrs. Epson continued her abuse, he'd be able to intervene. It wasn't really a question of if, he thought bitterly. There was little doubt that the woman would begin as soon as the door closed behind him.

Through the wall, he heard it.

The thin and quavering voice of the older woman began, "You're smarter than I gave you credit for. You'd do best to leave here and none too soon! It ain't fit that a gutter bred harlot should be lying in his bed while my poor mistress rots in her grave! If there was any justice in this world, they'd have hung him!"

Alex sighed. Why Mrs. Epson had decided to canonize Helena after her death, when the woman had reviled her with every breath while she lived, was a mystery to him. But he would have to pension her off. There was no excuse for her behavior and the vile things she'd said to Miss Mason, an innocent in all of it. His late wife, while she might not have been bred in the gutter as Miss Mason was accused of being, she'd have certainly qualified for the distinction of harlot. Helena had spread her thighs for every man on the estate while reviling his touch. Had he been less secure in his own abilities to provide a woman pleasure, he would have taken umbrage. But he'd learned early on that it wasn't pleasure Helena craved. She'd longed for punishment, for degradation, for things that he'd been unwilling to debase himself to provide.

There was no escaping the truth that something in Helena had been broken beyond repair. He was not a prude by any stretch of the imagination and had indulged in pleasures of the flesh when the desire struck him, but Helena had been unable to find her pleasure in anything but pain, humiliation, and cruelty—both the giving and receiving it. Recalling his late wife's behavior in the marriage bed only served to amplify the sweetness and innocence of the woman before him. It also reminded him fully why he needed her away from him as soon as possible. Any association with him would be ruinous for her. The entire country, high- and low-born alike, reviled him. It wasn't simply the doors of society matrons that would be shut to Miss Mason, but all doors. It could well extend to her brother, as well. Miss Mason would forgive him for destroying her reputation, but not her brother's. He'd seen the truth of their devotion the night before when she'd defended him so staunchly. It was the type of relationship siblings ought to have, not the base and revolting thing that had existed between his late wife and her stepbrother.

Dressing quickly, he stepped back into the bedchamber and delivered a cool and quelling glance to the housekeeper. "I will see to our horses and return for you," he said. "Mrs. Epson, you will leave this room before me. I cannot trust you not to harangue our guest further."

With the crotchety old woman before him, Alex left the bedchamber and headed for the stables. He could not afford to be in Miss Mason's presence enough to defend her at all times from Mrs. Epson. The best course of action for all of them was to see her returned to Bath and to her brother.

Chapter Nine

I T HAD BEEN some time since Mary had been riding. It had been a skill that Miss Darrow had insisted all of the girls at her school learn to master. Her reasoning had been quite sound: that it was not possible to know what sorts of positions they would obtain upon completing their schooling. Many of them would serve as governesses or companions in houses in the countryside and, to that end, they should know how to handle a horse. For Mary, riding had been something she had tolerated but had no great love for. Still, the mount Lord Wolverton had selected for her was docile enough. The rather placid mare seemed content to amble along at a sedate pace. As she could not place her foot in the stirrup, she was forced to simply utilize her knee hooked over the pommel to maintain balance. At the speed they were traveling, it wasn't proving to be too difficult. But Mary had not counted on her recent illness and just how weak it had left her. Her muscles trembled and quivered under the strain and, all too often, she'd feel that familiar tightness in her chest and could hear the faint wheezing of her breath. She was not as well as she'd thought, but to admit it now would delay her return to her brother. It would also necessitate staying longer in Lord Wolverton's presence, longer under the beguiling temptation of being kissed by him once more.

Putting on as brave a face as possible, Mary ignored her fatigue and her discomfort as much as she could while they traversed the meandering path through the woods. It was heavily lined with very old trees, each one more gnarled and twisted than the last. In spite of the fact that it was a relatively bright and warm day, Mary shivered. There was something ominous and foreboding about those woods, or perhaps it was simply the knowledge of what they were in search of that had her on edge.

"Are you warm enough?" Lord Wolverton asked. "I had thought the cloak would be adequate, but if you need mine—"

"It isn't the weather that made me shiver, my lord. It's my own too-vivid imagination and the idea of whatever might be lurking in these woods," she admitted. "You must think me quite foolish."

He glanced over at her, his expression one that she could not quite decipher. "Never that, Miss Mason. The last time you were in these woods you were fleeing for your very life... from those who meant you harm, and even from those of us who did not. I suppose, under the circumstances, it is only natural that you were uncertain which category I belonged to."

She rolled her eyes. "Or I could have been insensible with a raging fever. Surely, had I not been ill and been more capable of accurately assessing my situation, I would have recognized then that you meant me no harm!"

"Really? In the dark, in the woods, with two men on the road discussing your abduction and captivity and the man who'd been guarding you possibly in pursuit? I cannot imagine that your state of mind, fever or no, would have allowed you to see benevolence! And I was not benevolent. I did not seek to help you simply for the sake of it. Even now, I have ulterior motives."

She would not have classified them as such. He'd been quite upfront with her in discussing his need to find out who was truly responsible for killing his late wife and clearing his name. He was, she thought, a far more honorable man than he gave himself credit for being. It would do little good to say so, as he would only deny it. Instead, she stated something he could not refute. "Regardless of your intentions, Lord Wolverton, had you not come to my aid that night, I would have died. I owe you my very life and the circumstances surrounding that truly matter far less than the final outcome, I would think."

He looked back at her over his shoulder, arched one brow sardonically and replied, "Touché, Miss Mason."

"And I would also assert that you can hardly call your motives ulterior when you have never concealed them from the very start. You have been nothing but honest about your motives and your need to find proof—"

Mary paused, drawing back on the reins of her horse as she stared at a break in the path ahead. There was a large outcropping of rock and several trees growing out of it at a sharp angle. She recalled them well because as she'd run through the darkness she'd very nearly smashed into them. It had been a very narrowly avoided disaster. They were close, on the very cusp, it would seem, of locating her prison.

"Miss Mason?"

The earl's concern was evident in his tone and it pulled her from her reverie. "That way, I think," she said, and pointed toward the fork of the path furthest from them. "I recall those landmarks from my mad dash through the night." Her voice trembled and she berated herself mentally for it. She was not weak or cowardly. And yet, being in that place, she very much felt as if both terms could be applied to her.

"This is too much for you," he said. "I will return you to Wolfhaven and continue on my own."

"It is not too much for me… not as of yet. If I fear it is becoming too much, I will tell you. We cannot be but a few miles from the house, after all."

"We are not," he agreed, "But you have been ill, and this is—well, it can only be detrimental to your health to relive such negative events so shortly after a very serious illness. If you remember coming this way, then I am better off than when I started. It is all the confirmation I needed to know that my first inclinations were correct. There are two entrances to the mines and a rabbit warren of tunnels between them. But only one entrance lies that direction. I can investigate it on my own."

Mary looked back at him, and once more down the ominous path that would lead to her former prison. Perhaps it was cowardice or, perhaps, her illness had robbed her of the fortitude she expected from herself. Regardless, she felt immense relief at not having to face further reminders of those horrors for the time being. "Very well... I will return to Wolfhaven. I fear I must impose upon your hospitality a bit longer. I had thought I would be well enough to go on today, but I am fatigued and winded already, even from such a short ride. It would be impossible, I fear, to ride on to the city. I suppose we must wait then for our journey to Bath."

Alex nodded. "I am not completely without friends, Miss Mason, though the number is far smaller than it once was."

"The number is not smaller, my lord, you've simply winnowed the wheat from the chaff, as it were," she pointed out.

"Why, Miss Mason, that is positively biblical!" he replied with a grin. "It is also entirely accurate. As I was saying, I do have friends remaining, and one lives close enough by that I ought to be able to beg a reasonably comfortable closed carriage for our journey. Given your continued ailment, I think my open curricle or riding are simply out of the question."

"You are too kind, my lord," she said, as they turned their horses and headed back toward Wolfhaven.

As they rode, he asked, "I hesitate to press for more details, but when you were in that cell, and you made your escape, did you go very far within the tunnels? Were there any twists and turns?"

"Not really. It was not a very long distance, for I could see light at the end of it, dim as it was, from the moon. So, there could not have been any twists or turns then if I had an unobstructed view of the entrance," she reasoned.

Given that they were no longer seeking to cover terrain and identify something familiar to her, they made much better time on the return trip. It seemed that within minutes they were once more riding across the overgrown lawn of his estate. It was not as shabby as he'd made it sound. The walls were comprised of the same pale stone as most of the architecture in Bath but, here in the countryside, it was not as discolored by soot as those homes in the city were. While parts of the house were significantly older, the part that he currently resided in was much newer. The Palladian style structure had been constructed around the older sections. She could see that, in certain areas, the glass had been removed from the windows and replaced with boards.

"Glass tax," he said. "It was easier to remove the windows and sell them off than to pay taxes on them year after year. Perhaps, one day my fortunes will turn and I can see this home restored to its former glory."

"I certainly hope so, Lord Wolverton. It's a lovely house. Just what a country manor house ought to be," she replied.

As they neared the side entrance that was closest to the stables, a small, thin man appeared. He'd been skulking in nearby bushes. She felt Lord Wolverton tense beside her. Who was the man? A debtor, perhaps? But while he clearly recognized the man and was caught off guard by his presence, she did not sense anger or defensiveness in him. Mary glanced back at him curiously and wondered what sort of business he had with Lord Wolverton and if it involved his investigation into his late wife's ill fate.

"Let me see you inside, Miss Mason."

Mary could tell from his tone that it was not a request or even a suggestion. He did not want her to know what he was about or who he was dealing with. "Who is that man?" she asked.

"It's nothing you need concern yourself with," he replied firmly.

"On the contrary. I think I need to concern myself with it very much. It seems as if you are rather unhappy to have this person here and I would know why, Lord Wolverton. Is he pressing you for money? Or is this related to our mutual concerns regarding Lord Harrelson's affairs? Because if it is, I am entitled to know what it's about!"

Wolverton grimaced. "He's an employee, but not a respectable one. I have had to go to rather unsavory lengths to get the information that I require in order to prove my innocence, and he is part of that. He is a criminal, and I would prefer that you be exposed to no further criminal elements, especially not those that I am responsible for putting in your path. Let me get you inside and then I will see what has brought him here and send him on his way."

"You will relay all the information that he offers?"

"You have my word," Wolverton stated.

Mary nodded her agreement but said nothing further as Lord Wolverton lifted her down. In his arms again, pressed close to him with her hands clasped behind his neck, it was rather like being carried as a bride would have been. The thought made her blush, but not nearly so much as the yearning it stirred inside her. Somehow, in the course of their relatively short acquaintance, and despite the very unorthodox manner in which it had begun, she'd found herself quite smitten with him. She was not so foolish as to call it love. There were still far too many secrets between them for her to give it such credence. But the knowledge that it could be, that if nurtured and tended in just the right way those feelings could grow, that was very much on her mind as he carried her inside.

Hope was a futile thing and well she knew it. She was too lowborn for him, regardless of what his current standing was in society. And even were he to overlook such a thing, she did not possess the sort of fortune that he would require in a bride if he had any hope of setting his estates to rights. Mary was not so foolish as to think such things could or should be ignored. He had tenants who depended upon him. He had other tenants who had been shuffled off to heaven only knew what sort of landlords. There was far more at stake than simply her romantic inclinations. The world worked in certain ways and it had to. Marrying for love was all well and good when both parties were of the same class. He'd be forgiven for marrying someone "in trade" as it were, if only she were wealthy. But while Benedict was successful in his business, he had certainly not amassed the kind of riches that would make her lack of breeding acceptable. It was a terrible thing to have such irrepressible feelings for him while at the same time having such a firm and uncompromising understanding of precisely how the world worked. In short, hope would not die, even when she knew it to be utterly hopeless.

"Are you well, Miss Mason?" he asked, his voice heavy with concern.

"Quite well, Lord Wolverton, only a bit tired, I think," she lied. But then she knew he'd been asking after her physical health, and not the state of her heart. Bitter disappointment only qualified as an illness for those who were wealthy enough to be classified as eccentric. "If you could see me to my room, I think I shall rest for a bit."

"Of course," he agreed readily.

Mary managed to stifle her sigh, but only just, as he bore her up the stairs as if she weighed no more than a feather. Strong, handsome, and so very honorable, he'd been all that was kind and heroic to her. And she would be leaving him very soon. It was for the best, she knew, but she could not prevent a pang in her heart at the thought. But it would be better to do it now, make a clean break, and forget the burgeoning feelings she had for him, than to allow things to continue and truly have her heart broken.

ALEX DEPOSITED HER on the chair before the fire. He hadn't the strength to lay her upon the bed and actually walk away from her. Holding her closely, feeling the soft press of her body against him and the sweet way she'd clung to him had only intensified his craving for her. He needed her gone, though he knew that he would miss her terribly when she left. The house would feel empty again, perhaps more so than it had before.

He needed to speak with Davies and figure out what the man had learned. He would not have dared come directly to Wolfhaven unless the news was of great importance. To that end, Alex knew that he could not linger with Miss Mason. To do so would be to delay whatever news Davies wished to impart and also tempt him beyond what he could reasonably resist. "I'll return shortly," he said. He might have been fooling himself in thinking it, but he was certain that he saw a flash of disappointment in her eyes. It was quite possible that he only saw it because he wished to.

Leaving her, he headed down the stairs and back outside to where Davies waited. The man was skulking about, as if he literally did not know any other way of being except very poorly clandestine. "You have news?" Alex demanded.

"It's about the brother... I saw him in the city yesterday and followed him. He came here, my lord... to the abandoned salt mine on Harrelson's property. He knew that Miss Mason had been held there."

"Well, that was our suspicion and it certainly proved true enough. But that is not all you have learned or you would not be here," Alex said, his tone skeptical.

"No, my lord. I overheard him talking with the lady that was with him but I needed to go back to Bath and be certain that what I heard was right before I brung the information to you," the man hedged.

"You have been paid for the job, Davies. I'll not be giving you bonuses just because you've uncovered something of interest... that is what you were hired to do, after all," Alex reminded him archly.

Davies' eyes widened and he shook his head in protest. "Oh no, my lord... I didn't mean to... well, I wouldn't ask for more than already agreed upon. But what I learned is most impressive. It seems that Miss Mason's brother is not actually Benedict Mason at all but Benedict Middlethorp!"

Alex frowned. The name was familiar, teasing the edges of his mind. When realization dawned he shook his head in denial. "Surely you are mistaken, Davies! Miss Mason's brother could not be—"

"He is. Lord Benedict Middlethorp, Viscount Vale... the long-lost heir, kidnapped more than twenty years ago!"

They'd touched on it briefly the night before, during their midnight encounter in the library. Mary—Miss Mason—had admitted the possibility that Harrelson may well have been involved in the abduction that had initially brought her together with her brother under the cruel care of their adoptive parents.

"I'll be taking Miss Mason to Bath tomorrow. I assume that they are ensconced in the Vale townhouse?"

Davies nodded. "Yes, m'lord. It seems the whole family has accepted him without question! I know a pretty kitchen maid what works at a house in the Circus and she heard it straight from a maid that works for Lady Vale. He's the lost heir, right enough, and his uncle, who is the executer of the estates, has already petitioned the House of Lords to have him formally recognized."

"Find Hamilton. Focus all your efforts on him for now," Alex instructed. "I need to know what he's up to."

Davies nodded again and then slipped away, heading once more for the city. Stepping inside the house, Alex made a quick stop in the library to gather up the ledgers and correspondence he'd absconded with the night before. With those items in tow, he took the stairs to the bedchamber, where Mary Mason awaited him in a frustratingly platonic fashion.

Pausing outside, he knocked briskly on the chamber door and waited until she bade him enter. Seated before the hearth, the firelight glinted on her hair as she worked on hemming another of Helena's borrowed gowns. Stepping inside, he stopped there to simply take in the lovely picture she presented. It was a strange thing for him to be so much in the company of a woman whose presence he desired and who seemed to welcome his in return. Prior to his marriage, he'd been focused almost entirely upon his estates and setting things to rights following his father's poor management of them. While he'd never lacked for female attention and had enjoyed the physical aspects of intimacy with women frequently enough, their companionship in a non-carnal sense was not something he'd ever really understood.

After marrying Helena, he'd thought they would settle into their life together. But it had quickly become apparent that was not at all what she desired, and rather than force himself to endure her disinterest and complete displeasure with him, he'd left her to her own devices and she to his. But now, in the few short days when he'd been able to spend time in Mary's soothing presence, to appreciate the softness of her voice and the gentle expression of pleasure that always curved her lips when he entered the room, Alex was finally in a position to understand precisely what had been missing from his marriage. It wasn't simply that he and Miss Mason were attracted to one another, though it was clear that they both were despite the lack of wisdom in such a course of action, it was that they honestly rather liked one another.

"I will miss you when you are gone," he admitted softly. "I don't think I fully appreciated how much until this moment. This house has been very lonely and it has come alive with your presence." It was not the house. He had come alive with her presence, and he would feel the lack of it keenly.

She dropped her hands to her lap and the pale green muslin of the gown she was altering pooled about her. Her chin came up and her eyes glittered suspiciously with fiercely battled and unshed tears. "I shall miss you as well, Lord Wolverton. More than you can know." The admission did not ease the tension between them at all. Instead, it seemed to magnify the tension until it filled the room itself. As if to ease it and return them to something more manageable, she laughed, and declared in a much lighter tone, "But I shall not miss Mrs. Epson or her culinary torment."

Alex smiled at that. "We shall endeavor to carry on bravely without you then... I have news that may be of interest to you. It's regarding your brother, Mr. Benedict Mason. Or perhaps I should refer to him as Lord Benedict Middlethorp, Viscount Vale."

She gaped at him. "What did you say?"

"Your brother has been identified as the long-lost heir to the Vale Viscountcy. But I think you are more surprised that I am aware of it than that it has occurred. Was that not who you believed him to be when you came to Bath?"

Mary flushed guiltily. "I had thought that might be the case. I am surprised that he has found his family and also that the information is being bandied about so freely. I had not expected that he would just be readily accepted by them. I anticipated a great deal of resistance for him to be quite honest."

He stepped deeper into the room, seating himself in the chair opposite her. "I see. And your reasons for withholding that information from me?"

"I had no proof, Lord Wolverton," she replied. "I only had the same suspicions I'd had that brought me to Bath to start. But you may have proof. It could be that truth of my brother's identity is in those books you hold even now."

"And your identity, as well, perhaps?"

She shrugged. "I'd given very little thought to finding my own family. My adoptive mother enjoyed watching Benedict do menial tasks because she knew of his aristocratic origins. It was fulfilling to her in some perverse and cruel way to demean him because of it. It was different for me, so I can only assume that my own origins were not quite so exalted."

He took one of the journals and passed it to her. "Perhaps we should find out. There's no outward indication of which years each journal covers. We'll just have to go through both of them."

Chapter Ten

THEY SPENT HOURS going through the ledgers and various letters. Mary was exhausted when it was done, not physically, but emotionally. Those scribbled numbers and notations on the pages were representative of peoples' lives, of misery and humiliation, and heaven could only guess what kind of suffering might be attached to each one. It was at the beginning of the second ledger that she picked up, which predated the other one by a considerable number of years, that she found a notation that could have applied both to her and to Benedict, not in their current situation, but as children.

"Lord Wolverton," she said breathlessly. "I think... no, I'm certain that I've found something quite important."

"What is it, Miss Mason?"

"*Girl child, blonde, aged 2, sickly with a cough—buyer refused her thinking it consumption. FH sent her to his sister in the north who has V.*" Mary read it again. "The same cough that I have now, I've experienced it multiple times in my life... usually any time I've been exposed to extreme cold or damp. Given the conditions that were part of this abduction, I can only assume that the first time I was in their care wasn't very different. And 'V' must be Benedict then... V for Vale. It's dated 1798 which means Benedict would have been about 6 at the time, assuming my math is correct in relation to the time he was abducted."

"It certainly sounds reasonable. We'd be able to confirm it more easily if we knew who FH was. Perhaps when I take you to your brother tomorrow, he will be able to shed some light on that. Clearly, he has been able to do his own investigation and determine his identity to the satisfaction of all others involved. It would stand to reason that the identity of this mysterious FH was part of it," he mused.

"I'm sure you are right. I just cannot fathom what has happened to all of these people. There must be hundreds of them. And while the notations indicate that some were taken from their families as children and given to other families, childless ones, I assume, I find that I am more disturbed by those whose fate is more ambiguous at the end. Like this one—brunette, age 15, sold for one hundred pounds sterling at auction. Yet it does not say to whom she was sold nor what their purpose for her was. I cannot imagine that such a sum of money would have been paid—at auction no less—for a girl, if not to sell her into some truly horrific fate." Mary closed the book and set it aside. While she felt for that girl, was overwhelmed with sympathy for her, there was a very self-serving aspect of her horror. She realized, with shocking clarity, just how close she'd come to meeting a similar fate. It was terrifying.

Lord Wolverton's brows came together in a worried furrow. "This is not a fit task for you, Miss Mason. You are too kindhearted and your nature too given to empathy to read through these documents without it taking a significant toll on you. Set them aside and I will finish the rest later. We should stop now at any rate. I will need to travel a short distance to my friend's home and see about collecting a carriage that we might use to transport you safely tomorrow."

Mary nodded. "What will we do if he says no? I'm certain the curricle would not be too bad as long as I bundle up."

"Ambrose will not say no," he replied with a slight smile. "He is a true friend, the truest and, perhaps, only friend I possess these days."

"Not the only friend, my lord," she insisted. Immediately, she blushed. It was a forward thing to say, on top of all the other very forward things she had already said. And what on earth could a man such as the Earl of Wolverton want in a friend such as her? She was penniless. While her brother was wealthy in his own right thanks to his shrewd acumen for business and cards, she had no money of her own. With Benedict restored to the bosom of his proper family, she had to admit that she was somewhat concerned that there would no longer be a place for her in his life. Oh, he would see to her care. But she was a nobody, likely nothing better than a cast-off by-blow. Would she be an embarrassment to him now that he was a viscount? The answer to that was a definitive yes, she realized. Benedict would never admit it, but his newfound family would likely not appreciate her presence as a painful reminder of all the years he'd been stolen from them.

"You are troubled," he observed.

Mary shook her head. "Not really. Well, slightly, perhaps. I just wondered how Benedict's change in circumstance might—what if his new family does not wish him to associate with someone who is naught but a reminder of the painful years he was missing? And then there is the unknown nature of my own origins. I can only assume that I was low-born. It could well be that I am an embarrassment to him now. Certainly I would be an embarrassment to Lady Vale."

Alex gave a dismissive snort. "It is hardly worth considering, Miss Mason. Your brother has been quite devoted in his search for you. My man observed him at the salt mine where I believe you were held. He's been tracking you closely. Those are not the actions of a man who would be swayed so easily from those he loves. I think you'll find that his newfound family will be quite accepting of you. Otherwise he may very well choose not to accept them."

"I don't want that! I've no wish to come between him—"

"And people who would cast the blame of his abduction on an innocent child who was the victim of a similar fate? Or who would ask him to turn his back on the sister of his heart, who has been his truest companion and supporter for all the years of his absence from them?" Wolverton surmised, "If they are such people, Miss Mason, your brother is better off without them! Now, you must be tired. Mrs. Epson will bring you up some stew. Eat it if you wish. Toss it in the fireplace if you find it too inedible. I beg you do not pour it from the window as I've found her cooking kills the grass below."

Mary's jaw dropped. But then a laugh erupted from her. "Are you making jests now? I do believe you have taken leave of your senses, Lord Wolverton. Perhaps now it is you who is mad with fever?"

THE QUESTION, UTTERED on a musical laugh, could only be answered in the affirmative. He had quite taken leave of his senses. Without thought to the consequences or even the possibility of humiliating refusal, Alex leaned forward and captured her lips, still curved by a gentle smile. She did not push him away, but there was hesitation in her response. Her lips were still beneath his and unresponsive, but only for a moment. He recognized it for what it was—inexperience. Mary was not kissing him back because she wasn't entirely certain of what to do. But that hesitation was short lived. Within seconds, her actions mirrored his own and she pressed her lips gently against his, moving them in sweet supplication.

The kiss continued like that, not quite chaste but far from carnal, until he could no longer be satisfied by it. Only then did he urge her lips apart and invade the soft recesses of her mouth, sweeping his tongue against hers in a bold fashion that would surely shock her. But his Mary was not faint of heart, and she met him stroke for stroke, kissing him back with an urgency that belied her inexperience. If he'd thought himself tormented with desire before, he'd since seen the error of his ways. For this was the purest torture. Kissing her, the very act mimicking the physical intimacy that he craved with her, all the while knowing that he should not touch her, should not want her, and most assuredly should not pursue her.

And in spite of all that, he tugged her forward from the chair she occupied, pulling her onto his lap so that she straddled his thighs. All of which was accomplished without breaking the kiss. Her hands delved into his hair, holding him to her as if he had the will to leave. The kiss grew into a living thing all its own, their heartbeats synchronized in a rapid tattoo that belied their heightened states. Her skin flushed and as he touched her, his hands moved over that soft flesh as if he were touching the smoothest of satins.

It was the most natural thing in the world to let his hands wander, to touch her in a way that he knew no other man had. Cupping one breast in his palm, he felt her tense. For a moment, he feared he had pushed her too far. And part of him knew that he should hope for that, he should hope that he terrified her to the point of sensibility because, for him, all hope of it was lost. Kissing her again had robbed him of any hope of sanity, of being able to forget her once she was gone from him. Somehow, with her shy smile and her sweet but fierce nature, she'd invaded his very soul.

With his hand on her breast, her lips pressed to his, and her thighs spread over him, Alex was utterly lost. But even lost, he heard the clanking of the heavy keys Mrs. Epson wore on a belt about her waist. Alex broke the kiss, drawing back from her and rising quickly to his feet, he settled her once more in the chair she'd occupied earlier and moved away from her to look out the window as Mrs. Epson entered the room. The woman might have been in her dotage and nearly deaf, but she was clearly not blind. No sooner had she stepped into the room than she halted, looked from one to the other of them and then made a derisive sound that adequately expressed both her displeasure and disapproval.

For once, however, she said little enough. After placing the tray on the small table near the hearth, she gave them each a baleful stare and then turned to go. The door slammed loudly in her wake.

"Forgive me, Miss Mason. I should not have—that should not have happened again."

"No," she agreed. "It should not have. But it did. And as forward and wanton as I may sound for admitting it, I am not sorry. But even I recognize how unwise it would be to continue courting disaster, Lord Wolverton. You should see your friend about the carriage and, if possible, tomorrow I will return to my brother and we need never be faced with such temptations again."

It was precisely what he should do, and yet the idea of it left him feeling unsettled, as if the proper course and the right course of action were very different things. Still, he stepped back from the window and made for the door, pausing long enough to add, "I'm not sorry, either. Heaven knows I should be, for you deserve far better than a man such as me could ever offer."

He walked out, the door slamming once more. Without breaking stride, he made for the stables and rode hell bent for leather to a neighboring estate. Only a few miles cross country, it was a good seven miles by following the winding road. But he cut through the fields, taking jumps that bordered on reckless, and felt better for it. Riding had helped to exorcise her from his mind, at least momentarily.

As he reached Avondale Hall, Lord Ambrose's estate, the doors opened and Cornelius Garrett, Ambrose's son, came tearing out the door. The two were often at odds and it didn't surprise him in the least. Garrett gifted him with a derisive glance and then brushed past him without speaking. That, too, was not unusual. While Lord Ambrose had never seen fit to judge him based on gossip, Garrett certainly had. But then, he'd always thought the fellow a rather stuck up prig.

Knocking upon the door, the butler bade him enter and led him to the study where Lord Ambrose was reviewing correspondence at this desk. It was obvious that the man was unwell. His sallow countenance and the yellow cast to his eyes belied his condition.

"Wolverton! Good of you to visit!" Ambrose said. "I'm not down for long. Must get back to town you know! Can't let them have all the fun parties without me."

Alex crossed to the desk, examined the half-empty decanter of brandy and knew that it had likely been full at luncheon. "Perhaps you'd do better to let a few of those parties pass you by," he suggested mildly.

Ambrose waved away the suggestion like he would a buzzing insect. "You're beginning to sound like my tightly-wound son! Wound tighter than a clockmaker's pocket watch, that one! Had to send him away... won't be lectured to by a boy who is barely out of short pants."

"Your son is seven and twenty," Alex pointed out.

"He can't be," Ambrose protested.

"He was but a few years behind me at Eton. I assure you that he is," Alex said. "But I did not come to lecture you. I've come to beg a favor."

Ambrose nodded. "It's about bloody time. I can't stomach the idea of you living over there in that crumbling hovel, existing in penury! How much do you need?"

"I do not need your money," Alex protested. "I've come to borrow your carriage. There is a young woman who, through circumstances too terrible to divulge, has come into my care. I need to return her to her family in Bath but she is not well enough to ride horseback or in a curricle. A closed carriage would be best for her."

"And for her reputation, no doubt," Ambrose agreed, his silvered eyebrows arching upward in a mockery of shock. "I know better than to ask if you've had your way with her. You and my son are too much alike in that regard. You'll never have any fun of your own, Wolverton, but at least you will not begrudge me mine!"

"I do not think he begrudges your pleasures, Ambrose. I believe your son has concerns for your wellbeing. We all do. But I have accepted that you will do as you have always done, regardless of any physician's recommendation," Alex replied.

Ambrose waved a dismissive hand. "This girl... does this have anything to do with the recent death of Lord Harrelson? Funny how they call me a rogue and say I'm irredeemable and yet he's welcomed everywhere! Bounder!"

Alex made a face. "You are a rogue and you are irredeemable. You simply prefer to be irredeemable with willing and like-minded company."

Ambrose laughed heartily. "That I do, dear boy! Though I fear those days are behind me now... I prefer to imbibe freely and frighten young maidens with tales of what I might have done twenty years earlier." He laughed again, amused by his own wit, before sobering, as much as Ambrose ever could. "The carriage is yours, of course. And the money, too, if you ever have need of it. I would only ask one thing of you, Wolverton."

"And what is that?" Alex asked.

"Don't wallow in scandal and misery. Let the bastards think what they will of you and live your life on your own terms! After you've made Harrelson pay, that is!"

Alex looked at him from the corner of his eye. "You have not heard then, have you? Harrelson is dead. Poisoned by some charlatan fortune teller who worked for him—Madame Zula, who was likely one of his conspirators."

Ambrose nodded. "Hoisted on his own petard, as it were. I hope it was a painful death!"

At that, even Alex was taken aback. "So long as he's dead, does it truly matter how?"

"It does," Ambrose said heartily. "I'm dying, Wolverton. We both know it. My body is failing me and it's not a painless thing. Yet, I've lived the entirety of my life hurting only myself. Meanwhile, Harrelson has caused nothing but grief and misery for every person he's ever encountered. So, yes, I hope it was painful and humiliating, just as what I have to look forward to no doubt will be!"

It wasn't entirely true, Alex thought as he remembered the stormy countenance of Cornelius Garrett. He loved his father, and Alex knew that most of their disagreements stemmed from his attempts to get Ambrose to live a more moderate lifestyle. At one time, he'd thought it had been simply the family's reputation that was of concern to Cornelius. But as Lord Ambrose looked more frail and sickly at every meeting, he had begun to wonder if he had not misjudged Garrett on that count.

"Painful or not, he's dead now. But there are still questions to be answered. Hamilton's involvement is not yet clear. But what I do know is that Harrelson wasn't simply peddling secrets as we'd once suspected. He was peddling flesh as well. Kidnapping women and children and selling them into servitude to abbesses or to those who would keep them and abuse them in a more discreet manner."

Ambrose raised one eyebrow as he refilled his glass of brandy. "And how did you get this information?"

"I stole ledgers from Harrelson's estates," Alex admitted.

Ambrose shook his head. "Breaking the law will not aid your cause, Wolverton! Besides, you'll need more. Let me send some letters of inquiry to a few people I know... we should be able to come up with a trail of evidence on the receiving end of that merchandise which will support your claims nicely when you request your appeal. And now that Harrelson is no longer living, the blackmail that resulted in your conviction on the first go round should no longer be an issue. We will have this cleared away, my friend, if it is the last thing I ever do. It may well be, for that matter."

Alex frowned. "You need a physician! A good one and not one of our local quacks!"

An expression of what might have been wistfulness crossed Ambrose's face. "I fear it is far too late for that, in more ways than one. I've made peace with my fate, Wolverton. My son and heir requires no assistance from me... despite my own hardheadedness and indifference, he's managed to grow up as an honorable sort, if a bit priggish. There is nothing for me to do for him. Helping you is the closest I can come to atoning for my sins in this world. And so I shall go to meet my maker with receipt of a good deed in hand."

"There is time—"

"To what? Give up drinking? I've already given up women! Or perhaps they've given up on me," Ambrose mused. "No. I'll not deny myself every enjoyment in life when the outcome is all but set in stone. I'll see to this for you though. On that you have my word. And you have my carriage for as long as you shall need it... and my coachman, of course. See this young woman safely back to her family and allow me to handle things from here. With Harrelson dead, I see no impediment to your appeals!"

Alex rose and walked toward the desk. "Thank you for being my friend, Ambrose. Thank you for not turning your back on me when so many have."

"Nothing to thank me for, Wolverton. Had I not been drowning myself in drink and hussies at the time, it would never have come to this. Harrelson's engineering of the jury could have been averted and the truth would have won out. I failed you then, but I will not fail you now."

Alex nodded and turned to take his leave. At the door, he paused and asked, "Are you aware of a connection between Harrelson and the late Lord Vale?"

Ambrose's silvered eyebrows shot up again, but there was no mockery this time, only genuine surprise. "My dear boy, they were thick as thieves once upon a time. They tried to blackmail me, you know? Vale came to me and informed me that Harrelson had proof that I had sired a child with a lady of some repute. Her husband knew, of course. It was not a secret, but having it exposed could have been quite disastrous, indeed. I refused to pay, however, because I knew that if I did, I'd never stop paying. I did offer a duel though, to meet Vale first and Harrelson after should I survive. That was the end of it, so far as I know. But then they had a falling out, as I think Harrelson wished to edge Vale out of their joint business venture and keep the proceeds for himself. It all happened just before the boy went missing... Vale's heir. Why would you ask?"

"It seems that the missing Lord Vale has been reunited with his family. I just wondered if, perhaps, Harrelson might somehow have been involved in his initial disappearance and why," Alex admitted.

Ambrose considered his answer carefully. "The only thing that would surprise me about any of that would be Harrelson's choice to leave the boy alive. He has a cold and ruthless streak in him—had, I suppose."

Alex considered that. It was shocking and, perhaps, it meant that whoever was working for Harrelson at the time, FH as was mentioned in the ledgers, had taken some liberties himself in placing some of the children when deals fell through.

"There were notations in the ledgers identifying Harrelson's servant as FH. Do you know a name that is attached to those initials?"

"I do not, my boy… though I do recall Harrelson having some very disreputable-looking servants who accompanied him about town." Ambrose leaned back in his chair, "Tell me, Wolverton, is she pretty?"

"Pardon?"

"This girl you're set on reuniting with her family… is she pretty?" Ambrose demanded.

Alex had known Ambrose long enough to know exactly what the man was getting at, and he was not going to fall for it. "It's of no consequence."

"So she is pretty… sweet natured?"

"She's a lovely girl, gently-bred, and terribly traumatized. I want nothing more than to see her safely home," Alex insisted.

Lord Ambrose cackled at that, "Are you trying to convince me, Wolverton, or yourself?"

Alex grimaced. "You won't leave this alone, will you?"

"You're widowed, boy. Not dead. A pretty, young woman rescued from a terrible fate and immensely grateful to you—"

"I wouldn't dream of exploiting her gratitude or her trauma for my own benefit, Ambrose. As well you know!"

"I never said anything about exploiting. You're free to wed… she clearly needs someone to look after her. Why ever not? You're on the path to setting your fortunes to rights. You're a marrying kind of man, Wolverton… faithful as the day is long!"

"You say that rather like it's an insult," Alex mused.

"Well, not an insult, but certainly not something I've ever aspired to," Ambrose admitted. "My own wife, god rest her, was understanding enough. She tolerated me, even had a modicum of affection for me, I think. But she never loved me and I never loved her. But you are a romantic at heart. It's that more than Helena's faithlessness that wounded you, my boy. You could forgive her for anything except disabusing you of your romantic notions. Perhaps, this pretty young thing could help you rediscover them?"

"And in the meantime, shall we live in the four rooms of my house that are habitable and subsist on whatever the tenant farmers can spare and whatever I can eke out of the kitchen garden?" Alex demanded. "I'm not in a position to take a wife... and even if I were—"

"She's not high-born enough for you?"

"I don't give a whit about that," Alex retorted sharply. "If I married, if we had children... can you imagine what they would face given the scandal that is attached to my name? She'd never be accepted in society, polite or otherwise. I'd be damning her to a lonely existence, all but a prisoner in Wolfhaven Hall. Even if they do clear me of any wrongdoing and reverse the judgements against me, money alone will not halt the gossip and rumors, Ambrose. You know that."

"I do know that. Why do you think my son is such a prig? He's doing his damnedest to be anything but like me in the hopes of halting such gossip. But to hell with the lot of them, Alex. If you want to be with the girl, be with the girl! If you care for her as much as I suspect you do, then you wouldn't want to be anywhere but with each other anyway!"

"It's impossible."

"Nothing is impossible," Ambrose insisted. "Think on it, won't you?"

As if Alex had been able to think of much else since Mary Mason had come crashing through the woods that fateful night. He rose to his feet, nodded his head, "Thank you again, my friend."

With that parting comment, Alex left via the side door and made for the stables where his mount waited. He could have had a servant arrange for the carriage and his mount, but since his fall from grace, he'd grown rather used to seeing to his own needs. It scandalized Ambrose's servants, naturally, but Alex paid it no mind. He spoke to the coachman and made the necessary arrangements for him to arrive at Wolfhaven just past daybreak and see them to Bath. It would be a long journey and he needed to see to provisions for them. He was not flush by any means, but had enough coin to cover changing horses at the halfway mark and to provide a light luncheon for them.

With his business attended to, Alex headed home, heavy with the knowledge that this would be the last night he would have Mary Mason under his roof.

Chapter Eleven

DAVIES HAD GOTTEN back to the city late in the night, but he was up bright and early watching Number 27 Royal Crescent. He couldn't be entirely certain that Hamilton was in there, but even if he wasn't, he'd show up sooner or later. The mistress he kept there was a recluse, apparently, some sort of eccentric who never left the house, and if she did, she wore heavy veils that hid her face entirely. It was peculiar to the point that Davies had wondered if she had some reason to hide her face, a birthmark or some hideous scar perhaps. Whatever it was, he figured she'd have to be something special in other ways for Hamilton to tolerate it. The man was always coming and going from there. For such a posh address, there were dashedly few servants and not a single one of them could be plied with coin to gossip. He'd certainly tried. *Never met a more tight-lipped, pinch-faced housemaid in my life,* Davies thought.

No more had the thought crossed his mind than the door opened. Hamilton appeared, still wearing his evening clothes from the night before and looking fairly rumpled but quite pleased with himself. Davies allowed him to get several paces ahead of him before he emerged from his hiding place near the coal scuttle of a not quite as grand house on Church Street. Falling into step behind him, near enough to keep him in sight but not so near as to make the other man wary, Davies followed. Dressed in rough clothing, his face and hands smeared with dirt, he gave every impression of a workman heading for home or to the job, if he was on the slovenly side.

Perhaps, it was his certainty of his anonymity, his belief that a man as puffed up with his own importance as Hamilton would never stoop to notice the likes of him that made Davies careless. The coat he wore was the same one he'd worn when he followed the man two days earlier. The tune he whistled was familiar to Hamilton's ear, as well. Those things, more than anything else, pricked the unease of his quarry. There was no other explanation for why Hamilton rounded a corner and cut through a small alley between two terraces. By the time Davies followed suit, the other man had simply vanished.

Cursing under his breath, Davies scanned the street ahead but could not make out anyone amongst the few people strolling about that might be the gentleman in question. Turning, he headed back in the direction he'd first come to once more take up his watch at Number 27. If he followed the mistress, he'd eventually find his way back to Hamilton.

He'd no sooner rounded the corner than an angry shove forced him back against the stone wall of a back garden. The street was still dark, the long shadows of the tall townhouses making it dim and quiet. There was no one about to hear the whoosh of his breath leaving him as Hamilton punched him in the gut. Unable to talk or breathe, he doubled over, clutching at his middle and trying not to cast up his accounts.

"Who are you and why are you following me?"

Davies couldn't answer. The only sound that escaped him was a low, pained groan. Hamilton then hauled him up, lifting him off the ground by his throat. "Did Harrelson hire you? Well, you'll get no more money out of him. That bastard is dead!"

"I'm just off from work… heading home is all!" Davies managed to protest.

"And where is home then?" Hamilton challenged.

Davies had an answer for that. "I share a room with my cousin down on Manvers Street," he lied. "He works days on the docks during the day while I sleep!"

"And what do you do at night then? What sort of work keeps you out till morning?" the gentleman demanded, his gaze cold and full of fury.

"I light the lamps in the evening, then I have to go and douse them right at dawn, now don't I?" Davies shot back.

Hamilton's eyes narrowed. "You're lying. Because when I heard you whistle that same tune two days past, it was barely one in the afternoon," he said.

Davies struggled to free himself from the angry man's grasp, but Hamilton had withdrawn a small blade concealed in the shaft of his walking stick. The blade pressed against his throat. "I got a right to be out in the day like anyone else!" Davies protested.

"I'll ask again. Who are you working for?" Hamilton demanded. "Which of my enemies has set you on me?"

Recognizing the maddened glint in the other man's eyes, Davies knew that there was no answer to appease him. Truth or lies would get him killed. His only option was escape. "I'll tell you what you want to know, but not with the blade poking into my ribs!"

Hamilton lowered the weapon, "Go on."

With the weapon at the other man's side, Davies did the only thing that might give him a chance at survival. He dove to his right, as far from the menacing blade as possible. Running, he'd nearly reached the mouth of the alley when a rough hand hauled him back. But it didn't tug him to the ground. Instead, it tugged him backwards just as the blade pressed forward, slipping between his ribs and piercing his lung from behind.

It was almost painless, until the blade was withdrawn. Then the unbearable burning sensations began. He tried to breathe, to scream, but the blood was surging from the wound, filling his lungs, so that only a gurgling sound emerged from his lips.

Hamilton stepped back. "It doesn't matter who you worked for," he said. "You won't be reporting to them again. And should they send someone else to replace you, they will surely meet the same fate."

Davies sank slowly to his knees and then slumped to his side, his head resting on the hard stone. The last things he saw, before his eyes became fixed and sightless, were the heels of Hamilton's polished evening slippers as he strode away.

THE CARRIAGE RUMBLED along the highway toward the city of Bath. It was a very different journey than her departure from there had been, Mary reflected. Tossed into the back of a wagon like a sack of flour, with a hood tied over her head, hands and feet bound, and an uncertain fate awaiting her, she hadn't even considered the discomfort of that journey at the time. All of her attention, little of it as there had been given whatever drug they'd forced upon her, had been on what might be awaiting her when that rickety cart came to a stop.

Oddly enough, Mary found herself reluctant on her current journey as well, though for very different reasons. Despite everything, and despite her desire to see her brother and to let him know that she was well and had survived her ordeal, she had no real wish to be parted from Lord Wolverton. Over the course of their days together, she'd grown accustomed to his presence. It was impossible to say she had grown comfortable with his presence, though. For nothing could have been further from the truth. He made her heart race, sent butterflies swirling and soaring in her stomach. She was acutely aware of him on a primal level and could think of nothing save for the kisses they had shared—one chaste and one decidedly carnal. Ultimately, she wasn't certain whether she feared more of those encounters or craved them. Regardless, her will to resist diminished by the minute and if things went further than they had already, there was no hope of keeping either her heart or her virtue intact.

If things were different, if he wasn't haunted by the scandal and ruin of his wife's murder, if she weren't lacking in wealth or connections—there were dozens of questions and what ifs, and ultimately only one answer. It was impossible for them to have anything more than the brief interlude they had already shared, Mary thought sadly, accepting her fate. He would return her to Benedict and she would likely never see him again, much less have an opportunity to explore the surprisingly wanton element of her nature that he had called forth. Turning to look out the window, lest she get caught staring at him again, Mary must have let a sigh escape her.

"Are you well, Miss Mason? It is a bit early in the journey yet, but if you require a reprieve, you have only to say so," he offered, with all the solicitous concern of a true gentleman.

Mary shook her head. "I'm quite all right, Lord Wolverton. I was only thinking of what welcome might await us in Bath," she lied. "I can't help but wonder how my brother is settling in with his new family, and whether or not they will be as kind and gracious to me as you have been."

"I'm sure you have nothing to worry about. I do not know Lady Vale, as she has been much out of society since the abduction of her son so many years ago. I am familiar with Mr. Branson Middlethorp, however. He would be your brother's uncle. He's a fair man, though he can be somewhat intimidating. You mustn't let them worry you so. No doubt, your brother's happiness at seeing you safe will ease your way with his family," he offered.

"I certainly hope you are correct," she agreed. "I would hate to think that my presence would be unwelcome in his new life or create problems for him. And... perhaps I shouldn't speak of it, but there may be some way in which my brother, given his new position, might be able to repay your kindness to me—"

"I am not such a pauper, Miss Mason, that I would allow your brother to offer monetary compensation for assisting you!"

Mary flushed. "That wasn't at all what I meant. It's just that I know you are working so hard to prove you are innocent of your late wife's murder. If Benedict is truly accepted as Viscount Vale, and if this Mr. Middlethorp is as well respected as you say, then surely they could be valuable allies for you in your quest?"

He relaxed visibly, his face losing the angry tension that had tightened his jaw and narrowed his eyes. "If I am ever in need of their assistance, I will make the request at that time. It would be premature to ask them to do anything at this juncture."

She had wounded his pride, albeit unintentionally. Mary was all too aware that pride was one of the few things he had left. The poor state of his home, as well as the haphazard and scantily stocked larder was all the indication required. Of course, the latter might be more indicative of the quality of his servants. And yet, he turned himself out impeccably, even without the assistance of a valet. She knew from things that Mrs. Epson had let slip that he gardened and hunted to keep them fed, that when it was time to harvest the wheat and send it to market, he was in the fields swinging a scythe himself. How many other gentleman would do such? From things she'd overheard living above a gaming hell, she knew the answer was very few. How many whispered conversations had she heard between Benedict and his man of affairs about so-called gentleman who'd gambled away everything and ended their lives rather than pay their debts. That was not honor. But Lord Wolverton, his honor was unimpeachable in that regard.

"Whatever they, or I, could ever do for you, Lord Wolverton, you have only to ask and it will be done... I owe you my very life, after all," Mary said solemnly. But it wasn't her indebtedness to him that prompted such an offer. She was not so foolish as to think herself in love with him, not yet, but she was certainly smitten with him. If their circumstances had been different, it would have been only too easy to fall in love with him.

"You owe me nothing, Miss Mason. Your presence in my home has reminded me that there is far more to life than toil, hardship, and a potentially doomed quest for justice. I have laughed, smiled, and enjoyed pleasant company and pleasant conversation. I had not realized that those were the things I missed most from my old life until you. So I am in your debt, it would seem."

Mary fell silent, uncertain of what to say after that, but even more conflicted in her desire, inappropriate as it might have been, to remain at his side. They continued on in somewhat companionable silence, the borrowed traveling chariot making good time, much to her dismay.

Chapter Twelve

BENEDICT WAS SUFFERING through a tense and difficult meeting with Middlethorp. It wasn't the first and would likely not be the last. He needed brandy, but as it wasn't quite three in the afternoon, he felt it might be frowned upon.

"I will not do this, Middlethorp. I have a business of my own to manage and the family's estates appear to have flourished quite well with you at the helm. I see no need to change any of that simply because I am now a lord instead of a mister!" Benedict protested.

"And when I am gone? What then? Who will ensure that the estates continue to prosper for your children? If you do not do this now while I am still here to guide you—" Middlethorp shot back.

"Perhaps by then, I will have a better grasp on the finer points of animal husbandry and agriculture," Benedict snapped. "But until such time, I will gladly bow out. I'm ill-equipped to handle being a titled lord, much less a landowner, and we both know it!"

A knock at the door interrupted what was very likely to become a shouting match and both men recognized it for the reprieve it was. Middlethorp moved away from the desk to look out the window and Benedict barked an order bidding them enter. Immediately, he regretted his harsh tone. It was Lady Vale. *His mother.* "Forgive my tone," he offered. "I should not have been so abrupt."

"Nonsense. I know perfectly well how maddening Branson can be," she said. "But alas, I've come with rather distressing news. There's been a murder. A man was found just on the other side of our mews… stabbed in the chest. It's quite horrible! The magistrate is speaking to the servants now to see if perhaps one of them heard or saw something. I'm certain they will wish to speak with all of us as well. We might as well make up a guest room for the man at this point!"

Benedict didn't correct her. He couldn't. Between his shooting, Elizabeth's abduction, Mary's abduction, the murder and suicide of Lord Harrelson and Madame Zula, and then, of course, there was the strange matter of his apparent return from the grave—it was a wonder they weren't all being shuffled off to Bedlam. "We will make ourselves available at the magistrate's convenience. Where is Elizabeth?"

Lady Vale wrung her hands. "She's out. There were several errands that she needed to see to, and I had a few myself, so she kindly agreed to take care of them for me."

Middlethorp tossed his hands up in the air. "She's not your servant anymore, Sarah! Miss Masters is now betrothed to your son, Viscount Vale!"

Benedict watched her reaction. There was something more to her relationship with Branson than first appeared. While he had no wish to speculate about his mother's romantic inclinations, he couldn't help but think that the ever present anger between the pair of them was simply a mask for something else.

"I'm well aware of that, Branson! I didn't send her out to get the laundry, for heaven's sake! She was going to the milliner and I needed a bonnet repaired. Elizabeth offered to take it for me so I wouldn't have to go. She's a sweet girl and understands how very much I hate being the center of gossip!"

"I'm certain Elizabeth did not mind at all, Mother," Benedict said. "And Middlethorp, while I thank you for being so willing to rush to my bride-to-be's defense, if she requires defending, I assure you that I will see to it."

Branson snorted. "Well, there's one responsibility you won't shirk!"

"Enough," Lady Vale said firmly. "It won't do for us all to be at one another's throats when the magistrate walks in!"

"No, indeed," Benedict said, his eyes glued to the hallway behind his mother and the small, not so smartly dressed figure of the magistrate just beyond her. "He might believe we were all criminals and capable of murder."

Apparently his tone was revealing enough, for Lady Vale looked heavenward and sighed wearily before turning to greet the man. "Do come in, Mr. Hillyard. Might I offer you tea?"

"No, thank you, m'lady. I just need to ascertain the whereabouts of everyone this morning, between the hours of seven and eight. The lad who douses the lamps had gone through here by seven, and the body was not present at such time. But it did appear before the hour of eight when the Marquess of Reddington's man of affairs arrived. It's just a routine question, m'lady. No need to be up in arms about it. We're asking at every household on the street."

"I was still abed, Mr. Hillyard. It is my habit to sleep until at least nine and then have chocolate brought up. I will have breakfast afterward, around ten or so, and then begin my day," Lady Vale replied.

"I see. And you, Mr. Middlethorp?"

"I had gone riding with a friend... Mr. Sommersby," Middlethorp supplied readily.

Benedict knew it for a lie immediately, but why the man would have anything to hide was a mystery to him. Unless he'd been doing something he did not feel he could speak of in front of Lady Vale. Did Middlethorp have a mistress in the city?

"And you, Mr. Mason? Excuse me... Lord Vale?" Hillyard asked. It was clear that the slip had been quite intentional.

Benedict's expression remained bland. He'd been slipping from Elizabeth's chamber to his own, dodging chambermaids and footmen as he tried to keep from being discovered. It was hardly the sort of thing he would share, and most certainly not in front of his mother. "I must have been in my room... if not, I had made my way down here to the library to review some correspondence. We are still looking for my sister, after all. Sometimes, I find it difficult to sleep."

"I see," Hillyard said, nodding sagely. "I'm sure the servants will be able to corroborate everyone's stories. I'll just check with them again before I go."

THE CARRIAGE SLOWED and then halted before the exquisite townhome that was in the center of one of the three terraces that comprised the Circus. Grand and impressive, the rooms were two across, with one on either side of the central hall. Mary had seen it when she'd first come to Bath. She had made it a point to find out which of those homes belonged to Lady Vale and had spent a great deal of time observing it. In spite of her belief that Benedict was truly the lost heir to the Vale Viscountcy, the resemblance between her brother and Lady Vale had been *that* strong, it was a very strange thing to think he now resided within those walls.

Lord Wolverton alighted from the carriage first before turning back to assist her as the coachman retrieved the small bag of hastily altered garments from the small boot. It had rained through the afternoon and the pavement was dotted with puddles.

"Those bandages cannot get wet. I will carry you to the door," he said and then made to do just that, sweeping her into his arms.

Mary's breath caught as she realized it would likely be the last time she would ever be so close to him. She ducked her head, attempting to hide her reaction.

"Oh, dear heavens! Are you quite all right?"

The voice belonged to a young woman and Mary glanced in her direction. She recognized her immediately as Lady Vale's companion, but she was dressed very differently than she had been when Mary had last seen her. Wearing a fine walking dress of pale blue striped muslin with a matching spencer, she looked every inch a fashionable young woman.

But then the woman looked at her and her eyes widened. "You're Mary. You are Benedict's sister!"

Mary nodded. "Yes, I am Mary Mason. Please forgive me for arriving so. I have been ill and Lord Wolverton was kind enough to see me here to find my brother."

The woman nodded. "I am Elizabeth Masters... I am your brother's betrothed."

Mary blinked in surprise. That was news she hadn't quite expected. "I see. I wasn't aware that Benedict had formed any attachments."

Miss Masters smiled, but her gaze traveled from Lord Wolverton's face to Mary's own in a very knowing way. "It's been a very traumatic time for us all and in such times, I think that the intensity of one's feelings becomes heightened far more quickly," she suggested mildly. "But let us get you inside! Benedict is here and I know he is most eager to see you. Come! Come! This news is too joyous to keep him waiting."

Mary tightened her arms about Lord Wolverton's neck, perhaps more so than was necessary, as he climbed the steps. Just as the butler was opening the door, he placed her gently on her feet. She was immediately bereft at the loss of contact. Perhaps, she thought, it was best that they not see one another anymore. Her attachment to him was far too serious already and to further their acquaintance was simply courting disaster. But continuing to spend time with him, to deepen the connection she felt to him, or—heaven forbid—give in to the temptation and beg him once more to kiss her, would only lead them both down a path that ought to be denied.

Limping inside behind Miss Masters, she immediately heard raised voices from a room to their right. Miss Masters turned back to her. "Mr. Branson Middlethorp, your brother's uncle... they are far more alike than either of them realize and, as a result, have butted heads rather frequently since Benedict's identity was confirmed."

"Is he unhappy that Benedict has been confirmed to be Lord Vale, then?" Mary asked with concern. Had she inadvertently set her brother on a path that would cause him harm or unhappiness?

Miss Masters laughed, a musical sound that filled the small entryway. "Oh, good heavens! Not at all. Mr. Middlethorp could not be more thrilled. He's rather cross because your dear brother keeps insisting he is incapable of taking over the family estates. Personally, I rather agree with Mr. Middlethorp. Benedict is perfectly capable. He just simply needs to make peace with the idea of it. I think, and I would never say this to him, he feels somewhat intimidated by the prospect."

The butler cleared his throat. "I will announce the guests if it pleases you, Miss Masters."

"It does not please me," she replied. "I will take them in as I go. Miss Mason will need no introduction… and, oh dear, I do not believe I know who your gallant rescuer is!"

Mary blushed at the terrible lapse in manners. "I'm so terribly sorry. Miss Masters, may I present Lord Alexander Carnahan, Earl of Wolverton." Mary knew instantly that Miss Masters recognized his name. Her eyes widened and her face paled perceptibly. But she recovered quickly, pasting a smile on her face that was a tad too bright and far from sincere.

"Well, Lord Wolverton, it is a pleasure to make your acquaintance and I cannot tell you how grateful we are for your heroic rescue of my new sister. Please, let's convene to the library and see if this very glad news can stave off a bout of fisticuffs, shall we?"

Mary followed behind her, leaning heavily on Lord Wolverton's arm as they made their way to the other room. Miss Masters opened the door and they stepped into the dimly-lit chamber behind her. Benedict stood next to Lady Vale. Another man, a gentleman still quite fit and handsome, but with dark hair going to gray, stood near the window. Facing off against them was a smallish man in ill-fitting clothes and wearing a very satisfied smirk upon his thin face.

At their entrance, the room fell silent. It was so very quiet that a pin dropping on the carpet would have sounded like cannon fire, Mary thought. No sooner had the thought occurred, than Benedict made a sound that was unlike anything she'd ever heard. Had she not known him better, she would have thought it a sob. Without preamble, he closed the distance between them, swept her into his arms and hugged her so fiercely she feared her ribs would break.

"I thought you lost," he whispered, and there was something broken in his voice, something she had not heard since they were children.

"There were moments when I thought it as well," she admitted softly.

"Now see here—" the thin, weaselly man began.

"You see here, Hillyard," the older gentleman interrupted him. "This is a private family matter and you will take your leave!"

"I have not had my questions answered to my satisfaction!"

"And you will not today, regardless of whether you stand there braying like an ass or not," the gentleman stated, his language and his tone both quite shocking. "Now, off with you, or I will see you tossed out into the street."

The man, clearly taking the gentleman at his word, left though he grumbled under his breath as he did so. Finally, Benedict let her go, stepping back to look at her.

"Where have you been? We searched everywhere for you!" he said as his gaze traveled toward the man who stood beside her. There was suspicion in it and an abundance of caution.

It was Miss Masters who stepped in. "Benedict, she will tell us everything in good time. But for now, let us get her situated comfortably and offer some tea and food to our guests. I'm certain they must be exhausted and famished following their journey."

"Of course," he said. "Forgive me, Mary, I'm just so glad to have you here with us again."

With Lord Wolverton's assistance, Mary made her way to the settee that Lady Vale gestured toward with a graceful sweep of her hand. "Poor, dear girl! How worried we have all been for you!"

Miss Masters rang for tea and Mr. Middlethorp watched them curiously, but it was clearly Lord Wolverton who held his attention. It appeared to her that Benedict's newfound uncle was a man who missed very little.

Wanting to get the worst of it over with, Mary began, "I came to Bath because I encountered Lady Vale in London—"

"We know all that," Benedict said. "Your things were still with Mrs. Simms and, as sorry as I am to admit it to you, we read your journal. I had hoped it would offer some insight into who might have taken you but, alas, it did not."

Mary frowned, not out of anger, but confusion. "So you knew that I came here to investigate your past? That I suspected you were Lord Vale?"

"Yes," Benedict offered. "We're clear on everything up until the abduction itself. We know you were taken from the street in front of Madame Zula's, likely taken to the same warehouse they took Elizabeth to, and then to an abandoned mine on Lord Harrelson's property. But you escaped and then all trace of you vanished."

"Well that is where Lord Wolverton comes in," Mary answered.

"Wolverton?" Lady Vale gasped, drawing back in horror.

"Yes," Mary said. "Lord Wolverton found me in the woods after I escaped. I was injured and suffering from an ailment of the lungs. He took me to his home and cared for me until I was well enough to travel here."

Benedict's brows drew together. "Who resides in this house?"

Wolverton had been silent to that point, allowing his identity and the scandal attached to it to settle over those gathered like a pall. "My estate is impoverished, Lord Vale. I was alone there with Miss Mason save for my housekeeper and stable master. There are a couple of other servants but they do not live on the property. They come and go from their own homes."

Another gasp from Lady Vale and a thunderous glower from Mr. Middlethorp only underscored the tension in the room following that admission. Mary looked imploringly at Benedict. "I understand that it is improper but under the circumstances, it was simply not possible for a chaperone to be procured. I was too ill to travel and there was no one else to tend me if he left! Surely you see that despite the circumstances, any impropriety was secondary to the dire nature of the situation we found ourselves in."

"Miss Mason," Lady Vale began, then paused as if to collect her thoughts. "In your previous life, and please forgive me if what I'm about to say makes me seem cold to your circumstances, for I am not! But when you were the sister of a businessman who had no connections to polite society, then such things might have passed without comment. But Benedict is no longer simply a businessman. He is now a lord! A peer of the realm and you are his adopted sister. Whatever scandal touches you, touches us all."

"Then should I have lain there on the ground, bleeding and burning with fever, refusing any offer of salvation until a chaperone could be obtained?" Mary snapped.

"My dear, I meant no offense. And I am not suggesting that anything you have done was without cause or in any way imprudent! The question now is not about what has been done, but about what is left to do!" Lady Vale insisted. "I'm certain that Lord Wolverton, in spite of his past, understands what the honorable course of action is here."

"What about his past?" Benedict demanded.

"There were rumors about the first wife," Middlethorp said. Both his tone and his expression were utterly inscrutable.

Wolverton shook his head. "I was tried for murdering my wife, Lord Vale. Let us call a spade a spade in this instance and have no more vague references or allusions. I was acquitted of the charges. But in civil proceedings, heavy fines were levied against me and a settlement awarded to my late wife's family. Hence the impoverished nature of my home."

Lady Vale looked pointedly at Benedict. "Under the circumstance, and I'm certain that Lord Wolverton understands the proper course of action here, perhaps a special license can be procured?"

"A special license?" Mary asked. "What in heaven's name do you mean, Lady Vale?"

"My dear, there is only one way to come back from such an indelicate sort of foible as this... and that is marriage. Society will forgive many things once a union is sanctioned by the church!"

Mary spared a glance at Lord Wolverton, stoic and utterly silent as a room full of strangers plotted their lives together. He didn't want it and even if he had, she would never allow it to happen in such a way. The very idea that he might feel forced or coerced left her feeling sick to her stomach at the thought. "You are all making a great number of assumptions—"

"Miss Mason," Lord Wolverton said. "This is not unexpected. I realize it is not what you might wish for, but if your brother is insistent, and should gossip spread that would necessitate our marrying, I will certainly agree. It is the most expedient way to preserve certain aspects of your reputation, though I fear it may suffer in other ways."

Benedict rose to his feet, an angry glare twisting his normally handsome features. "So you think to marry my sister? I'll not compound one stroke of bad luck by heaping poor judgement upon it! There will be no marriage!"

"I had not assumed there would be," Lord Wolverton stated emphatically. "I understand that I have put Miss Mason in an untenable position. Had there been another option that would have resulted in saving her life, I would have taken it. And regardless of my loss in the civil trial, I am innocent of the crime."

"Then who did it?" This question came from Middlethorp. It wasn't angry and accusatory as the others had been, but reflective and curious.

"Lord Harrelson," Mary stated softly. "I think we are all victims of Lord Harrelson here, in one way or another. And we have some proof of his perfidy in other areas, if not in this one."

Whether it was the truth of her words or the quiet conviction with which she uttered them, a hush once more fell over the room. Tension was still there, evident in Lord Wolverton's rigid posture and the fact that Benedict had his hands balled into fists at his sides, as if ready to take a swing at the slightest provocation.

"You asked to hear what happened, and if you will all stop making assumptions and trying to plan how best to avoid a scandal that may never even occur, I will tell you," Mary said. "There is much information to be offered and I think it may help to answer questions that we all have... questions that were born twenty some years ago, Benedict, when you were taken from your mother's arms."

"Very well," Middlethorp said just as the maid entered bearing a tray of tea and small sandwiched and cakes. "Let us begin then."

Mary looked back to Lord Wolverton, noting the hard line of his jaw and the firm set of his chin. They had wounded him carelessly, she thought, as if accusations against him were as commonplace as breathing. She supposed they were, really, but it was grossly unfair. Her own suspicions of him from earlier came rushing to her mind, along with no small amount of shame. She'd been just as judgmental and mean-spirited as others had toward him.

Resisting the urge to simply throw herself at his feet and beg forgiveness, Mary said, "Perhaps you should start with why you suspected Lord Harrelson's involvement in Lady Helena's murder."

Chapter Thirteen

THE NOTE SHE'D received from Albie that morning had sent Helena into a panic. He'd insisted that they were being followed, watched. Then he'd confessed to her that he'd dispatched a man he believed to be Harrelson's spy. It was the latter part of the letter that had set her on edge, of course. He'd told her she would have to engineer her own return to Wolverton, that it was too dangerous for them to be together now.

It was the culmination of all of Helena's worst fears. She had been in love with Albie since she was a little girl, worshipping him. Together, they'd learned and explored their passions in secret. If the small, sane part of her whispered that it wasn't love at all, but obsession, she ignored that as she had ignored all prudent warnings in her life. Instead, Helena grasped the one thought that had been with her, a constant fear since her girlhood. Albie was leaving her. She was being abandoned by the one person who had sworn never to desert her.

He insisted in his letter that it wasn't so, that he would always love her and would never be far away. Then he made promises that it was only temporary and as soon as the possibility for discovery lessened, she would once again be in his arms. *Lies*, she thought bitterly. He swore that as soon as they'd managed to tamp down any suspicions or gossip over her return, everything would go according to their original plan.

They'd known, of course, that Wolverton believed Albie and Harrelson to be responsible for her "death." It had never been of any real

concern to them given that her poor, widowed husband was so
horribly discredited in the eyes of the world that he would never be
able to get anyone to listen to him. But that was before Harrelson's
untimely end. Now, with no notion where his books with all his filthy
secrets were, they had no way of making others kowtow to them as he
had. In essence, they were cast adrift.

Anger, fear, and pure, blind panic—all of those things had driven
her to this small rebellion of taking a sedan chair out in the middle of
the day. She was desperate to get to Albie, to have him offer her
reassurance. So she'd summoned a Bath chair and was on her way to
his rooms near Avon Street. He stayed in that little hovel, so he said, to
keep abreast of the goings-on with Harrelson's other hirelings. She
knew the truth, of course. Albie had always loved the cards and
couldn't get credit to gamble anywhere respectable.

But her journey was cut abruptly short when she saw a familiar
coat of arms traveling along Brock Street and onto the Circus. Her
breath caught.

"Follow that carriage," she snapped at the chairmen.

They followed her direction, grunting as they increased their
speed. Luckily, the carriage slowed and then halted directly in front of
one of the Palladian townhouses that comprised the only address in
Bath more fashionable than the veritable prison she existed in.
Immediately, she recognized it as Lady Vale's residence. The reclusive
Lady Vale and the debauched Lord Ambrose were unlikely friends. Of
course, anything was possible. Her own husband's friendship with the
aging rogue had always been a puzzle to her, as well. It appeared there
was more to Lord Ambrose than the drinking and whoring that he was
known for.

"Stop here," she hissed at the chairman again and, immediately,
they did as she asked, stopping near the end of one of the curved
terraces that comprised the Circus.

Helena bit back a gasp as a familiar figure emerged from the carriage. It was not Lord Ambrose at all, but Alexander. He was holding
on to some ridiculous slip of a girl as if she were the great love of his

life. Not that she'd ever desired his love or devotion, Helena thought bitterly. But it had stung to see his disgust of her written so plainly upon his face. From the tender way he held that girl, whoever she might be, it was clear that he was certainly not repulsed by her. An unreasonable anger filled her—at Albie, at Harrelson, at her worthless stepfather who had never lost an opportunity in private to tell her that she was destined to be a whore, just like her mother. That anger extended to Wolverton and by virtue of association, the woman who had clearly managed to capture his heart.

Albie had wanted her to reunite with Alexander, she thought, seizing upon the seeds of a plan. Now that she'd seen her poor, aggrieved husband so clearly smitten with someone else, she rather fancied a reconciliation herself. It wasn't that she wanted him, or even that she wanted him to want her. She simply couldn't abide the thought that he might find someone to be happy with. That, she would not stand for.

As if with the snap of the fingers, Helena's mood and plans changed. A cold smile curved her lips beneath the heavy, black veil. Albie would be furious if she acted without him, but it had been his suggestion, after all. And it wouldn't hurt him to suffer a little, too.

"Turn around," she instructed the chairmen. "I need to be at home. There is much to be done."

The chairmen shared a glance with one another as they turned the conveyance. It wasn't the first time they had been summoned to carry the madwoman to whatever destination she chose. She was always a bit wild and unpredictable, not to mention incredibly moody. But if home was what she wanted that was where they'd take her. They got their coin just the same.

ALEX HAD NOT expected that Mary's return would go without some degree of difficulty. He was a widower, regardless of the circumstances which created that status, and she had been alone in his home with him for many days. Part of him wished they would force the issue, that they would demand without quarter that he do the *honorable* thing and marry her. Then she would be his and he would be able to stop fighting the damnable desire he felt for her. But whatever they thought of him, he knew what the truly honorable thing to do was. He had to let her go. To tie her to him, with the black cloud hanging over him and the scandal that dogged his every step—how long would it take for her to grow to hate him when she lived a life of penury in a crumbling estate?

"My late wife, prior to our marriage, was Helena Hamilton."

It wasn't Lady Vale who gasped at that admission, but Miss Masters. He glanced at her in surprise. "You knew her?" Alex asked.

"We moved in the same circles when I was younger... before my turn of fortune," she answered. To Lord Vale, she said softly, "She was Freddy's sister."

Vale seemed to consider that carefully, before finally allowing his clenched fists to relax and once more taking a seat. "Go on."

"Helena is, by law, half-sister to Freddy and to Albert Hamilton. By blood, she is no relation to them at all," Alex asserted.

Miss Masters nodded. "It's true. Freddy's mother, Lady Samford, was a terrible flirt... and much worse if rumors are to be believed."

"And Lady Samford is the younger sister of Lord Harrelson," Alex explained. "I was approached about a match with Helena. I had not been much to town with my father's illness. The estates needed tending and, frankly, navigating society to find a bride seemed a poor use of my time. I was reluctant, at first. There were rumors about her, that she was a bit wild and fast. But it was a good match with a favorable contract and the promise of land adjoining my estate."

"And Helena Hamilton was a remarkably beautiful woman. One who might make any man take a foolish course of action," Middlethorp said.

"True enough, though my marriage to Helena was never imagined to be anything other than a business arrangement," Alex replied. "I had reason to believe, prior to the marriage and as it continued, that

Helena was actually involved in a romantic way with her stepbrother, Albert. We had argued about it… not about her faithlessness, so much as her recklessness. My only concern at that point was that she should be discreet. I had given up hope of anything else with her."

"And yet you claim that it was Harrelson who killed her?" Benedict demanded. "You have just announced your rather convincing motive."

"I don't know that it was Harrelson. I think the more probable scenario is that Albert Hamilton killed her and then Harrelson helped him to direct suspicion at me. And as to what will likely be your next question, I believe that Hamilton was assisting him in a rather unscrupulous enterprise of blackmail and slavery."

Middlethorp nodded. "I don't discount what you say. Harrelson is certainly capable of it and we have reason to believe that Fredrick Hamilton is also involved in the mess, though perhaps not in the same manner that his brother is… or was. But how does that account for your conviction in civil trial?"

It was a question that he'd known they would ask. "That is where the blackmail enters the equation. My trial was rushed, completed before the House of Lords was in session. There were the very minimum number of lords present to serve as a jury and the vast majority of them were being blackmailed into submission by Harrelson. I've amassed proof in many of those cases, but not all. Certainly enough that I can take that information, along with what I have recently learned, and begin the process of appeal."

"Lord Wolverton has obtained some journals, ledgers really, as well as some letters from Lord Harrelson's study that corroborate most of what he'd suspected all along," Mary said. "Those ledgers detail all of the women and children that he had abducted throughout the years… including me. It appears he was not keeping such adequate records when you were taken, Benedict."

Lord Vale rose and crossed to the desk where he retrieved a book. "We have something similar from Madame Zula. Perhaps if we compare them we shall have enough information to locate some of these people and possibly improve their situations... as for my abduction, it appears that mine was the starting point for Harrelson in this particular enterprise. It was through the unfortunate events of that night that he realized people would pay for children... for any number of reasons."

"There are mentions in the journal of someone whose initials are FH. Do you know who that is?" Alex demanded.

"Fenton Hardwick," Miss Masters answered. "He was a lackey, a brute really, who worked for Harrelson and conducted most of the abductions, including my own."

"That rough-looking man who followed you!" Mary said. As if realizing what she'd given away, she flushed with embarrassment, her cheeks turning a lovely shade of pink. "When I was trying to determine whether or not it was possible that Benedict might, in fact, be Lord Vale, I was doing rather shady things myself, Lady Vale, including following you and Miss Masters. That was how I was led to Madame Zula. But while following you, I observed a man who kept close watch on you and he talked rather familiarly with Madame Zula's manservant."

"That would be him," Vale agreed.

"I know you all have more questions, but Miss Mason is still recovering. The bandages on her feet will need to be changed and she needs to rest. Any questions can wait, I think," Alex said. If his tone was more forceful than necessary, no one, save for Miss Masters, paid it any heed.

"What is wrong with her feet?" Vale demanded.

"I ran barefoot through the woods for miles, Benedict, over stones and twigs and heaven knows what else. Cuts and bruises. Nothing more," she said dismissively.

"I will help you upstairs," he said.

"I think Lord Wolverton should stay, if possible!" Mary blurted out.

Everyone in the room looked at her as if she'd gone mad, himself included. Alex shook his head. "Miss Mason, while I appreciate the gesture, that would be impossible—"

"Nonsense," Miss Masters said. "We have room. And since we clearly have much to discuss if we are ever to solve all of these ridiculous mysteries, it only makes sense you would stay close at hand. Don't you agree, Lady Vale?"

Lady Vale, put thoroughly on the spot, blustered but failed to produce an intelligible reply.

"I agree completely," Middlethorp said. "I'll send a man to your estate to fetch clothing for you, as it appears you did not come equipped for a lengthy visit."

Alex was stuck. "Very well, though I daresay my aging and rebellious housekeeper would rather burn my things than pack them."

"Then I shall send my valet. He will know just what to do. I'm assuming the stairs would be too difficult for Miss Mason alone. If you will both come with me, I will show you to your rooms," Middlethorp continued, completely ignoring the scandalized expression from Lady Vale and the rather mutinous one from her son. It was only Miss Masters, rising from her chair and placing a staying hand on her betrothed's arm, that prevented another eruption of temper. Whether Vale had some insight into the impure nature of his feelings toward Miss Mason or not, it was clear the man wanted Alex nowhere near his sister. He couldn't blame the man for that.

Chapter Fourteen

"WHAT THE DEVIL are you about, Elizabeth?" Benedict demanded.

"Yes, Miss Masters," Lady Vale snapped, "What are you about? That man is said to have killed his wife!"

"That man saved Mary's life. And has cared for her very tenderly it would seem. We have all been victims of Harrelson's schemes. Is it so shocking to think that he might have engineered Lord Wolverton's legal and financial difficulties in order to protect his nephew and protégé? Although, I find it likely that there is a more mercenary reason at heart. Freddy married an heiress because the family was terribly in debt. I overheard him once discussing it with Albert, and that debt was owed to Lord Harrelson."

"I still fail to see the connection between that and Lord Wolverton," Lady Vale insisted.

It was Benedict who answered. "I recall the trials. Both criminal and civil. It was all anyone talked about in the club. If I recall correctly, there were any number of wagers on it in the betting book. And no one won a single note from it because the outcome was so surprising. Anything that had gone to Lord Wolverton as part of the marriage settlement, and anything that he owned that was not entailed, was stripped from him and given directly to the Hamilton family."

Lady Vale gasped. "Do you really think he would have seen his niece married off to a man just to see her dead and claim the man's holdings?"

Elizabeth nodded. "I do think that. I think that there is very little

Harrelson would not have done. I do agree with Lord Wolverton's assessment that it wasn't planned that way per se, but when the opportunity arose, he would have taken it straightaway."

"I don't like it," Benedict said firmly. "He was very proprietary with her. And she seemed… different."

"Taken, you mean," Elizabeth said. "She is rather taken with him. And he with her, I think. And you are both being the worst of hypocrites. Every person in this room is scandal-ridden, and most of us have courted that scandal of our own accord! Lord Wolverton, if what he asserts is, in fact, the truth, has been an innocent victim all along. We owe it to him and we owe it to your sister to help him prove his case."

"I still don't like it," Benedict repeated. "I'm not disagreeing with you, but I don't like it."

"She's your sister. Of course you don't. But she's only just returned to you, Benedict," Elizabeth added. "Don't be so wrong-headed that you drive her away!"

Lady Vale let out a long-suffering sigh. "We'll never be accepted in society. Ever."

"And you have shunned society yourself for the past twenty years," Benedict pointed out. "What's a few more?"

"Very well, but if we're all murdered in our beds, it'll be entirely upon your head, Elizabeth Masters," Lady Vale warned.

"Perhaps, we should start a betting book of our own?" Elizabeth suggested with amusement. "I daresay that the only threats we face at present originate outside of this house."

"THESE CHAMBERS ARE smaller and typically we would not use them for guests," Mr. Middlethorp said. "But at present, the house is a bit fuller than it typically has been, so we must make do. Naturally, a man of your station should command better accommodations, Lord Wolverton, and after I return to London, you'll be able to take my room in the family quarters below."

"I'll be quite comfortable here," Alex said. It was a lie, of course. He had no notion what Middlethorp was thinking in placing him in the room directly across the hall from Miss Mason. To protest the arrangement would make him look like a snobbish prig or would bring into question how honorably he had behaved toward Mary. In short, his only option was to accept the room assignment.

"I knew your father," Middlethorp said casually. "Years ago. Good man. Very sorely missed, I think."

"That he is, Mr. Middlethorp," Alex agreed. Had his father lived, he would never have made the mistake he had of marrying Helena. For one, his father would have advised against it and rightly so; secondly, he would have been in society, likely in London. It was fanciful thinking to believe that he might have innocently crossed paths with Mary Mason, but the thought was there nonetheless. In some ways, he felt they had been destined to meet, even if they were not to be together.

The man nodded again. "It appears that you and Miss Mason have developed quite the rapport during your time together. She's a lovely girl."

"She is. And she has been through a terrible ordeal. It would take the worst sort of blackguard to take advantage of a woman in her situation," Alex said, his words and tone heavily laced with warning.

"So it would. But I'm a military man, Wolverton, or I was. And I learned that sometimes the strongest of bonds are formed under the worst of circumstances. I shall see you at dinner."

Alex watched Middlethorp walk away. It didn't matter that the man had just given his not so subtle blessing to Alex's pursuit of Mary Mason. It wasn't his place to do so, after all. But it worried him that he'd been so obvious in his feelings for her. If he did not curb his response to her and the transparency of his affections, he could very well ruin her.

Cursing under his breath, he turned and entered the room he'd been given for the duration of his stay. It was small, the bed narrow, and the furniture simple. But it was bright and clean, and there wasn't a speck of dust to be found unless it was one he'd brought with him. How his definition of luxury had transformed, he thought bitterly.

A moment later, a footman knocked softly at the door and entered with fresh water. "Mr. Middlethorp thought you might wish to refresh yourself after your journey, my lord."

"Put it there," Alex said, pointing to the simple wash basin. "Thank you."

The footman nodded and left as quickly as he'd entered. Immediately, Alex removed his cravat and coat, his waistcoat and then stripped his shirt off over his head. He washed away the dust and grime from his face first and was midway through washing his chest when another knock sounded. Expecting another servant, he called out and bade them enter.

At the soft gasp, he looked up and found Mary Mason standing in the doorway, blushing furiously. But she didn't look away. Instead, it appeared her gaze was locked firmly upon his naked flesh. It was the very antithesis of what he should do, and yet Alex turned to face her fully, allowing her to look her fill.

"Did you need something from me?" he asked. There was a wealth of meaning in that phrase and while he understood it perfectly, he could see that she did not.

Abruptly she cut her gaze to the floor. "I wanted to bring the ledgers back to you. I had packed them in my bag this morning since you did not bring one."

Alex strode forward, taking the books from her. "You should not be in here. You should not trust me."

"Why ever not? You have been all that is honorable!" she protested.

"In deed, yes, but not in my thoughts, Mary Mason. In my thoughts, I have been more wicked than you can possibly imagine. Return to your room, and do not seek me out unless we are in the company of others. You have more trust in me than I have in myself at this time," he said roughly. "Go."

She did. He watched her turn and flee across the hall, her door closing softly behind her. Alex cursed again and wished for the thousandth time that his life was different, that he was free to pursue her in the way that he ought to, the way he wanted. *If she is still free when my properties are returned and my name is cleared,* he vowed to himself, *I will come for her and hell itself will not stop me.*

MARY RETREATED HASTILY to her own room. Closing the door behind her, she leaned against it and drew in a deep, shuddering breath. There was a very imprudent and, perhaps, slightly wanton part of her that had longed to challenge him, to demand that he show her just how wicked his thoughts had been. The very idea of it left her trembling and breathless.

He'd lifted and carried her so frequently over the last few days, and with such ease, she'd been left with little doubt of his considerable strength. That was a very different thing when confronted with his bare chest. The breadth of his shoulders, the firm contours of well-defined muscles and the light dusting of crisp, brown hair that bisected his ridged abdomen had been a shock to the senses. It also added an entirely new dimension to her rather abbreviated fantasies of him. While she understood the essential elements of carnal activity, having grown up largely in the countryside and then indulging in many whispered conversations with the girls at school, there was a great deal of it that was a mystery to her. She'd wondered how it would feel to be crushed against a man as he kissed her, how different a man's body might feel from her own. And while some of those questions had been answered by the brief kisses and sensual interludes they'd shared, only more questions had arisen.

Her curiosity had been piqued by him, as had her desire. But ultimately, she was a coward. Rather than facing him with certainty when he'd told her the truth of his own desires, she'd fled like a scared rabbit. Frustrated by the situation, by her own desires, her fear of consequences, his need to adhere to the mandates of propriety, Mary moved to the bed and slumped down upon it dejectedly.

"It would be so much easier if he would just seduce me," she whispered to the empty room. "Because I simply lack the knowledge to manage any sort of seduction of him."

Mary laid back on the pillows and stared up at the ceiling wishing desperately that she could be more bold with him. She'd had the audacity to come to Bath alone, to lie to her brother in order to investigate his origins without his knowledge! Of course, that had not gone as intended but, still, she had done it. Why did she lack any sort of courage when it came to advancing her relationship with Lord Wolverton?

Because he might reject her. That was ultimately it, Mary realized. And whether he did it out of his impeccable sense of honor, or whether he did it because he simply could not align himself in any meaningful way with someone as potentially low-born as she was, made little difference. It would be humiliating regardless and after all that had occurred, she had little enough dignity left to spare.

A soft knock at the door had her heart pounding. Mary sat up, called out for the person to enter, and knew a moment of bitter disappointment when it was only Miss Masters and not Lord Wolverton. Apparently, she did not hide her response very well because Miss Masters laughed.

"Is my presence truly so unwelcome then?" the other woman asked.

"Not at all," Mary insisted, feeling even more embarrassed and terribly out of her depth. "I was simply—I wasn't expecting you, Miss Masters, but you are more than welcome."

Miss Masters entered the room fully, several gowns draped over her arms. "I see. But I am not as welcome as Lord Wolverton might have been. Isn't that who you expected?"

"Not expected," Mary answered.

"Hoped, then," Miss Masters continued. "I must admit that I was rather taken aback when I heard his name. And I'm certain I did not conceal it well. For that, I am terribly sorry, because whatever may have been said about him in the past, no man who cared for you and tended to you as carefully and tenderly as he has could be guilty of such crimes."

"He is not guilty," Mary said adamantly. "I'm certain of it. Even before we studied the ledgers and found the true depths of evil to which Harrelson had sunk, I knew that he was incapable of what he'd been accused of. But I think Benedict is not so certain and I worry that he will make trouble for Lord Wolverton, Miss Masters."

"We are to be sisters. You will call me Elizabeth and I will call you Mary. I already have been at any rate, a habit I picked up from Benedict, I suppose," the other woman said. "These gowns are Lady Vale's from some time ago. But they are not so terribly out of fashion, I think, and should suffice until we can get some things made up for you. She is somewhat taller than you, however."

Mary laughed at that. "As is everyone! I thank her ladyship for the gowns."

Elizabeth nodded. "I will tell her you said so. Now, I recommend this lovely periwinkle one for dinner. I'll send a maid to help you take it up. As for your brother and Lord Wolverton, you leave Benedict to me."

"And now, I must give you my thanks," Mary replied.

Elizabeth waved away the gratitude as she made for the door. As she reached it, she turned back. "I nearly drove Benedict away. I refused him reputedly because I believed that things in my past made me unsuitable for him. But he was remarkably persistent and I am now so very grateful for that. Do not let Lord Wolverton push you away because of his past, Mary. It's obvious that he cares for you and it is equally obvious that you care for him!"

"It isn't only his past, Elizabeth. Benedict is high-born, but I am not. There is nothing in the records we found to indicate that I am anything more than a child plucked from one poverty-ridden slum and placed in another. What on earth could I offer Lord Wolverton?"

"Love, Mary. You could offer him love... and I think, perhaps, he may need that more than anything else," Elizabeth said, and then slipped out the door.

The words hung in the air, echoing long after Elizabeth Masters was gone. Even when the maid arrived to assist Mary with taking up the dinner gown she'd been provided with, she could not put that soft rebuke from her mind.

Chapter Fifteen

DINNER WAS A strained affair. Benedict sat at the head of the table with Miss Masters to his right and Lord Wolverton to his left. Lady Vale sat next to him, while Mary sat next to Miss Masters and Mr. Middlethorp sat at the opposite end. As the table was not overly large despite the grandeur of the room, it did not feel as if they were having to shout the length of it to engage in conversation. The first course was completed with only the most stilted and painful conversation. By the second course, enough wine had been imbibed that those present had begun to relax to some small degree.

"Tell me, Wolverton, about the trial," Mr. Middlethorp suggested as he carved a bit of the glazed ham that graced the table. He offered a selection of it to Mary and she declined. She was over full already from the small amount she had eaten in the first course.

"What is it you would wish to know, Mr. Middlethorp?"

"Call me Branson," he insisted. "We have very little use for formality in this household. We are much too involved in one another's business to stand on such ceremony. Wouldn't you agree?"

Mary watched Lord Wolverton out of the corner of her eye. He gave a brief nod and continued, "Very well, Branson. I will answer any questions you have about the trial. If I know the answer, that is."

"Who were the lords presiding over your jury?"

"Fulton, Standifer, Montcray, Villiers, Andover, Sutcliffe, Whitlow and Farnsworth. There were others that I did not know well. Those men I have studied and at least six of those eight had rather unsavory dealings with Harrelson," Wolverton explained, before sipping his wine.

Branson Middlethorp frowned. "Obviously, I am not a member of the House of Lords nor have I ever been permitted within their hallowed halls. But I have friends who are and I keep myself quite well informed of the proceedings. To my knowledge, not a one of those you mentioned has ever been a truly active member. They shirk their duties shamelessly… but for your trial. Curious, indeed."

"At least four of those have considerable gaming debts," Benedict stated. "And I am in a position to know, as those debts were incurred at my establishment."

"I will make for London and find out what I can," Branson remarked casually. "But it will not be until the day after tomorrow as that odious little magistrate is coming back tomorrow."

"The man who was here this afternoon?" Mary asked.

"Yes, Mr. Hillyard," Lady Vale replied easily. "There was a murder only a few streets away. A workman by the name of Davies, I think it was. I can't imagine why he thinks we might know something about it."

Wolverton went completely still, the tension from him a palpable thing. "Did you say Davies, Lady Vale?"

"I did. Surely, you are not acquainted with him, Lord Wolverton," she replied.

Mary noted the frown that furrowed his brow. He was obviously distressed and she wanted nothing more than to try and soothe his worries, but that would only cause further tensions between him and everyone else in the house.

"He worked for me," Wolverton finally said. "I very much fear that I sent that poor man to his death."

"Is it the man who came to Wolfhaven Hall yesterday?" Mary asked, recalling the small, skinny man with the furtive manner. Surely, it was not he who had been murdered only a few yards away from them. What was the possibility of that being a random occurrence? Very slim, she realized.

"Yes," Wolverton answered. "He was a petty thief and a criminal, but he was very good at ferreting out information. I had sent him to Bath to discover if your brother was still in the city so that I might inform him of your rescue. He reported to me just yesterday that he had, in fact, been recognized as Lord Vale and that he was in residence here. I had then sent him back to the city with instructions to watch Albert Hamilton and report to me on his activities. This cannot have been just happenstance. Hamilton must be involved."

"I reached the same conclusion... well, that it wasn't a random event and that, somehow, whatever violence had befallen the poor man was related to the shady business we have found ourselves mired in," Mary said. "I am terribly sorry, Lord Wolverton, but you must not assume guilt or responsibility for this."

"How can I not?"

"Because you did not murder him. It is likely that Albert Hamilton killed the man and the guilt should fall solely upon his shoulders. If this man was a criminal, I can only assume that he knew there would be danger in this task and took it on regardless."

Those surprisingly kind words came from Benedict. Given that he had been cold to the point of hostility up to then, Mary was quite surprised by it. But she seconded her brother's point. "I find it is always best to lay blame where it is actually due, Wolverton. Had you any inkling that he would be in that much danger, you would likely have found a different course. We cannot be accountable for that which we do not know."

"You are kind to say so," Wolverton replied, addressing the comment to them both.

After that, the meal continued in a very subdued manner, but it was at least companionable. They had just completed the dessert course when the men rose to take brandy and cigars in the library, and the ladies were to retreat to the drawing room for sherry and polite conversation. It was an odd thing for Mary, for those social conventions to be upheld when, for what seemed like an eternity, her life had been darkness and fear. Would she ever feel "normal" again? Did she even want to? She had never been especially naïve, but she had always depended far too much on Benedict to protect her. It had been an eye-opening discovery in many ways to realize that she could actually protect herself. Regardless of the trauma, that was not something she would give up or allow herself to forget.

As they neared the drawing room which was located at the front of the house, facing the street, there was a great commotion outside. The sound of a woman's screams ripped through the darkness, loud and terrified. Even in the library, the gentleman heard it and emerged again immediately.

"What on heaven's name is going on out there?" Lady Vale asked.

"I mean to find out," Mr. Middlethorp said firmly and headed for the door.

Benedict and Lord Wolverton fell in step behind him, while Mary huddled in the entryway with Lady Vale and Elizabeth, awaiting word on what might be happening.

"I must be entirely honest," Mary admitted rather ruefully, "I had not thought Bath such a fertile ground for criminal activity!"

"There are unscrupulous individuals amongst all classes," Elizabeth said sagely. "I find that gentlemen are only better at hiding their darker natures than their poorer counterparts. Even then, the truth will always come out."

ALEX STEPPED OUT into the darkness, he and Lord Vale moving forward to flank Mr. Middlethorp. It was quite possible that those screams had been nothing more than the bait in a trap, luring them into an ambush. At this stage of the game, he could no longer predict what Hamilton might do. Clearly, Harrelson meeting his end had set something in motion that none of them could fully grasp.

"Do you see anything?" Vale asked.

"Nothing," Middlethorp responded. "But it was nearby. I'm certain of it."

"Well, it is quiet enough now," Alex replied. "I think we should go inside. I dislike leaving the ladies unattended. I cannot help but feel that this was nothing more than an attempt at distraction."

Middlethorp nodded. "I quite agree."

As they turned back toward the house, the screams sounded again. In unison, they turned toward the other end of the terrace, where it opened up onto Bennett Street and the Assembly Rooms beyond. There was a woman, running toward them, wearing a pale gown that billowed behind her as she ran. She was wild-eyed, her dark hair flying behind her. There was something strangely familiar about her, something that teased his mind. It was that, more than anything, that held Alex rooted to the spot, watching her approach as she screamed in apparent terror.

The nearer she drew to them, the more Alex's heart pounded in his chest. It wasn't possible. It simply could not be. And yet, he knew it was. Recognition hit him with the force of a hammer, knocking him backwards as he recoiled from the truth of it. The woman rushing toward them was none other than his dead wife. Helena had returned to torment him once more, it seemed.

She careened wildly down the street, to and fro, occasionally looking behind her as if she were being pursued. And yet, the only person disturbing the peacefulness of the night was her. Alex recognized it instantly for what it was—a ruse.

It was instinct and breeding more than anything that prompted him to step forward as she stumbled near them. He caught her as she overbalanced and began tumbling toward the hard paving stones. Her face was dirty and bruised, her hair a tangled mass. She collapsed against him in a manner that was befitting any of the finest stages in London. But then, Helena had always had a penchant for dramatics.

"Alexander," she cried. "Can it be you? Truly?"

"I have hardly altered my appearance," he replied coolly.

"My dearest husband! I saw the coach pass by my window earlier. I had thought it was Ambrose. I knew that if I could get to him, he would return me to you," she said breathlessly, continuing on as if his previous reply had not been laced with both sarcasm and disbelief.

"But to find you here instead… God be praised."

He was fairly certain Helena had never praised God in her life. "Where have you been all this time, Helena? It's been more than a year!"

"I was Harrelson's prisoner," she whispered on a broken sob. "I found out about the women he had abducted and he locked me away. He said that he couldn't bring himself to kill me. I was always his favorite, you know."

Another lie. "Harrelson has been dead for days," Alex pointed out. "Why has it taken you this long to come forward?"

"I was locked in an attic room in a townhouse near here. I saw the coach from the window. The servants Harrelson had paid to hold me prisoner had all fled but one," she shuddered delicately. "He intended to use the time alone with me to satisfy his dark desires for me." That statement was accompanied with a sidelong glance at the other gentlemen present. Even in her current state, Helena found it impossible to be anything other than a coquette.

Middlethorp cleared his throat. "Let us take her inside and then sort the fact from the fiction, Wolverton."

"Carry me, my darling," Helena said. "I fear I haven't the strength to walk."

Alex looked down at her, at the slyness of her gaze even as she schooled her face into a mask of fear and desperation. How he hated her in that moment! For the first time, he wished her truly dead and it shamed him more than a little.

"I'll fetch a footman to do so," Vale offered.

"Yes, please do," Alex replied.

Helena's face fell. For anyone who did not know her, she would give every appearance of a woman brokenhearted. "Why do you revile me so, Husband? I did not abandon you by choice! I was locked away from you!"

Nothing further was said as a footman came forward and lifted Helena into his arms, carrying her inside the house. Middlethorp and Vale both looked at Alex. But it was Vale who spoke first, "That is not something I would have bet on. Ever. If your wife is not dead, Wolverton, whose body did you find in the woods?"

"I can only assume one of Harrelson's many abductees," he answered. It was the most logical solution. "This cannot be happening!"

"It is happening. And for my sister's sake, I hope you held fast to the honor she attributes to you. For if you've made her an adulteress, it will not be my wrath you should fear," Vale warned softly.

MARY WATCHED THE footman carrying in the unknown woman. She was instantly overwhelmed with empathy, noting the woman's bruises and her torn, dirty gown. Had it been just a week since Lord Wolverton had found her in a similar fashion? A week that had altered her forever. *A man who had altered her forever*, a traitorous voice whispered in her mind. While she hated to acknowledge it, the fact remained that whatever happened between her and Lord Wolverton at the end, her feelings for him would be part of her forever—her feelings and the tantalizing fantasies of what might have been.

Beside her, Elizabeth Masters gasped in shock. Mary glanced at her and saw that she was looking at the woman not with horror but with recognition. "You know her?"

Elizabeth turned to face Mary and her expression shifted to one of what could only be described as pity. Unshed tears shimmered in her eyes as she uttered brokenly, "I do know her. Miss Mason—Mary— that woman is Lady Helena Carnahan, the Countess of Wolverton."

Mary glanced once more at the bedraggled but undeniably beautiful woman who was being tended to by a maid and a footman. Her gaze drifted toward the men who had entered and stood stock still in the entryway. Benedict looked angry, Middlethorp was inscrutable as always, but it was Wolverton who held her attention. He looked directly at her, and what she saw in him nearly broke her heart. There was bitterness and resentment but, above all, there was resignation. For better or worse, Helena was his wife, and whether he despised her or cherished her, his honor would not allow him to cast her aside no matter what she might have done.

It was all too much. Everything seemed to crash in upon her at once. It felt as though the room was spinning, as if the floor itself was rushing up to greet her. The world went black and Mary sank gratefully into the respite that darkness provided.

Chapter Sixteen

HELENA HAD WATCHED the other woman faint, the petite blonde that Alexander had carried so tenderly earlier that day. She covered her face with her hands and let out a soft sob to cover the smirk that twisted her lips upward. From the moment she had returned home that afternoon, she'd been in whirlwind of activity. She'd had her maid take one of her older dresses out to the garden and literally roll it in the dirt. After all, she could not return from an abduction dressed in her finest, could she? The footman placed her on a lovely upholstered settee and a glass of fortifying brandy was placed in her hands. Normally, it was not a lady's drink but, under the circumstances, it was clear that something as delicate as sherry just would not do.

Cautiously, Helena took a sip of the liquid and the burn took her by surprise. She no longer had to feign tears. Her eyes burned with them until her vision blurred. It was still clear enough to see the other younger gentleman gently pick up the delicately-pretty blonde and carry her up the stairs. Who was she? Helena mused on that question as a vicious need to see the woman suffer filled her. For herself, she had never been liked. Helena was not the kind of woman people liked. She was the kind of woman they desired or envied. Those sweet-natured creatures that others felt compelled to cosset had always been held in contempt by her. This one was no different.

Everyone seemed so concerned for the other woman. And yet, given the circumstances, Helena knew that it was she who should have captured their attention. She had made certain of it. While she had numerous bruises on her body from Albie's latest attentions, visible bruises on her face, those that would garner sympathy and lend credence to her tale, had been harder to come by. She'd demanded that one of the footmen strike her and he'd simply walked out. The man had literally left the house without a backward glance. Ultimately, she'd managed it herself by repeatedly hitting her cheek against the bed posts. They weren't overly serious but they only had to be convincing, after all.

"My dear Lady Vale, please forgive me for the upheaval I have caused in your home! I was desperate for help and after seeing Lord Ambrose's carriage travel this way—" Helena broke off abruptly, descending once more into broken sobs. She had considered what she would say very carefully, laying all the blame on Harrelson and none on Albie, at least for now. It would all be worth it. Watching the little blonde's heart break right before her very eyes because dear, *honorable* Alexander was no longer a free man had already made it more than worth her efforts. Taking her hands from her face, she drew a deep, fortifying breath and made a great show of gathering her composure. "I apologize for being so emotional! You just cannot know the relief I feel to finally be free of that wretched place!"

"You were imprisoned in a townhouse in a fashionable part of Bath. I'd hardly call it wretched," Alex pointed out.

Helena's eyes cut to him sharply. "You are so cold, Husband! Have you not searched for me? Have you given no thought to where I have been or what I may have suffered while away from your protection?" She knew that feigning ignorance of the ruse of her death was her only way forward. Immediately, Alexander fell to stony silence, that same muscle working in his jaw as he bit his tongue and attempted to be all that was right and proper. How she despised him for that!

"You are unaware that the world believes you dead? That a woman beaten beyond recognition, but wearing your gown and your wedding ring, was discovered on Lord Wolverton's property?"

The question had been posed by the older gentleman. Naturally, Helena had taken an instant dislike to him. He was too shrewd, his expressions too unreadable. She'd never been one to tolerate a man she could not easily manipulate. "How would I know such things, sir? Lord Harrelson, more wicked than I could ever have imagined, locked me away and I have not exchanged a word with anyone in my family, nor seen a newssheet in all that time! The servants barely spoke to me and then it was only to issue orders! Oh, Alexander, how you must have mourned thinking me dead!"

"I was preoccupied with proving my innocence of your murder," Alex replied, his tone clipped and the chill of it all but tangible. "Sadly, I failed in that task. While not convicted of the crime, in civil court all of my assets were stripped from me and then summarily handed over to your uncle-by-marriage."

Helena smiled then, using the beauty of it to her advantage. "Well, that can all be undone, my darling... here I am, alive and well and returned to you. We have only but to petition the courts!"

And there it was, Helena thought with a smile, watching the realization sink in on him. He could accept her as his wife once more and have all of the lovely money he had so longed for to put his estates to rights, or he could disavow her, forfeit it all, and live in poverty with his miniature blonde. "Alexander, please take me to your room."

"Lord Wolverton is not staying in chambers appropriate to your station, my lady," the older man said. "And under the circumstances, I can only think that you might enjoy some private time without having to attend to a husband. I shall vacate my room immediately and have it prepared for you. I think it will be much more to your liking."

Helena smiled, though her jaw tightened and her teeth clenched tightly together at being thwarted on such a minor point. She would not have Alexander running free through the house to make advances on the tiny trollop that had so captured his heart. "But I have missed you so, my darling. I don't care where we stay as long as we are together."

"You need a doctor and rest," Alex said. "As we never shared a chamber before your disappearance, I hardly think doing so now would be beneficial to your recovery. Excuse me. There is something I must attend to."

Helena watched him sweep from the room and noted that every-one's sympathetic gaze followed him. But it was her they were supposed to pity. To that end, she began weeping again, softly, as if her heart were broken. "Alexander does not love me anymore! His affections are engaged elsewhere, are they not?"

The younger of the two women remaining in the room turned to her then. There was something familiar about the girl. Helena frowned as she tried to place her.

"Lady Wolverton, I see you are struggling to recall how we know one another," she said. "I am Elizabeth Masters. We were neighbors and, for a time, your brother, Freddy, courted me rather ardently. That is, until he went to London and found himself engaged to another."

Helena smiled to camouflage her clenched teeth. Of course, he had. Freddy had needed to bag himself an heiress and that still hadn't gotten them out of debt to Harrelson. Only the inheritance left to her by her maternal grandfather could do that. It was that dire need for funds that had given birth to the elaborate scheme to fake her death. Harrelson had promised that if they did so, the funds granted to Wolverton as part of the marriage contract would be wrested from him and returned to her family. It had all seemed so simple when he laid it out. But they hadn't dreamed that she'd need to stay "dead" for quite so long. Alexander had surprised them all by not ending his own miserable life after being spared the indignity of hanging. Now, here she was, once more playing wife to the miserable bore while being silently judged by Freddy's jilted lover.

"Miss Masters, of course, I remember you," Helena said sweetly. "I am terribly ashamed of my brother's abominable behavior toward you!"

"Oh, being jilted by him and utterly ruined wasn't nearly as horri-ble as him soliciting Lord Harrelson to have me abducted so that he might keep me as his unwilling mistress," Miss Masters replied coolly. "You're a liar, Lady Wolverton, born of a family of them it would seem. I have no notion what you are playing at here, but I will not see my betrothed's sister wounded by you, nor anyone else in this house, including your poor husband."

Helena drew back as if she'd been struck. In truth, she found herself rather admiring Miss Masters and her forthright manner. "Your betrothed? Have you snared yourself an aging bachelor then?"

"My betrothed is Lord Benedict Middlethorp, Viscount Vale… also taken from his home as a child and his life upended by your uncle, Lord Harrelson," Miss Masters continued. "You may claim you are his victim but, for my money, you will have to prove it, because I remember you far better than you remember me, it would seem. You, Albert, and Harrelson were as thick as thieves, the lot of you, with Freddy always floating around the periphery. I'll have a footman show you to your room. I find I am rather fatigued now. Excuse me."

When the woman left, Helena looked back at Lady Vale who had stood silently through it all. "Well, your daughter-in-law-to-be is quite free with accusations and taking command of your house, Lady Vale."

"It is her home. I am happy to have my son in it with me once more and betrothed to a woman he adores. I trust Miss Masters completely and have found her opinions and perceptions of others to be both accurate and invaluable. You are remarkably calm, Lady Wolverton, for someone who just escaped after being held captive for a year. As a woman who has shed more than her share of tears in life, I found yours to be a bit too pretty. It does quite stretch the bounds of credulity. Good evening, madam."

Left alone, everyone in the house having turned away from her, Helena felt panic rising. They were supposed to have believed her. Everyone always had believed her, no matter how wild the tale. She'd been lying and scheming her entire life and it had never failed to produce the desired effect. *Until now.* It was something else to lay at Alexander's door, and perhaps that of the pretty blonde, as well. Lord Vale's sister, if she had inferred correctly from what Miss Masters had said.

Fury swept through her, but she tamped it down. It was not the time to have a tantrum, not when everyone was already so set against her. She needed to gain their sympathy first and as the woman scorned, that shouldn't be difficult.

"Is my room ready? I am so very tired," she said to the nearest footman.

"I'll help you up to it, m'lady."

HE'D FLED THE drawing room and Helena's presence because his temper would not allow him to remain. She had utterly ruined his life with her deception, and he had little doubt that she had been party to whatever schemes Harrelson and Hamilton had concocted. Now, she had managed to ruin him once more by returning. Fury was too mild a term to describe what he felt, but it was all that he could lay claim to in that moment. It appeared she had robbed him of sense, as well. If there were any possibility that Helena was being truthful—but, of course, that was impossible. Helena had lied with the same casual ease with which she drew breath. From the moment he'd met her, it had been one elaborately concocted tale after another. And all of it, it seemed, had been driving toward that very moment. Had they planned to fake her death from the outset? There were answers he simply did not have, and more questions seemed to arise with every passing second.

Running his fingers through his hair in a gesture of impatience, Alex paced the hall as he tried to make sense of it all. When he had finally managed to amass enough proof to clear his name and be free of all the chaos and destruction she had wrought in his life, she had returned to once again decimate any chance at happiness for the people surrounding her. There had been a chance, slim as it was, that he would have found himself in a position to actually pursue a woman he desired, a woman that, if he were to be honest, he loved. Mary Mason had invaded every fiber of his being, but there was no longer any possibility of having her in his life in an honorable fashion.

Alex turned again, stalking across the narrow hall. He paused outside Mary's door, his hand poised only a scant inch from knocking. What could he say to her? He didn't even fully understand what was happening himself. How could he, after all? Helena was alive. He didn't believe for even one second that Harrelson had held her prisoner. It was obvious that whatever scheme they'd been about had collapsed with Harrelson's death and she was simply scrambling.

He stood there for a long moment, debating whether to knock, debating whether or not to disturb her when he had no right to do so. Reluctantly, Alex dropped his hand and stepped back. He would not dishonor her by making declarations of his feelings for her while the woman he was bound to for the remainder of his days waited below stairs. Bitterness rose up in him, bitterness and resentment so consuming that it nearly overwhelmed him. Along with it came the shocking realization that he'd have rather lived out his days as a reputed murderer, shunned by society, than to spend another day as Helena's husband.

Turning, he crossed the narrow distance back to his own room. Alex's hand closed over the door handle to his own modest chamber, but before the door could swing inward, the one behind him opened. He heard her voice, and closed his eyes as regret washed through him.

"Lord Wolverton?"

He closed his eyes and prayed for strength. It was a test of his will not to simply turn and take her in his arms, knowing that it would be the very last time. "Forgive me, Miss Mason, I did not mean to disturb you."

She let out a laugh, but it was not a happy noise nor was there any sort of amusement in the sound. It was hard, brittle and full of the very same feelings that now consumed him.

After she had composed herself to some degree, she admitted with a rueful note to her voice, "I am afraid I cannot help but be disturbed... your wife—"

"I beg you, do not call her that," he implored. It only underscored the hopelessness of his current situation and the unhappiness of his future. "I cannot abide the sound of it."

"Helena, then," she conceded. "No doubt referring to her by your title would be just as distressing. I must confess that I am deeply shocked by her presence here. I understand that yours was not a happy union." Her voice was soft, tinged with regret, with empathy and with a tenderness for him that made him ache. "But I've given it a considerable amount of thought in the last quarter hour—heaven knows it feels as if it's been so much longer than that—and I'm glad of her return. I'm glad that you will be able to finally restore your reputation and that your honor will no longer be called into question by every person you meet. It isn't happening in the way you envisioned, but it is what you wanted, after all."

What he wanted. Alex shook his head. "If there is one thing that her return has brought me, Miss Mason, it is clarity. And I understand now that, until it was taken from me in its entirety, I had no idea just how much I wanted something else." He paused, drew a deep breath and met her gaze levelly. He could see the tears in her eyes, the tracks of them upon her cheeks. Were they for him? "I had paused just a moment ago, persuaded myself that I should not knock upon your door because I am not free to do so. But there are things I must say to you, and I know that I will never have the opportunity again—"

She held up her hands, pleading with eyes still damp with tears. "Lord Wolverton, I beg of you—"

"No, Miss Mason. I may not be free to have what I want, but I will acknowledge that I wanted it," he said firmly. Whether it was to her benefit or detriment, he did not know, but he would not let her go without telling her the truth of his feelings for her. "In the days I have spent with you, indeed, from the very moment I first laid eyes upon you, I've desired you. Even when I knew it was wrong, when you were at your weakest and most vulnerable, it shames me to admit how much you stirred me. But that is nothing compared to what I felt when I kissed you that first time. But it isn't simply a physical attraction. I feel it to the very depths of my soul, and there is nothing I will regret more in this life than that we will never have the option to explore that, to build something from it."

She shook her head. "We should not say such things to one anoth-er... not now, when nothing could ever come of it."

"If I do not say them now, they will never be said. I offer them with no expectation other than that. When I kissed you, I did so because I could not do anything else. It was never my intent to trifle with you, or to take advantage of our situation."

"I know that," she replied insistently. "Of course, I know it. Given the situation that we found ourselves in, and given that my own behavior was hardly beyond reproach—if it is a time for confessions, Lord Wolverton, then here is mine! I am even now cursing you for your honor. I am cursing you because I wanted so much more than just a few stolen kisses... and I am cursing your wife. It marks me a wicked person to admit it, but I do wish her dead. I wish that had not simply been some fabrication! And I fear for you because I do not believe that she was kept from you unwillingly. I think she is a liar and a manipulator, and I fear what she may have in store for you."

Alex felt his gut clench, his breath knocked from him as surely as if she had struck him. To know that she would have willingly granted him all the liberties he had so desired to take was both a blessing and a curse, one that would haunt him eternally. "I have no faith in her innocence either, but I am at a loss as to how to proceed. I wish that I were free to tell you that I love you."

"I will not tell you that I love you either. But we will both know it just the same," she admitted softly. "I've tried to deny it, to dissuade myself from it. We haven't known one another long enough. We met in such extreme circumstances. We've had such forced intimacy in our relationship that it's given rise to the illusion of feelings—I've told myself all of those things. And I believed them, until I heard her name, and knew that you belonged to someone else. I'm leaving for London tomorrow. Benedict is making all of the arrangements because I cannot stay here under the same roof as your wife."

"We will leave. I will take Helena and return to Wolfhaven Hall tomorrow. You need not put yourself through such a rigorous journey simply to avoid our company," he replied. It was too soon for her to travel such a great distance and far too dangerous given her recent illness.

"You cannot. You will have the magistrate to deal with, and you'll need to contact your solicitors and begin the legal proceedings. It's better this way," she said. "I wish you well, Lord Wolverton, as much as I wish your wife to the devil, as apparently I have a sinner's heart."

She moved to retreat to her room, but he could not allow it. He wasn't ready to watch her walk away from him for the last time. Reaching out, Alex grasped her wrist and pulled her back to him until her body was pressed to his and all he had to do was dip his head slightly to be able to capture her lips.

"Do not," she said breathlessly. "It was one thing to allow your kisses while we were still at Wolfhaven Hall… but now, here, with her downstairs, I cannot. Regardless of the circumstances of your marriage, you are still married. And it would be disastrous for either of us to forget that fact even for a moment."

Unable to refute her words, Alex let her go, stepping back and allowing her to enter her room. When the door closed softly, the click of it rang as resolutely as any pistol shot. But he wasn't giving up. There had to be some way, whether by divorce or annulment, that he could be free of her. If it was divorce, all of the moneys that came with the marriage settlement would remain with her family, but the estates that had been stripped from him would be returned. It would not be a luxurious lifestyle by the standards of most, but it would be enough.

Cursing Helena again, he wondered what it was that had prompted her return. Entering his chamber, one word suddenly rang in his mind, eclipsing everything else. *Davies*. He'd set Davies to watch Hamilton and it was likely Hamilton had killed him. Albert had abandoned her to save his own skin rather than be taken for murder. That was why Helena had fabricated her elaborate resurrection. Of course, it didn't matter. Legally, regardless of how immoral, perfidious and unconscionable that she was, she was still his wife. To that end, he was tied to her forever.

If he could prove that Hamilton was guilty of Davies' murder, assuming he could find him, he did not question that the man would turn on Helena without a qualm if it meant a lesser punishment for himself. He needed to speak to Branson Middlethorp.

MARY CLOSED THE door behind her and leaned back against it. It might have been better if she'd thought her feelings for him were entirely one-sided. To know that he longed for the same thing she did and would be forever denied it only intensified the heartache for her. At least she would be free to move on, to perhaps find someone else with whom to share her life, while he would be forever trapped with the vile Helena.

She didn't weep. In truth, she'd have been crying more for lost possibilities than for anything truly lost in the moment. They had not explored their feelings for one another, and had not made declarations of those feelings until they both knew doing so was utterly futile. *Because there should have been more time.*

Why had Helena turned up on the same day they'd arrived in Bath? How was it possible that she'd managed to escape her captors and flee in the exact direction of her abandoned husband? It was all too convenient, frankly. Helena had to have known they had arrived and if that was the case, then she had to have been close enough to see them. It was unlikely she would have seen the Ambrose crest on the door of the carriage if she'd been locked away in the upper floors of a house. She'd have to have been outside near the street or, at the very least, peering through a window no higher than the first floor. That hardly coincided with her description of being imprisoned. Given that Mary had firsthand experience with being imprisoned, she felt she had a certain amount of expertise on the subject.

Stepping away from the door, she moved to the bed and considered how best to proceed. *Miss Masters. Elizabeth.* Benedict would help, but he would ask far too many questions about her motives. He did not appear to be supportive of any feelings that might have developed between her and Lord Wolverton, but Elizabeth was another matter entirely. From the very moment they had met out front, it seemed that she had sensed the undercurrent between them and had given her very hearty approval.

She would still have to leave in the morning. Withstanding the temptation of being in such close proximity to him, coupled with the desperation brought on by their current situation, was simply too much for her.

A knock on the door had her heart pounding in her chest. Part of her hoped that it was Wolverton and part of her feared that it was. Calling out, she said, "You may enter."

The door opened and, as if she'd been summoned, Miss Masters entered. "I wanted to check on you after... well, after everything. I cannot imagine how awful this must be for you both." Elizabeth stepped deeper into the room and closed the door behind her, closing the distance until she could sit on the edge of Mary's bed. It was rather like the late night chats she'd had with the other girls at school, Mary thought.

Mary sighed. "Were we really so terribly obvious?"

Elizabeth smiled. "I think when you are as happily and desperately in love as I am with your brother, then you tend to look for it and find it in others. It was obvious to me immediately that he cared for you. I didn't know that it was love... not until I saw his reaction to his wife's return. It is the answer to all of his problems as far as his legal and financial woes, yet there was nothing in his face but bitter disappointment. And then he looked at you, and I saw something else. I saw longing. I think, if he were free to do so, he would offer for you. I also believe that if he were free to do so, you would accept."

"Without hesitation," Mary admitted. "I was drawn to him immediately. Strange as it was, when I was in his presence, I was never afraid of him. Of course, when I was alone, my imagination would get the better of me. There is something I must ask of you."

"Anything," Elizabeth said. "Whatever you need."

"I know that we are all quite aware that Lady Wolverton has lied horribly. I do not for one moment believe that she has been Harrelson's prisoner," Mary replied. "But she said that she'd recognized Lord Ambrose's carriage. The only identifying mark upon it is his coat of arms and that is on the doors. It would be visible from the lower floors of the house, the ground floor and, perhaps, the first floor, but anything on the second or third, given how narrow the streets are, she could never have seen!"

Elizabeth's eyes widened in surprise. "I had not considered it, but you are quite right. It would be impossible! So how did she know?"

Mary shrugged. "Either she was given free rein of the house or she was not in the house at all. She might have been out and about on the street."

An odd expression crossed Elizabeth's features and her lips parted as if to speak. But she hesitated.

"What is it?" Mary demanded. "If there is something that you think may help, no matter how small it is, please, I beg of you, tell me!"

"When I was approaching and I saw your carriage, just beyond, near the end of the terrace, was a Bath chair and the woman who was in it wore black and was heavily veiled. So heavily veiled that it appeared off, as if she were trying to conceal her identity rather than just showcase her mourning. Perhaps, if we can find the right chairmen, and get them in close enough proximity to Lady Wolverton, they might recognize her voice. It would do nothing save prove that she had the means and ability to return to her husband and did not. It would also completely negate her statement that she did not know he had been blamed for her death."

"It would cast suspicion on her... enough that, perhaps, he might be able to free himself of her," Mary whispered.

"I will tell Benedict and then we will discuss this with Lord Wolverton—"

"No! I don't want to give him false hope. And I don't want him to feel... well, he and I have said our goodbyes, as it were. I'd rather not have him think that I am still working on ways to circumvent his marriage when there is no guarantee that it will even be effective. Let's see what can be discovered first. I will wait for word at the King's Head tomorrow evening if you need to reach me."

"Are you certain you must leave, Mary? I think staying here and seeing this through might be for the best," Elizabeth suggested gently.

"I cannot. If I stay, I will do something that I will regret, and that he will regret, as well. It is better for all of us if I go, at least for now," Mary insisted. "First thing in the morning, you'll start speaking to the chairmen?"

"Not even then. I'm going to send Benedict out to canvas the area and talk to them tonight. They should all be out and waiting for the mass exodus from the Assembly Rooms." Elizabeth nodded, "Yes. The sooner the better, I think. Sleep well, and if anything is discovered, I will wake you."

Mary watched her leave and then settled back onto the pillows. There was very little for her to pack. The few gowns and possessions she'd had with her at Mrs. Simms were already safely folded into her valise. The borrowed gowns that had been Helena's, well, she couldn't stomach the thought of ever touching them again much less wearing them.

Closing her eyes, Mary willed sleep to come and her tears to stay at bay. She failed on both counts.

Chapter Seventeen

ALBERT HAMILTON LAUGHED, smiled and played the part of a gentleman as he made his way through the Assembly Rooms. It was slightly scandalous to have been in society so soon after the death of his uncle. His purpose in being there was twofold. First, he needed to put on a calm and collected facade for the world to witness. In short, he needed not to look like a murderer. Secondly, he needed to know what was being said about the murder itself. Society loved nothing better than gossip, after all, and the lot of them would be standing about, engaging in hysterics about how they might all be murdered in their beds. If only they knew that he was wandering amongst them at that very moment, he thought caustically.

He loathed the lot of them, and yet he needed to fit in, to blend in and be part of their world. To that end, he'd reached a very painful conclusion. He would have to untether himself from Helena's desperate clutches. She'd sent the note round earlier informing him that she'd preemptively gone back to Wolverton because he'd shown up in Bath. It was a bloody nightmare. She should have waited until they could formulate a better plan; one that he could be sure would not incriminate him in anyway. In one regard, he and Helena would always be similar. They would each take care of themselves before anyone else. While he adored her, admired her willingness to dirty her hands and her complete lack of morality, and he certainly enjoyed her wanton and abandoned nature in the bedchamber, in the end, he would sacrifice her to save his own hide.

Rumors were rampant that evening. Lord Vale's miraculous return and, now, Lady Wolverton's dramatic escape from an unknown captor to return to the loving arms of her husband—those topics were on the lips of every man and woman present. From the oldest to the youngest, and even to the dull, staid companions lurking in plain dresses in the corners, they all whispered about them. She'd made a grave error in judgement in returning in such a public fashion. But then, she'd always enjoyed dramatics.

Making his way toward the doors, chatting casually with all those he passed, he made certain to give the appearance of a man with not a care in the world. Once he'd made it outside, he didn't bother with a sedan chair. He intended to walk the short distance to the house in Royal Crescent. He would go through it room by room to be certain there was nothing there that could tie him to the place. A few well-placed coins and the servants would disappear, leaving the house dark and deserted and no one the wiser. At least the house was in Harrelson's name. It would become Freddy's misery.

Making his way along the street, he passed a blonde-haired man—a gentleman, obviously—speaking to a sedan chair driver. He paid them no more heed than that and continued on his way, oblivious to the fact that their conversation would incriminate him as well as his lover.

BENEDICT HAD BEEN less than pleased to make his way out into the darkness in the wee hours of the night to question the men who carted Bath's leading citizens about in sedan chairs. When Elizabeth had knocked upon his door, he had thought it would be for much more enjoyable activities than the one he currently found himself engaged in. He cursed under his breath as he made his way along the rows of sedans chairs lining the streets outside the Assembly Rooms. While many people utilized carriages, the sedan chairs were a far more convenient mode of transportation on the narrow, crowded streets. Those gathered for the evening's entertainments would be emerging soon, seeking transportation home. To that end, he was running out of time to question the remaining operators of the many sedan chairs lining the street.

He had his doubts about whether or not that avenue of investigation would bear fruit, but he'd told her he would see to it and so he was. Approaching another of the chairmen, he said, "I'm looking for information."

The chairman gave him a look that said information could be had, but only for a price. "Aye, sir, if I have it."

"Have you transported a woman here in this area, today specifically, who wore a dark and heavy veil?"

"Oh, aye. Been transporting her about the city for nigh on a year now. Not every day, but every few days like, we'll be fetched by one of her servants and will take her to the baths, or a shop. Sometimes we take her to an address near Avon Street, which is right odd for a lady of her standing... always at odd times though, when there's fewer folks about."

Benedict hadn't expected to actually find the man. "Where do you fetch her from? What address?"

"She's at Number 27 Royal Crescent," the driver said.

Had it really been that easy? "What's her name?"

"Don't know it. She weren't the kind to talk much and her servants always just summoned us to the address and never said who we'd be transporting. Didn't give it much thought at the time, but I reckon it were right odd now that I think on it."

Of course, his first estimation had been right. A woman hiding her identity and the fact that she still numbered amongst the living would have taken steps to conceal such details.

"What shops did you take her to?"

"We always set her down outside the Pump Room or at the end of Milson Street. But I reckon she came back with boxes from that fancy milliner's shop there one day."

"Bertrand's?"

"Aye, sir, that one. I could take you to the house if you like."

"No, thank you," Benedict said. "The address in Avon Street... do you know who lives there?"

"A man… a gentleman from the looks of him, well turned out. But don't know his name. Dark haired and tall, but—" The man broke off abruptly. "It was that gentleman what passed us a moment ago. I didn't make the connection right off, but I'd say he's headed home now. Or to one of the many taverns or bawdy houses near there! I could take you there."

Benedict shook his head, but produced several coins from his pocket and passed them to the man. "You've been more than helpful. I may have to have a magistrate speak to you about this woman. Where can you be found?"

"I'm here most every night," the man said. "Name is Jeb, sir."

"Thank you, Jeb."

Benedict left the row of chairmen and made his way back along Brock Street to the Circus. Mary and Elizabeth had been correct. While that didn't surprise him, the ease with which he had discovered the man transporting Lady Wolverton around the city did shock him. It seemed to him that her decision to plunge back into Wolverton's life must have been impulsive. Otherwise, Hamilton, or possibly Lady Wolverton herself, would have tidied up such loose ends. Harrelson's death had left them scrambling and the subsequent confusion and lack of leadership had likely contributed to Hamilton's actions in the death of Wolverton's employee, Mr. Davies.

Returning to the house, he found Elizabeth waiting for him in the hall. "Well?"

Benedict removed his coat. "I found him. He confirmed that not only did he bring her by here today, but that he's been transporting her over the entire city for the past year. And he's always asked to fetch her from Royal Crescent. Later, when the streets are more deserted and I'm unlikely to be seen, I'll go to that address and uncover what I can."

"Take Wolverton with you," Elizabeth suggested.

Benedict balked at that immediately. "Why on earth would I do that? I cannot abide the man."

Elizabeth looked at him rather disapprovingly. "Because his life is hanging in the balance here... as is your sister's future happiness," she said softly. "You only dislike him because you know that Mary has feelings for him. You're being an utter hypocrite. You revile him for feeling about your sister the same way that you feel about me!"

"I love you. I don't know that he loves her!" The protest was sharper than he'd intended for it to be and significantly louder.

She stepped closer to him, placing a staying hand on his arm. "Then perhaps taking Lord Wolverton with you would offer you an opportunity to assess his motives and his intentions. It might be just the thing to let you determine the character of the man your sister loves!"

Benedict struggled to find an argument for that. When he failed, he let out a sigh and replied, "Well played, my darling. Well played."

Elizabeth leaned in, the scent of her perfume teasing his senses. Her breath was warm against his ear as she whispered, "Let us find a way to occupy your time until you are to embark upon your larcenous nighttime activities. It might even improve your mood."

"You're simply trying to distract me from my intense dislike of the man," he complained.

"Is it working?" she asked with a smile.

"Of course, it is," he admitted. "I'm helpless to resist you. You are a wicked woman, Elizabeth Masters."

"Then let us go and be wicked together, Lord Vale," she teased and danced away from him to the stairs.

Benedict followed her, eager to be alone with her and to show her precisely how wicked he was.

HELENA WATCHED THE couple disappear up the stairs. She noted how they couldn't stop touching one another, whispering sweetly in one another's ear. A part of her envied Elizabeth Masters in that moment. What would it be like to savor such a tender touch? What would it be like to not be haunted by dark cravings and vicious moods that would always make her question the presence of love in her life? She was driven by a need to push others away, utterly convinced that they would abandon her regardless, and so she attacked them until they were left with no other choice but to do just that. Isn't that how she wound up ensconced in the midst of the Vale townhouse, beset with suspicion and disbelief? She'd had no faith in Albie's promise that it was only a temporary setback, and she'd done something reckless in response. Now, she was paying the price for it, or would soon enough.

Her gaze drifted toward the couple again, as they paused to share a kiss at the top of the stairs. She both envied it and was revolted by it. Or perhaps, it was simply her nerves or her distaste for all of them that left her feeling on the verge of casting up her accounts. There was one undeniable fact in all of it, however. It was just as Albie had warned. Her own impulsiveness had sealed her fate. They would prove, without question, that her tale of abduction was a lie and then heaven knew what would happen. She'd be arrested for a fraud and hanged, or she'd have given Alexander precisely the ammunition he needed to see them divorced or annulled. She had rushed headlong with her plan which hadn't been a plan at all. Now she was well and truly caught and there was no way out.

A flood of emotions filled her. Anger, fear, resentment—above all resentment. It bubbled inside her, rising to the surface and creating a vicious need to lash out. She needed a place to direct her anger, a way to free herself from it even temporarily. But there was also a need to create the maximum amount of damage. All of the people in that house were contributing to her downfall. But there was one person, that if she hurt her, it would hurt everyone else. Mary Mason. It would break Alexander's heart, as he had clearly fallen in love with the girl. It would destroy Lord Vale, who was so protective of the girl and had only just been reunited with her. And watching him suffer would inflict so much pain on Lady Vale and Elizabeth Masters that she couldn't stop the wicked smile that curved her lips at the thought of it. As for Mr. Middlethorp, no doubt he'd feel responsible. That was his way, after all.

But it wasn't just that it would hurt the others. It was pettiness. Alexander was like a toy to her, one she had never wanted, until someone else did.

"She will pay for this, and they will all pay with her," Helena muttered. "Whatever happens to me, I will not allow that wretched creature to take what should have been mine."

With those whispered words, Helena eased back into the shadows and made her way to the study. If there was one thing she understood, it was men. And if there was a weapon to be had in the house, it would be that masculine domain.

Chapter Eighteen

ALEX WAS AWAKE and in misery. He didn't want to let Mary leave, even if he knew it was the best possible course of action for them both. In just over a week, he'd grown not just accustomed to her presence, but dependent upon it. The intimacy they'd enjoyed at Wolfhaven, interrupted only occasionally by Mrs. Epson's foul temper, had provided them greater time together than what he'd experienced with Helena in their courtship, and possibly even their marriage. He certainly knew Mary better than he'd ever known his wife. Even when she'd lied, when she'd hidden information from him about her brother and his suspected identity, he'd not questioned her integrity. There was a light in her, a goodness, that was impossible to deny and impossible to ignore. And he was going to lose it forever.

Biting back a curse, Alex rose and stalked to the door. He'd confront Helena, demand a divorce and be done with it all. Money and scandal be damned. But as he yanked the door open, he found himself face to face with Lord Benedict Middlethorp, Viscount Vale.

"Going somewhere?" Vale asked.

"I had thought to have a confrontation with my wife and demand a divorce so that I might marry your sister," Alex snapped.

Vale arched one golden brow. "A rather ambitious undertaking for four in the morning… perhaps a bit of larceny, first?"

Alex frowned. "What did you have in mind?"

"Elizabeth, my intended, and Mary, almost your intended, had a conversation earlier and realized that Helena had to have lied about seeing the carriage. She could not have recognized the coat of arms if she'd been looking at it from the upper floors where she was supposedly locked away. After some investigating on my part, at the behest of my betrothed, I stumbled upon a sedan chair porter who recognized my description of Lady Wolverton based on what Elizabeth saw today. He's given me an address. And it's only two streets over. In Royal Crescent."

"What are we waiting for?" Alex demanded.

"For you to put on your boots," Vale said, gesturing to Alex's stockinged feet.

Cursing under his breath yet again, Alex retreated into the chamber, donned his boots and his coat, ignoring his cravat and disheveled waistcoat. "I meant what I said. If there is any way possible to extricate myself from this, I mean to marry her."

Vale inclined his head. "And if you extricate yourself from this, and Mary consents, I will not attempt to stop you. Elizabeth insisted that your intentions or, at the very least, your affections, for my sister were genuine and honorable. It appears she was correct... again. I don't mean to let her know that just yet, if you please. She gets rather insufferable about that sort of thing."

They said nothing further on the matter, but slipped quietly from the house and kept to the shadows as much as possible as they made their way to Royal Crescent. By mutual and unspoken agreement, they used the servants' entrance. If Vale was surprised when Alex produced the same lock picking tools he'd used to gain entrance to Harrelson's home, it was displayed by nothing more than an arched brow and a quirk of his lips that might have been a grin.

Once inside, they moved quietly, making their way past the servants' quarters and through the kitchens until they could take a narrow staircase, thankfully free of creaks, up to the ground floor. They moved silently down the corridor, past the dining room and toward the morning room just beyond it. There was a small writing desk in the corner. Lighting the single candle atop it, they went through the contents quickly, finding nothing of any import. It was all lists for the market and bills from the butcher. But it was Helena's handwriting.

Alex recognized it easily enough.

Taking the main staircase, they bypassed the drawing room and music room on that floor and headed to the second instead and what would likely have been Helena's chamber. As they neared it, the door opened. They ducked back into an alcove and waited. After a moment, Albert Hamilton appeared, carrying an armload of clothes and a heavily-stuffed valise. He stopped mid-stride as some of the items fell from his heavily-burdened arms to the carpet at his feet.

Hamilton cursed as he stooped to gather the things, just as Alex stepped forward. "A rather hasty and furtive exit, Hamilton. But then, I'd expect little better from you."

Hamilton looked up, met his gaze, and the other man's jaw steeled with anger. "What do you want, Wolverton?"

"I want you and Helena to pay for ruining my life. Harrelson already has, it would seem," Alex replied evenly. His tone was cold and sharp, his gaze steady and his fists clenched at his sides. "And then there's the little matter of your involvement in the abduction scheme that proved so very lucrative for Harrelson and managed to harm someone I hold very dear."

"I don't know what you're talking about," he denied.

"What about Davies? Do you recall him? About yay high," Alex said, holding his hand up to chest height, "Skinny fellow. Rough spoken. You shoved a knife between his ribs, apparently."

Hamilton rose, but it wasn't to face the accusations. Instead, he tossed the valise and ran. But he didn't know that Vale was there, as well, still hidden in the shadows. The other man rushed forward, taking Hamilton to the ground easily.

"A couple of those cravats should do nicely at tying him up," Wolverton said, snatching a few from the floor and dropping them next to Vale.

"We've no authority to arrest him. It's abduction," Vale pointed out.

"You keep forgetting something... you are a lord. A peer of the realm. They won't take you to prison for it," Wolverton stated coldly.

"I know that for certain."

Vale sighed, looped the neckcloth over Hamilton's wrists and bound them tightly. When it was done, he hauled Albert up. "And now what do we do with him?"

"We take him back with us and call that magistrate, Hillyard, to come and interrogate him," Wolverton said, pausing to pick up the valise. "He would not have come here in the dark of night to collect his things if there was not something in them that could incriminate him."

"Go to hell," Hamilton said. And jerking his head toward Vale, he added, "And take this gutter-raised bastard with you!"

Vale only laughed at that. "We'll meet you there, then!"

The three of them left, Vale holding on to Hamilton primarily because Alex didn't trust himself not to strangle the bastard. Looking at him made his stomach turn as he thought of all the misery that had been wrought on so many, himself included, thanks to Hamilton's and Helena's self-serving greed.

It was nearing dawn as they reached the Vale townhouse once more. The servants were beginning to stir, heating water for washing and beginning the preparations for breakfast. Once inside the house, they passed maids and footmen going about their morning routines. All of them appeared utterly confounded to have the rest of the household up and about at such an ungodly hour. Of course, it likely didn't help that they were bringing a prisoner with them.

To one of the footman, Vale directed, "Go and fetch Magistrate Hillyard. We have need of him."

"Yes, my lord," the servant replied and dashed off immediately.

Ushering Hamilton, who was sullen and recalcitrant, toward the library, they found Middlethorp awaiting them there. "I see the two of you have put aside your differences… for the moment at least. I take it this is the erstwhile Albert Hamilton?"

"It is," Alex confirmed. "We went to investigate the house that the sedan chair porter had identified as Helena's and found him attempting to flee into the night with his things."

Middlethorp nodded. "I see. Hamilton, this is your only chance to tell us everything. If you do not, and the magistrate takes you, I will do everything in my considerable power to see you punished to the full extent of the law. In case you are confused, that does mean seeing you hanged… and Lady Wolverton, as well. If you have any honor at all, you will speak now."

"You think I'll take the blame and let her walk away from all this?" Hamilton laughed. "She's not a hapless victim. Who do you think bludgeoned that poor maid that was discovered next to Wolverton's falling down chapel? It wasn't me. And Harrelson would never have killed a woman that he could sell for a profit!"

Middlethorp frowned. "Have a pair of footmen fetch her down, willingly or otherwise. I'd rather not have to relay the accusations they will make against one another. It's better to confront them together."

Dropping Hamilton unceremoniously onto his rump in one of the chairs, Benedict rang the bell pull and when the butler arrived, issued the appropriate instructions. Watching it all, Alex considered the possibilities. Would they grant him a divorce? Adultery was clearly grounds, but framing him for a murder that didn't happen would surely sway both the church and the court to his cause, would it not?

⚜

MARY HANDED HER small bag to the coachman. She was making free of Lord Ambrose's carriage to get her as far as the King's Head and would then take the mail coach the rest of the way to London. The maid had retreated to the kitchen to fetch some food and provisions for the journey as the cook had insisted they not eat any of the filth served at coaching inns.

As she stepped into the darkened interior of the carriage, helped up by a footman, a sensation of foreboding filled her. The shades of the carriage were drawn so that no light penetrated it, but she did not need it to know, instantly, that she was not alone.

"Do not make a sound or I will shoot you right where you stand."

The voice belonged to Helena, yet it was devoid of the dramatics and hysterics of the prior evening. Instead, it was cold and calculating. There was no feeling in her voice at all, and that was all the assurance Mary needed that the woman meant precisely that. She considered, briefly, simply falling backwards out the door and hoping for the best. But the paving stones, carriage wheels and horses' hooves were just as deadly, if not more so, than the pistol that Helena had trained on her. It glinted in the dim light, the barrel aimed directly at her.

Uncertain if her actions were born of cowardice or wisdom, Mary eased deeper into the carriage and settled onto the seat. Mary was careful to arrange her skirts so she wouldn't trip on them if she had a chance to overpower the other woman or make her escape. Though given that Helena was considerably taller and likely outweighed her by a stone at least, the possibility seemed rather remote.

"What is it that you want of me?" Mary asked softly, after the door had shut behind her.

"My name is Lady Wolverton... I realize my husband now fancies himself in love with you, but he is still my husband and you will show me the respect due my position."

Mary gritted her teeth. "Very well. What is it that you want of me, Lady Wolverton?"

After a moment of tense silence, she gestured with the pistol. "Knock on the ceiling and urge the driver on. We haven't all day to sit here."

Reluctantly, Mary did as she'd been told and the carriage lurched forward, the wheels rumbling over the cobbled street.

Across the expanse of the carriage, the other woman smiled, her teeth gleaming in the dimness like those of a predator. "That's better. It's always good to know one's place, I think. And you, outside your rather weak connection to Lord Vale, are nothing more than a gutter-born trollop."

Mary refused to be baited by her. "I asked what you wanted of me. I did not ask for your opinion of me. I am to assume that there is some reason you have concealed yourself within this carriage as I use it to leave the city. Is that it? Safe passage out of Bath?"

"Oh, no, my dear. If that was all I wanted it would have been easy enough to arrange," Helena replied drolly. "No. I want something much more unique to our particular situation. You see, I hate my husband. Loathe him, really. And despite his unimpeachable honor, he is rather hopelessly and obviously besotted with you!"

"And I am leaving, so I fail to see what that has to do with anything!" Mary snapped.

Helena laughed. "Well, let me put it in terms you might understand. I want to cause him pain. To see him suffer unimaginably, I must take everything from him. And I tried that. We managed to take his wealth, his land, his reputation—and then he found you. There is finally something he cannot live without. You see, when I kill you, and I shall, it will finally break him!"

The woman was utterly unhinged. "You are mad. Completely mad."

"Perhaps. But I have killed before. After all, there had to be a body for poor, dear Alexander to find on his property, didn't there? We'll get far enough out of town that I can put a pistol ball right between your pretty, brown eyes... then the other gun I have tucked in beside me will see an end to the coachman. Then I'll drive myself on to London, throw myself on the mercy of my relatives. While I'm not overly keen on the idea of going to America, there are certainly wealthy enough men to be had there."

In the other woman's mad ramblings, Mary seized upon one fact. There was another gun. If she could manage to get Helena to fire wildly, and miss her, then she might have a chance. It was the only way, but the risk was great. Mary desperately did not want to die. The guilt of it would destroy all of those she loved, both Benedict and Lord Wolverton. *Alexander.* If she was going to risk her life to spare his conscience, then she would not stand on that ridiculous formality that she'd used to maintain distance between them. Had he not kissed her passionately? Had he not told her how much he cared for her and that it was she whom he wished to be with? And if it were not for the wicked, evil woman seated across from her—a woman whose only pursuits in life were to inflict pain and misery upon others—they might have found their happiness together.

"You will never get away with this," Mary insisted. "I would think that Wolverton would avenge me. And even if he should fail to do so, you cannot think that my brother would not! Benedict will hunt you to the ends of the earth!"

Helena laughed bitterly. "You are such a naïve, little fool! Wolverton may. Out of some misguided sense of honor, he may, in fact, feel the need to see me brought to justice! But your brother... no, my dear. Men who are in love are led around by their cocks. And Miss Elizabeth Masters has your brother's firmly in hand. He'll look for me for a bit. And then he will grow lonely and miss her, and then you will be a distant memory—nothing more than a sad and fleeting thought that crosses his mind from time to time. Tell me, did you fuck my husband?"

The words were not unknown to her. She'd heard such foulness from their parents when she was younger. But it had been years. Benedict had worked so very hard to shield her from such ugliness. It was unfathomable to her that a woman such as Helena, who'd been born and raised into polite society, would actively engage in and seek such ugliness for herself. "Now who sounds like a gutter-born trollop?" Mary asked, unable to keep the scorn from her voice.

Helena smiled then. "Well, clearly, you're nothing but a little prude. No doubt, Alexander was a perfect gentleman and you were a perfectly behaved, shriveled spinster. How delightfully boring you all are. It's a pity, really! You're perfect for one another."

"Why do you hate him so? He's an honorable man who made every effort to be a good and faithful husband. What is there to despise in that?"

Helena cocked her head to the side. "Because he saw me. He was not blinded by my beauty. He was not swept away with the need to possess me. He looked at me and thought that I was... acceptable. And when he thought me dead, he simply went on with his life. Had it not been for the lack of money, he would have married some other woman and forgotten me entirely! That is unforgivable, Miss Mason. Whether I desired him or not, he was supposed to want me... he was supposed to crave me and worship me above all others. But I don't suppose a mouse like you could ever understand that."

"All of this—this—this death and destruction and utter mayhem, and it is for nothing but your vanity?" Mary all but shouted.

"Yes," Helena replied steadily. "For my vanity, for my pride, for my gluttony and greed and lust. For my wrath. Every sin I have committed has brought me here to this day, and I will not hesitate. Remember that, mouse."

Chapter Nineteen

A HARRIED MAID entered the library and all of the men present, Hamilton included, looked up expectantly. But there were no footmen following on her heels and Helena was nowhere to be seen.

"Where is Lady Wolverton?" Alex asked.

The maid shook her head as she bobbed a rather clumsy curtsy. "Forgive me, my lord, but I don't know where she is. The footmen said her room was empty and I went to see for myself. It's vacant as can be and there's no sign of her in the breakfast room, the morning room, the garden or anywhere else. It's as if she simply vanished!"

"Bloody hell." The curse came from Vale, and while it was hardly appropriate language, the sentiment mirrored Alex's own feelings perfectly.

Hamilton smirked. "I see my little bird has flown the coop."

"That means nothing in terms of your own fate," Alex stated firmly. "You see, I have Harrelson's journals. And in them, I have records of payments to you. So with or without her to corroborate the claims, you're done for."

"And how will you prove you're not a murderer then? If she's gone, you'll be as guilty as ever in the eyes of the law."

"Not exactly," Vale said. "You see, my betrothed is an old acquaintance of yours and of Lady Wolverton's. She can attest, without question, to the fact that Lady Wolverton is alive and well and has been residing in Bath for the past year. I'm afraid you're quite done for."

Hamilton's face paled. "Your betrothed?"

"Yes," Vale answered firmly. "I believe that you were assisting Harrelson in abducting her for your brother's enjoyment. Miss Elizabeth Masters?"

Hamilton began to struggle against his bonds. "I had nothing to do with it!"

"Harrelson's ledgers would prove otherwise," Alex said. "All you have to do is tell the truth, Hamilton. If you do, I will ask that you be transported rather than hanged."

"I'd rather be hanged!" Hamilton shouted as he bared his teeth in a growl. "I'll not be shipped off to some dirty, filthy colony to work like a common laborer!"

Alex said nothing. He had worked like a common laborer and hadn't left the country to do so. Since he'd lost his fortune, he'd been out in the gardens, in the fields, mucking stalls, and patching roofs whenever and wherever he had to, because paying someone else to do so was no longer an option for him.

The door opened again and another maid entered, this one carrying a small hamper from the kitchen and wearing a cloak as if she'd been intending to travel. "Forgive me, my lords and Mr. Middlethorp, sir... but the carriage is gone and Miss Mason with it. I went to fetch the basket of food from cook, and when I came back, it had already left. I would not have let her travel alone! I swear it!"

Cold dread swept through Alex. If Helena was missing and Mary had suddenly disappeared in the carriage without her chaperone, it wasn't a great stretch of the imagination to think they were together, and not willingly on Mary's part.

"Where was she headed?"

"London, via the main road," Vale said. "She was to stop at the King's Head in Wickham for the night before continuing on tomorrow."

"I'll head toward Pulteney Bridge and you come around the other side. Perhaps, we can head them off before they get out of the city," Alex said.

Middlethorp had opened the bottom drawer of the desk and drew out a box. "There is more, gentlemen, and I fear it does not bode well for Miss Mason. The brace of pistols kept in here is now missing. I doubt Miss Mason would have taken them. I cannot say the same of Lady Wolverton."

It wasn't Vale who cursed that time, but Alex himself as he dashed from the house. He didn't bother with a sedan chair or a horse. In the city, he'd be faster on foot. Heading toward the parade grounds via Landsdowne Street, he prayed for a sight of them. If something happened to her, he'd never forgive himself. And he would finally be guilty of the crime he'd already been convicted of, because he would see Helena dead by his own hands before the day was done.

THEY HAD MADE it to Pulteney Bridge, but an overturned cart was blocking their way across to the main road to London. The driver called back, "We'll have to turn around, but it'll take a bit as the street is so congested. Hold tight, miss, and you'll be on your way soon enough!"

Helena had tensed the moment the coach stopped. "Is this some sort of trick?" she asked, her words hissing out between clenched teeth.

"As I had no notion you would be in my carriage, I'd have hardly possessed the foresight to engineer an ambush for you. Now would I?" Mary replied caustically. She could see that Helena was on edge. The delay was making her nervous and the more nervous she was, the more likely she was to make an error in judgement. It was the only chance Mary had to outmaneuver her and escape.

"You would do well, Miss Mason, to recall which one of us is armed!" the other woman snapped. "Tell the coachmen to get this thing turned around and to do it now. I will not be trapped here with the likes of you!"

Mary would have refused but Lady Wolverton raised the pistol, pointing it directly at her in a manner that left no question as to whether or not she would happily fire the shot at that very moment. Rising to her feet, she tapped on the roof of the carriage, "You must turn around now," she called out. "I cannot wait longer here!"

"But, miss, there is no room!" the coachman protested.

"Find the room, now!" Mary replied without pause. She'd never spoken so to a servant in her life, not that she'd had the opportunity to be exposed to many.

The driver grumbled, his words unintelligible over the din of the street. But slowly, the carriage began to turn, the wheels cutting and the horses' hooves moving over the street. The wheels lifted up over the edge of the rut they had been in, worn there by all the coaches and carts that preceded it. It was the opportunity Mary had been waiting for. The jolt sent her careening toward the door and it jostled Helena so that she could not hold the pistol steady. Without a thought of hesitation, Mary forced the door open and leapt free of the carriage. She landed on the road in an undignified heap, but she didn't care. Rising quickly, ignoring the pain in her hip from where she had landed, she moved with all the haste her bandaged feet would allow. They were tucked into a pair of boots borrowed from Elizabeth and while they offered some protection, it was still terribly painful.

Weaving her way through the throng of traffic, she made her way toward the shops. She could hear gasps behind her. No doubt, Helena was in pursuit, pistol at the ready. The woman was utterly mad. That much had become glaringly apparent during their brief exchange. Rounding the corner of the bridge, away from the shops, Mary made her way toward the Abbey and the Pump Rooms, hoping to get lost in the throng of other well-dressed ladies. She had only just cleared the bridge and was looking down at the river below when a pistol shot rang out. There were screams, and one woman fainted dead away, as everyone scrambled for cover.

Mary stood stock still, waiting to feel the burn of the pistol ball tearing through her skin. She didn't doubt that Helena had the other gun and that it was trained on her at that very moment. She could all but feel the weight of it.

"Turn around. I want to see your face when I end your miserable life," the other woman commanded.

Reluctantly, Mary did as she was bid, but turned toward the river, bringing her one step closer to the balustrade that separated her from the drop. If the opportunity presented itself, she would jump. She was a strong swimmer and it was her only chance at survival. With her battered feet, there would be no hope of outrunning Helena. The water would even the playing field, so to speak.

ALEX'S HEART THUNDERED in his chest, less from running through the streets than from the sound of a single gunshot echoing through the narrowed streets. Emerging from the alley shortcut he'd taken, he came out directly across from the Guildhall. Looking to his left, he could see Helena holding a pistol. Two steps forward, and he'd cleared the building giving him a full view of the street. Only a short distance before Helena was Mary, facing off against her with no weapon. The pistol trained on her glinted in Helena's hand and fear stuttered his heart. She would not hesitate to shoot Mary. Of that much, he was certain.

There was too much open space between him and Helena to hope of being able to catch her unawares. His only hope would be to draw her ire, to pray that she would turn the pistol on him and allow Mary a chance to escape.

Taking another step forward, Alex called out, "Helena, there is no need for this!"

Her head snapped toward him. "There is every need for this! I will not be replaced by her, of all people... some low-born wretch who hasn't the breeding to even speak my name, much less take my husband."

"A husband you never wanted," he pointed out. "You have hated me from the start... I think because I was not Albie."

"I didn't hate you for not being Albert," she said dismissively. "I hate you because you are not like us. I hate you for having such a wretchedly firm sense of honor that you would never be swayed to our way of thinking, of living, no matter what I offered you. You did not grovel at my feet because I was beautiful and you desired me above all others."

"Then I will grovel now," he offered.

She screeched in reply. It was the only apt description he could muster for the sound that she emitted.

"I don't want it! I don't want it and I don't want you! But you want her and that's why I will see an end to her right now!"

"If you're going to kill me then get on with it. I'd rather that than listen to any further insane ravings of a madwoman!" Mary snapped.

If he hadn't been completely terrified at that moment, Mary's cavalier behavior would have driven him to that point. No one knew better than he how quickly Helena's moods could turn or just how vicious she could be.

"Helena, please... Miss Mason has nothing to do with this. It's between you and me. Let her go. We will climb into Lord Ambrose's carriage together and make for Wolfhaven. I will be your captive audience for any grievances you feel compelled to air," he offered.

Helena moved closer to Mary, until they were only an arm's length from one another. "I don't think so, Alexander. I think Miss Mason has everything to do with it... I saw how you looked at her. And even now, you've run through the streets like a lunatic in the hopes of saving her! You would never have done those things for me!"

"I would have. I did. Helena, I have worked tirelessly from the moment I thought you had perished to find the people responsible and bring them to justice!" Alex protested. As he did, he inched closer, closing the distance between him and his wife. If he could just put himself between her and Mary, he no longer cared what might happen to him. But he would not allow Mary to be harmed, not when he had the power to prevent it.

Helena surged forward, gripping Mary's hand and tugging the woman back against her. The pistol was now pressed firmly to Mary's head and in Helena's eyes he saw nothing but madness. She was entirely beyond reason.

"Stop it!" Helena shouted. "Just stop! You never loved me. You never wanted me!"

"We never loved one another," he answered evenly, hoping that agreeing with her would defuse the situation to some degree. "It's true. We married because it was an advantageous match and our feelings, for one another or for anyone else we might have formed attachments to, never entered into it. But Helena, if you do this, you will go to prison... if not prison, it's quite possible that you will be committed to an asylum. That is not a place you wish to be. Ever."

Helena laughed wildly. "You don't understand anything, Alexander. I know what is going to happen to me. I knew from the moment I took the guns from the library that I was sealing my fate... and I don't mind at all. Because I'll be sealing yours, too. For the rest of your life, you will mourn the lovely Miss Mason and what might have been! And you will regret to your dying day that the body you found at that chapel was not actually mine. After all this time, I will finally give you a reason for all the hatred and derision you have shown me."

He was still too far from them. There was no way he could reach Mary before Helena fired the gun. It was a fear unlike anything he'd ever known, to stand there and know beyond the shadow of a doubt that Helena had already set her course. She'd left the Vale house bent on destruction and there was no power on earth that would dissuade her. His only hope, and it was a fervent prayer from his heart, was that the gun might misfire.

Chapter Twenty

MARY SAW THE intent in his gaze. It was immediately and terrifyingly clear to her that he intended to do something impossibly reckless and heroic—something that would have disastrous consequences. She could not and would not allow him to sacrifice his life for her, not when there was another way. Her plan, impetuous and likely fatally flawed, at least offered a slim chance that one of them might survive.

Mary looked at Alexander Carnahan, Lord Wolverton, and committed everything about him to memory, knowing it might be the last time she looked upon him before death claimed her. She hoped that he might see in her gaze just how much she felt for him. Regret swamped her. If she had it to do over again, Mary knew that she would have done things very differently. She would not have hesitated. She would not have run from him. She would not have insisted that he return her to Bath and her brother. Instead, she would have stayed with him at Wolfhaven, and either willingly been seduced or mustered the courage to do a bit of seducing of her own. But there was no more time to think of such things. Her moment was at hand and action was required.

Taking a deep breath, as much for courage as for what was to come, Mary hurled herself backward with as much force as possible. The momentum carried both her and Helena to the balustrade that kept careless passersby from tumbling into the Avon below. With their combined weight and the awkward lack of balance due to Helena having one arm wrapped about her neck and the pistol pointed at her head, there was simply no way to recover. She felt the other woman teetering, grasping at her as if Mary could somehow keep them on firm ground.

Helena screamed, flailing for purchase as they fell. The gun discharged, firing harmlessly toward the sky as they plunged backward toward the rushing river. The impact as they struck the water was staggering. It was rather like hitting a brick wall. Disoriented at first, Mary finally managed to find the light. She swam for it with all she was worth, finally breaking the surface and drawing in air until her lungs were full to bursting. Then the water dragged her down, sweeping her downriver.

The current tugged mercilessly at her skirts, trapping her legs. But Mary recalled the lessons of her youth, first from Benedict and later from Miss Darrow who had insisted that all of her girls know how to swim. She didn't fight the water, knowing that to struggle against it would only leave her weak and exhausted. If she could keep her nerves in check and her wits about her, the river would eventually wash her to the shores and she would be safe.

Instead of trying to direct her body in the heavy current, she focused on breathing. Every time she bobbed to the surface, she drew another deep breath and simply allowed the water to carry her. There would be bumps and bruises aplenty, especially as they tumbled over the weir and beyond. Out of the corner of her eye, Mary saw Helena. The other woman's struggles had ceased, as well, but not because she'd managed to achieve any sort of calmness in the water.

Helena floated face down in the water, her gown billowing around her and her dark hair fanning out. The current swept Mary toward her. Panic did set in then. Even in death, she thought Helena might find some way to take her down with her. But the water carried Mary past her, sweeping her over the terraces of the weir. Mary used the ledges to push herself out of the center of it and toward the side where a group of people had gathered. Men were reaching out for her, trying to grasp her and pull her from the water. Desperately, she reached out, trying to snag one of their outstretched arms. When it happened, when she felt a firm hand grasp her wrist and haul her toward the bank, she let out a startled sob.

Lying on the grass of the parade ground, wet and shivering, her hair and her gown plastered to her skin, Mary looked up at the sky above and then let her eyes drift closed. In the distance, she could hear someone calling her name. She recognized it as Alexander, but as she gasped for air and tried to fight the bitter cold from the water, darkness crept in. Exhaustion claimed her and Mary's eyes fluttered closed on one thought. They were safe. For the moment, at least, they were both safe.

⊱⊰

HIS HEART WAS in his throat when he reached her. Mary lay upon the grass, her wet gown clinging to her and her face as pale as death. Stripping off his coat, he placed it over her. Alex placed his fingers at her neck, just below her jaw, and felt the steady thrum of her pulse. It was faster than it should have been, but strong and steady.

Without a second thought, he lifted her into his arms and made the arduous trek back up to the street. Climbing the narrow, moss and algae-covered stairs that led up from the river to the bridge above, he found Lord Ambrose's carriage still there and the coachman looking on in horror. "Take us back to the Circus," he shouted and placed Mary inside the carriage, levering himself inside afterward.

He'd no more than gotten her back into his arms, pressing her against him and willing the warmth of his body into hers, when the carriage lurched forward. "You will not die. Not after all that we have been through," he whispered, his voice sharp and angry. "I simply will not allow it."

Her eyes fluttered open then. Alex found himself gazing into their dark depths, rendered nearly black in the confines of the carriage. "I certainly will not," she agreed, her voice raspy from the river water she'd likely swallowed. "Not for a considerable length of time, at any rate."

"Just so long as you let me go first," Alex replied. "I think I've seen you at death's door once too often already."

"Why must I always be damp and cold? Just once, I'd like to almost die from being too warm and too cozy. Is that possible?"

He smiled. "I think, perhaps, you've struck your head again."

She frowned. "Helena is dead. I saw her body in water... do you think... will they be able to retrieve it?"

"Are you concerned for her proper burial?" he asked incredulously.

Mary shook her head. "No. I'm only concerned that you have the proof you require to finally clear your name. If her body is lost to the river, then it is only the word of others that she still lived. I want you to finally be free of it all."

Alex couldn't resist it. He kissed her then. It wasn't a gesture of passion, but one of tenderness, one that he hoped might show her how much he cherished her. "I am free. I will never be as free as I am with you in my arms. Now that there are no remaining reasons to deny it, I will say without hesitation, I love you. As soon as it is humanly possible, I mean to make you my wife."

Her eyes drifted closed again, but her lips curved in a slight smile. Within minutes, they had reached the Vale home. Alex handed her down to the waiting coachman and then disembarked himself. Once his feet were firmly planted on the pavement, he reached for her again. With her tucked safely in his arms, he strode up the steps to the door that was currently being held open by the butler.

In the hall, he heard Miss Masters and Lady Vale gasp in horror. "Whatever happened?"

"She and Helena struggled and fell into the river," he said, offering the short version of the tale. "We have to get her warm as soon as possible. She's been in these wet things too long already!"

"Get her upstairs to the guest room," Lady Vale said, rushing ahead of him. Alex followed hot on his heels. Once inside, he placed Mary on the bed and began removing her cloak and the sodden garments beneath. Immediately, he felt feminine hands tugging him away.

"You are not in the country in your abandoned mausoleum, Lord Wolverton," Lady Vale snapped. "In this house, we will do things the proper way. Miss Masters and I will see to her."

Before he could utter a protest, he was shoved out the door and it was closed firmly in his face. In the corridor, put rather firmly in his place, Alex was at a loss what to do. Of course, he reasoned someone should send for her brother. But as he descended the stairs he could hear Mr. Middlethorp issuing orders to the footmen to do just that. He was, in that moment, completely extraneous.

Middlethorp turned to go back to the library and caught sight of him. "Banished you, did they?"

"Something to that effect," Alex answered.

"Come along and we'll have some brandy. It's a bit early in the day, but I daresay the day has already warranted it. Of course, you haven't been to bed yet, so one could argue that it's actually late for you."

He hadn't felt the exhaustion until that moment. When it was presented to him in that way, when he had a moment to entertain just how long it had been since he had slept, Alex wondered how he was even upright, much less putting one foot in front of the other. Yet, he knew that even if he were to close his eyes, sleep would not come. Not yet. Not when he was still uncertain of Mary's wellbeing. Once he knew she was well, then perhaps.

Gratefully, he accepted the cut crystal glass and sipped the warming liquid. It was damned fine brandy, certainly better than he'd been able to afford for some time. He savored the spreading warmth and the sweet, complex flavor as it settled on his tongue.

"There is no substitute for a fine brandy… unless it's a woman," Middlethorp said. "And I'm assuming that there is no woman more vital to your happiness and satisfaction at this time than Miss Mason is."

"I have done a disservice to her in being so obvious with my affections," Alex replied.

Middlethorp chuckled softly, but it was not a humorous sound.

There was a wealth of pain in it. Enough so that Alex glanced up at him and caught the flicker of intense sadness in the other man's gaze before it shuttered entirely.

"It is not as if you have made a cake of yourself in society for her. She will not be ruined by what has occurred in this house... and given the amount of gossip already swirling about her, with the kidnapping, the identity of her adopted brother, and whatever occurred today," Middlethorp lifted his hands in exasperation. "Your degree of indiscretion in exhibiting your attachment to her is hardly the worst thing people will discuss."

"No, I suppose it is not. Helena is dead, by the way."

"I assumed so," Middlethorp replied. "The magistrate is currently questioning Albert Hamilton. The man is singing like a bird at present. He has incriminated Harrelson, Helena, his brother, Fredrick, and everyone but himself. He insists that he is nothing more than an innocent bystander lured into their schemes and threatened on pain of death if he spoke the truth."

An ugly epithet escaped Alex then. "Will the magistrate buy it?"

"Unlikely," Middlethorp said. "But the magistrate isn't the issue. Albert's not a peer, but he is the younger brother of one. It is likely that his family will pull enough strings to get him off with a lighter sentence, but I do not think he will escape the consequences of his actions entirely. Tell me what occurred today."

"Helena secreted herself in the carriage and held Mary at gunpoint. There was an overturned cart on Pulteney Bridge that stifled traffic, giving Mary an opportunity to jump from the carriage. Helena pursued her, intending to shoot her before my very eyes... and at the last possible second, Mary managed to tip them both over the balustrade and into the river below. Helena drowned in the Avon."

"Her body has been recovered?"

Alex frowned. "Yes. Others were removing her from the water... I did not stay to see it taken care of. I wanted to get Mary here and get her warm. I suppose I ought to go back."

"I'll send someone to take care of it," Middlethorp offered. "I asked after her body because it will be key in proving that you are not the murderer they claimed you to be. If you have any hope of having the decisions of the courts reversed, your property returned to you and to finally put all the gossip to rest, then there will need to be witnesses who can identify Helena."

"How many witnesses would be required?"

Middlethorp shrugged. "I can only assume that any number of the genteel set leaving the Baths would have recognized your wife. She was marked as a great beauty by society... and she did not make herself unobtrusive in the least."

At that moment, Lord Vale entered. "What happened?"

"Mary fell into the river with Lady Wolverton," Middlethorp offered succinctly. "Mary has survived but Lady Wolverton has succumbed. She is upstairs, being tended to by your mother and your betrothed. No doubt, they will have her warm, stuffed with hot tea and biscuits. She will be fine."

Vale sank into the other chair that faced the desk and reached for the bottle of brandy. He didn't even bother with a glass but drank straight from the decanter. Under the circumstances, the breech in etiquette was hardly worth commenting on.

"So, you're finally the widower, after all," Vale said after a moment.

"It would seem so," Alex agreed.

"This changes nothing as far as I'm concerned. Mary is in too fragile a state to make such monumental decisions right now, given all that she's been through," Vale continued. "I think it best if you return to Wolfhaven Hall while we sort all of this out."

Alex's brows shot up at essentially being dismissed. "Excuse me?"

"You should go" Vale said. "Before Mary wakes. It will only create problems for her if you remain."

It took a moment for Alex to understand precisely what had been said. "If you have concerns that my intentions are dishonorable, you may rest assured that I mean to propose to her."

"But you will not do it today," Vale insisted. "You will not do it until the entire debacle with your late wife and her grasping relatives is resolved. I am not forbidding you to marry her. But I am quite firm that you will not do so until your affairs are in order and until she has had sufficient time to recover."

Hot fury washed through him. "And were your affairs perfectly in order when you proposed to Elizabeth Masters, Lord Vale? Though we both know I only use that title as a courtesy as you are just as much at the mercy of the House of Lords as I am!"

Vale had the decency to flush guiltily. "Whether or not I had a title, I still had the means to support Elizabeth! She would not have gone from living in relative comfort to eking out a meager existence in a falling down hovel! Can you honestly say that you can see to Mary's comfort there? She is fragile!"

"She is stronger than you give her credit for," Alex said, rising to his feet. "She is stronger than you and I put together. The very fact that she has survived all that she has been forced to endure and that her own resourcefulness is largely to thank for it should be proof enough of it!"

"And is that what you will offer her when your honeymoon is done? A home devoid of servants because you lack the ability to pay them? My sister, who weighs less than five stone soaking wet, will have to use her resourcefulness to scrub your floors and wash your clothes. I will not have it, Wolverton, and if you love her, you will not either. Wait until you have the answers you seek from the powers that be! My sister has suffered enough poverty, pain, and uncertainty in her life without foolishly marrying into more of it."

Alex wanted to protest. He wanted to state that he had waited long enough for his chance at happiness. But there was a part of him that recognized the wisdom of Vale's words. But God above, he resented them. "And when she asks where I've gone, what will you tell her? That I've abandoned her?"

"I will tell her that you are working to secure your fortune and your property, and urge her to be patient," Vale replied. "This is not villainy on my part, Wolverton. I am looking after her because it is my duty to do so."

"Is that all it is? Really? She spoke of you, of your devotion to one another. Is it really that, Vale, or is it that you're so dependent upon your sister worshipping you that you'd stand in the way of her happiness?" Alex demanded.

Vale rose from his chair, fists at the ready. "If you're suggesting that my relationship with Mary is in anyway improper—"

"I am not suggesting any such thing! In spite of what my late wife and her stepbrother have done, I know that isn't commonplace and it is beneath the both of you!" Alex had risen from his own chair, ready to exchange blows if needed. "What I'm suggesting is that you've been her hero and her savior for so long that you find yourself reluctant to grant that role to anyone else. It's your ego that's in the way!"

Vale eased back at that. "Maybe I am. But is that what you want? For her to marry you because you saved her? Do you want her head clouded with such things, or do you want to be certain that it's really you she cares for and not just the impossible events that have sur-rounded the two of you and muddled her thinking? Now is not the time, Wolverton, and if you'll take a moment and consider it, you'll see that I'm right!"

It wouldn't have been so painful if it hadn't mirrored thoughts of his own. From abduction, rescue, illness, another kidnapping and hostage situation with Helena, Mary's life had been nothing but upheaval. He had been the first bastion of safety she'd known after weeks of uncertainty. What if it was that which was the basis of her feelings for him? One loveless marriage had been enough for him.

"How long?"

Vale relaxed visibly. "Get your affairs settled and then court her as she deserves."

Alex nodded. "Then I'll be off. You can send my things to Wolf-haven. I'll be making for London to get things sorted out."

Walking out the door, knowing that Mary was above stairs and would soon realize he'd left without even saying goodbye—it was the hardest thing he'd ever done. But perhaps, Vale was correct. If he looked at her again, if he had to look into her eyes as they said goodbye yet again, he would not have the strength. Alex prayed that fortune would smile upon him, that the wheels of justice would move with the same sense of urgency in returning his property as they had when they had seized it all from him.

Chapter Twenty-One

"WHAT DO YOU mean he's gone?" Mary demanded. Her heart had dropped, sinking into her stomach, when her brother told her that Alex had left. He had told her he loved her. He had sworn that they would be together. Perhaps not in those exact words, and perhaps her memory of it was a bit fuzzy as she'd only just escaped drowning, but he had! She was certain of it.

A muscle ticked in Benedict's jaw as he looked away. "It's for the best… at least for now. It will take months if not years before he has his finances sorted—"

"I don't care about his finances! He would not simply have left me, Benedict! He loves me. He said so," she whispered fiercely, shaking her head in dismay. "How can a man make such declarations and then simply walk away? That isn't like him."

"To be fair, Mary, you do not know him that well. None of us do. Would it be so awful for you to wait a while before entangling yourself with him in a permanent fashion?"

There was something in her brother's tone and in the way he steadfastly refused to look her in the eyes. Suspicion was an ugly thing, but it reared inside her. "What did you do?"

"Mary—"

"Tell me, Benedict! What did you do?" she demanded again, all but shouting. In all of her life, she had never raised her voice to him, never been anything but grateful and obedient as he'd sacrificed so much for her. But that only made the betrayal cut even deeper. Had he really sabotaged her chance at happiness?

"Fine," Benedict said on a heavy sigh. "I insisted that he wait until his finances and legal woes were taken care of and he could make a respectable offer for you."

It cut her to the quick. "You had no right."

"I have every right! You are my responsibility—"

"I am a grown woman! I am twenty-five years old and perfectly capable of making my own choices."

"You don't know him—"

"And do you know Elizabeth, then? You've only just met her within the last two weeks, after all, and yet you are betrothed! And I daresay you behaved far less honorably toward her than Alexander Carnahan behaved toward me!"

He drew back as if she'd struck him. "Mary, you are overwrought."

"No. I'm not overwrought. I'm not hysterical. I'm not going to have the vapors or fall into a faint. While I may be physically at a disadvantage in many ways, Benedict, when it comes to my understanding of the world, we came from the same hovel—from the same drunken, rage-filled, filthy hovel! This was not about what was best for me. If it was, you would have asked for my opinion first!" she snapped.

He had the decency, at least, to look moderately shamed by that. But Mary was far from done. "Do you really think that my feelings for him, and his for me, are less valid and less urgent than what you feel for Elizabeth? If I told you—or did as you have done and went behind your back! If I told her that she should not marry you until she has her reputation perfectly restored or until you have the title entirely secured... what would you say to that, Benedict?"

"The situation is entirely different!" Benedict protested.

"No. Our anatomy is different. Because you are male and I am female, you assume that the rules should be applied differently! I'm not having it." Mary rose from the bed and pulled her traveling gown from the wardrobe.

"What the devil are you doing?"

She arched one pale brow at him. "What does it look like I'm do-

THE MYSTERY OF MISS MASON

ing? I mean to go after him."

"He's off to London. You'd never be able to track him down."

Mary laughed bitterly. "You stand here, in the home of the woman who gave birth to you because of my ability to *track people down*. Or have you forgotten that you'd have never discovered who you truly are if I hadn't come to Bath to investigate?"

"And got yourself abducted and very narrowly avoided a fate that could potentially have been worse than death!" he snapped back at her. "Mary, be reasonable. You have been ill. Only hours ago you very nearly died."

"Fine. I'll be perfectly reasonable. I will not travel to London alone. You may escort me or I shall ask Mr. Middlethorp to do so." It was a rare thing for her to dig her heels in quite so viciously, but it was also a rare circumstance.

"I will take you to London!" Benedict shouted. "I will take you and I will find bloody Wolverton for you! When did you become this obstinate?"

"I've always been this obstinate, Benedict," she insisted. "We just rarely ever wanted different things for me. He loves me. And there is nothing that he would not do to see me safe and happy. Can you not see that?"

"You'll be poor," he replied.

"As I have been before. If marrying Elizabeth meant giving up all of your wealth, would you?"

His gaze settled on hers and she saw a flash of understanding finally break through his stubborn male pride. "I would do whatever was necessary to be with her."

"As would I to be with him. And I know you said you'd take me, but it would be very difficult to convince him to elope to Gretna Green with me if you are staring daggers at his back. If it's just the same, I'd rather go alone. If I leave now, I might be able to make the posting inn at Wickham. Perhaps he will have stopped there himself."

"Can he afford a bloody inn?"

"Probably not. You should have thought of that before you asked him to leave," she said.

Benedict rolled his eyes. "You'll need funds for your journey—and your elopement," he added somewhat bitterly. "I'll have it waiting for you in the study."

Mary smiled. "I love you, Benedict. I really, really do. But I'm not a little girl anymore, even though half the time I despair of looking like one."

"If he ever gives you cause to regret this—"

"He will not," Mary said, and she had complete faith in that. She believed it entirely. "I'm certain we will disagree. I'm even more certain that he will, at times, be as high-handed and managing as you are and I will have to put him in his place, just as I did you! And I relish the very thought of it. No one, Benedict, knows better than the two of us how precious it is to find love... not when the first half of our lives was so lacking in it. Now get out of here so that I can change and go chase down the man I love like the scandalous creature I've become."

Benedict shuddered at the thought, but said nothing further as he left the room.

Mary immediately stripped off her nightrail and donned a chemise and stays. A single petticoat followed and the traveling gown she had worn when she first came to Bath. It had been just over a month since she'd come to the city, a fortnight since she'd been abducted. How time could appear so fluid, with events being so fresh in her mind and also feel as if eons had passed, was a mystery to her. *Because her life was so incredibly different from the beginning of that journey to the end of it.*

Twisting her hair up into a simple knot, she shoved pins in it as one of the maids entered and began packing the few gowns she possessed into her valise. "Lord Vale ordered the coach round for you, miss. It should be here directly."

Mary thanked the girl and left the room. In the corridor, she ran into Elizabeth. The other woman hugged her quickly. "I wish you the very best of luck, my dear. And I am appalled at your brother's managing behavior."

A smile curved Mary's lips. "He is doing what he always does—

what he perceives to be best for me. It just so happens that, for once, we disagree on that course of action. But I do think he has seen the error of his ways. I meant to ask earlier, what happened to Mr. Hamilton?"

"He's been taken by the magistrate to the gaol. And it's quite likely that he will stay there. Given what happened with Lady Wolverton today, he may succeed in laying everything at her door, but perhaps not. Mr. Hillyard was quite unconvinced by his stories. Benedict has already stated that he will front the costs for trying him for both Mr. Davies' murder and his role in the kidnapping scheme that Harrelson was operating, so we shall see."

Mary nodded, relieved to have one loose end tied up. "And Frederick, his brother? And the other women and children who were taken? What of them?"

"Middlethorp is piecing it together. He has friends at Bow Street and in the Home Office. Obviously, we will not be able to find them all, but if there are any that can be rescued or require rescuing, we will do so. But stop worrying about this and go after that man. I knew from the moment I saw you together that he adored you!" Elizabeth protested.

"He does," Mary said. "And I adore him. I only hope this hasn't ruined anything for us."

"The course of true love does not run smooth, but it does always run. Infinitely and without thought to any obstacle in its path. Go and catch yourself an earl, my dear."

Chapter Twenty-Two

THE INN AT Wickham was crowded but Alex had managed to snag the last room for himself. It was small and cramped, tucked up under the eaves with a narrow bed and a chimney that smoked, but at least it was private. He was in no mood for company and the boisterous taproom had grated on his nerves the moment he walked in.

He missed her already. He was angry at himself for leaving her, but equally angry because every point Vale had made in favor of delaying the match had been valid. It was an assault on his pride and his dignity that he couldn't provide for her in the way that she deserved. And while the promise of an end to his financial hardships was nigh, he had no guarantee of when it would occur, or if everything that had been taken would be returned or only a portion of it. It was very possible that even after the House of Lords had made their decisions, he might still be poor by the standards of the nobility. She would be denied the society that her brother would now be welcomed into because he couldn't afford it.

Cursing, Alex stripped off his dusty coat and waistcoat. The cravat came next and the lot of it was tossed upon the single chair in the room. He didn't care that he had nothing else to wear and that the clothes would be horribly rumpled the following morning. Those were the very least of his concerns.

Crossing to the basin, he tipped the pitcher of water and filled the bowl so that he could wash some of the grime of the road from his body. If he had any sense about him, he would have gotten a bottle from the taproom before coming up. There weren't enough spirits in the entire establishment to tempt him once more into the company of others.

There was a knock on the door and Alex cursed. It was likely the maid bringing up dinner. Grabbing his shirt, he tugged it on and then opened the door. Immediately he stopped, struck completely speechless by the sight that greeted him. Mary, with her blonde hair tucked under her bonnet and wearing a simple traveling costume of green wool, stood before him, her small hand poised as if she'd meant to knock again.

"I was hoping I'd catch you here," she said softly. "It wasn't quite noon when I left Bath and thought you might stop for the night here."

"It's a good stopping point, half the journey behind and half ahead." Realizing just how inane the conversation had become, he got to the point straightaway. His confusion evident in his tone, he asked, "Why are you here?"

"Because you said you wanted to marry me," she replied. "And I really want to be married to you. And my brother is an idiot."

"His reasons are valid—"

"His reasons are his reasons, Alexander Carnahan, but I have reasons of my own. Will you invite me in to hear them or must I shout them in the corridor?" she asked with a sweet smile and cold steel in her gaze.

Alex stepped back and held the door wide for her to enter. "Come in. I don't suppose I need to tell you that this is incredibly improper."

"As was the fact that you tended me while I was ill. I've been abducted and held captive, for the likely purpose of being auctioned off to a brothel, and my adopted brother is the long-lost son of a misanthropic viscount who has been reunited with his family after two decades. Not to mention that the wife of the man I love tried to murder me in full view of the Pump Room and the Abbey in the center of Bath today. I think we have scandal covered, Lord Wolverton."

He had to bite his lip to keep from grinning at her caustic and clearly irritated tone. "When you put it in those terms, well... that doesn't change the fact that your brother was quite adamant about our waiting to be married."

"And I was quite adamant when I told him I would not wait," she replied softly, but then her confidence faltered, and uncertainty blazed in her eyes for just a moment. "Unless… do you want to be married to me now? Under the circumstances, having finally just become a widower, in fact, perhaps marriage is not something you wish to enter into again so soon. Given the behavior of your previous wife, one can certainly understand any hesitation on your part."

"I've never been more certain of anything in my life. I want you to be my wife more than I have ever wanted anything else," Alex replied, his voice roughened with desire, longing, with the faint stirrings of hope.

"I have no fortune," she said.

"I could not care less."

"My name will be synonymous with scandal and society will cut us entirely," Mary continued.

"And I've never much cared for society anyway. I'd far rather rusticate in the country."

"I will likely be called upon to offer testimony in several very high profile court proceedings related to Lord Harrelson and his many schemes."

"As will I," he replied.

She looked at him levelly, her brows furrowed and her lips pinched into a tight line. "Then why in heaven's name would you have been stupid enough to think that those were valid reasons for me not to marry you?"

"I really don't quite know… other than to say that I was impossibly stupid," Alex agreed.

"I've made a decision, by the way." As she uttered this proclamation, she removed her bonnet and placed it on the chair. Then her hands came up to tackle the buttons of her spencer. When that garment joined the bonnet and his discarded items, she reached behind her and untied the laces of her gown until it gaped at her breasts and slipped low over one shoulder. "To avoid any further questions about whether or not marrying me now is an honorable thing to do, I'm going to seduce you."

Utterly entranced, Alex stared at that softly rounded shoulder bared to him save for the thin strap of her chemise. "And are you well acquainted with seduction then?"

"I might require some advice on the matter," she said as she slid the puffed sleeves of the gown over her arms. The fabric fell to her hips, catching there for just the briefest second before she shimmied slightly and it dropped to the floor to pool at her feet. "I'm assuming that the removal of one's clothing is usually a step in the right direction."

His mouth had gone as dry as parchment as he looked at her standing before him in her very sensible undergarments. Clearing his throat, he managed a reply that would allow their banter to continue for a bit longer. "I would say that is a rather universal truth. Nudity and seduction certainly go hand in hand."

Alex's gaze locked on her small and delicate fingers as she tugged at the laces of her stays, loosening them until the garment simply fell away. The shift she wore beneath revealed far more than it hid. The linen was so fine and sheer that he could see the curves of her breasts and the darker shadow of rose-colored nipples that had haunted his dreams.

Her petticoat came next, joining her discarded gown on the floor. When she wore only that thin shift and every part of her was bared by the gossamer-like fabric, she paused.

"Is seduction typically so one-sided? Or do you remove your clothing as well?"

It was a challenge, and one that prompted a smile from him despite the state of aroused agony he found himself in. "By definition, yes, seduction is rather one-sided. But as I am already thoroughly seduced, I think we can dispense with the standard protocol." With that, he reached for the hem of his shirt and stripped it off. His boots followed and then he was stalking toward her, closing the small amount of space between them until he could feel the heat of her skin and soft press of her breasts against him. Her bravado had faltered by then, her lower lip trembled slightly and her brown eyes were wide. "You can still change your mind. It may well ruin me forever, but you can."

"No. I can't. Today, just before I took both Helena and myself over that balustrade and into the river, my greatest regret was that I didn't explore the feelings I had for you at Wolfhaven. That I ran like a scared rabbit when you kissed me. So, while I lack the knowledge to lead any further in this particular arena, I will not be bowing out."

Alex lifted her into his arms and carried her to the small bed. But he didn't lay her down upon it. Instead, he seated himself on the edge of it and settled her across his thighs. The position had the advantage of putting them eye to eye. It gave them a moment to take one another's measure, as if sizing up an opponent rather than a lover. It also caused the thin chemise she wore to ride up, bunching around her hips until her thighs and the gentle curves of her bottom were entirely bare. One less barrier between them, one less obstacle to keep him from the treasures of her body and the pleasure that awaited them both.

"Kiss me," she said. "And stop all this infernal thinking that only rattles my nerves further."

He did. Alex was helpless to do anything else. Capturing her lips, the kiss was gentle but still potent. His lips moved over hers and she answered by mimicking those same touches. Unable to resist the temptation of her parted lips, he slipped his tongue between them, stroking it gently against hers. Soft sighs gave way to moans. Her arms locked about his neck, her hands pressing firmly against his shoulders as her breath shuddered from her. His hands did ample exploring of their own, coasting along the satiny skin of her thighs, her shapely calves, and then delving beneath the simple linen that still covered most of her charms.

It was only the promise of sweeter torment that induced him to break the kiss. The slender column of her throat, the lovely and perfect curve of her shoulder. Tugging at the thin straps of her chemise, he pulled the garment lower until one lush breast was bared to him. Her head fell back and she arched toward him in obvious invitation.

THE MEMORY OF his hand on her breast, even though it had only been the briefest of caresses, had inflamed her. But it wasn't his hand she felt on that tender flesh in that moment. It was the wet heat of his mouth closing over the budded peak. The sensation overwhelmed her, the pleasure of it swarming her senses but also inciting a deep longing inside her. She ached for him, for his touch, for the fulfillment of being his in every way that she possibly could.

Thought fled as the pleasure grew. She simply could not hold on to rational thought anymore. In fact, she could not have formed words for the life of her. Instead, she simply held on to him, offering herself up to the sweet torment of his lips on her skin, of the slight sting of his teeth and the soothing, gentle strokes of his tongue.

At some point, he stripped away her chemise, the thin garment simply drifting to the floor, forgotten and ignored. Naked, seated astride his powerful thighs, there was no embarrassment or hesitation. It felt strangely natural to be so with him. But his remaining clothing became a source of frustration. Compelled by both curiosity and desire, she reached for the fall of his trousers, but Alex caught her hand.

"Not yet," he said. "I've only a shred of control left and if you touch me…"

"Would that be so terrible?" she asked.

His smile was just a bit wicked as he said, "Yes. It would. It's your turn to be seduced now."

Before Mary could question what he meant, he had moved them so that she was reclining on the bed and he was on top of her, but still pressed very intimately between her thighs. But then he was kissing her breasts again, teasing each furled nipple with his questing mouth until she couldn't think. She could only feel.

Then his hands were on her thighs, stroking them slowly and sensually until he reached the apex and touched the curls that shielded her sex. A gasp escaped her, but not of fear. It was anticipation and eagerness to finally know his touch. Mary parted her thighs further, an act of complete trust and surrender, an invitation for him to complete their joining. She could feel the heat building inside her, unfurling, and then he touched her intimately. He parted her flesh and stroked one fingertip over a sensitive bud of flesh that made her cry out.

He touched her again and again, coaxing a chorus of moans and cries from her. Her body had bowed beneath his, arching into his touch, seeking something that she could not quite fathom. And then it happened. The unbearable tension that had drawn her muscles taut and left her shuddering beneath him simply snapped. Her body pulsed with it, sending waves of intense pleasure rushing through her until she collapsed on the bed once more, panting and breathless.

"I think you are much better at seduction than I am," she finally managed and startled a laugh from him.

"I don't know. You availed yourself quite well, I think," he teased.

"Don't make me wait any longer. I want you to make love to me. I want to be yours," she urged him. It was a desperate plea, and some of her fear crept in. It wasn't fear of what they were about to do, or of the unknown given her lack of experience. It was the fear that something else would happen to keep them apart. Mary felt as if the fates had pushed them together just long enough for her heart to be engaged and had then done everything possible to tear them apart.

Alex rose just long enough to shed the last remnants of his clothing. Naked, he joined her once more, their bodies molded together in an intimate embrace. "You will always be mine," he vowed.

The release he'd given her had eased her desire, offering some respite from the relentless yearning, but it was still there, simmering just below the surface. As he entered her, it was neither pleasant nor unpleasant. Foreign, yes, entirely. Then there was the briefest moment of discomfort. And yet when their bodies were fully joined, when she was connected to him in a way she never had been with any other and would never be, she met his gaze. And as their eyes locked, he moved within her, surging forward and then withdrawing.

That slight movement was a revelation. The tension that had filled her before appeared again, more intense and more insistent than before. Every surge, every stroke of his flesh within her ratcheted that tension higher. But now, she understood what awaited her beyond it. And when it peaked, Mary welcomed it eagerly, calling out his name with abandon. Only seconds later, he followed her over that precipice.

In the aftermath of it, still trembling and breathless, Mary clung to him and vowed that nothing would ever come between them again.

Epilogue

M ARY PICKED UP the small posy of flowers from the table beside the bed and sniffed them with a smile. They would wilt soon, but for now they were lovely.

"Perhaps I can dry them? Or take some of them and press them into a book to keep them forever?"

Alex rolled onto his side and looked at her steadily. "You may do whichever pleases you most, Lady Wolverton."

They had married that morning, three days after she'd "seduced" him at the inn. They'd obtained a special license, paid for in large part by her brother's largesse. The ceremony had taken place at St Pancras in the old church, and had been attended by Miss Euphemia Darrow and by Alex's solicitor. He'd offered to wait until Benedict and Elizabeth could arrive, but Mary had declined. The idea of delaying the start of their life together for any reason was simply beyond her. She hadn't wanted to provide an opportunity for anything else to go awry.

Placing the flowers on the table once more, she held her left hand up to the light. The ring on her third finger was something of a surprise given her husband's rather limited finances. The large emerald was flanked on either side by a single sapphire and a diamond. It wasn't heavy or overly ornate, but it was lavishly expensive and very beautiful. It seemed Ambrose had kept it tucked away in his London home, locked up with Alexander's other family heirlooms that he'd considered too precious to part with. London, far from any bailiffs or bill collectors who might come calling at Wolfhaven, had seemed the best option. At receiving news of their coming nuptials, Ambrose had sent a letter to his man of affairs and had him fetch it for Alex just in time for the wedding. "You could have sold this ring and lived much more comfortably. In fact, it's rather silly of you not to have done so," she admonished.

"My finances will work themselves out soon enough," he said and absently stroked the curve of her hip with the tips of his fingers. "That ring belonged to my mother and had been in her family for years. Now it belongs to you."

It tickled slightly but it also reignited the passion they had shared only a short time earlier. "Stop that. I'm being serious. We should talk about how we're going to live. I have a bit of money, but not much. And once the dust has settled, I know that Benedict would provide a dowry for me."

Alex sighed. "I don't care about money. Middlethorp has called in a few favors and now there is to be a special session of the House to hear the appeal of my case and, hopefully, reverse their earlier ruling… as well as settle the matter of your brother's title once and for all."

Mary sat up then. "When did you find this out?"

"This morning… just before we went to the church."

She huffed out a breath, incapable of hiding her irritation. "And you didn't think to share that with me?"

He wrapped his arms around her and pulled her back down until her cheek was pressed against his shoulder. Mary tried to hold on to her ire, but it faded quickly.

"I wanted to tell you. I meant to, in fact, but we had the church and the wedding, and then we had the consummation… so many tasks, my dearest!"

She lifted her head, gaping at him slightly in horrified amusement. "A task is it?"

He grinned. "It does require a good bit of exertion."

Mary laughed and then tucked herself once more in at his side. "Do you really think they will return everything to you?"

"Not everything. A good deal, yes. I imagine things will still be a bit lean for us for a while, but several of the estates are quite profitable.

Those profits can be invested in the others to improve their productivity," he offered. "Will you mind very much that I'll simply be less poor instead of terribly wealthy?"

She sighed dramatically. "I suppose I shall just have to content myself with being married to a man I love, who seduces me quite regularly, much to my delight, and who tells me on a daily basis that he adores the ground I walk upon. We must all make sacrifices."

He was laughing as he flipped them entirely and had her pinned beneath him. "Minx."

"Scoundrel," she countered.

He kissed her neck, his teeth scraping gently along that one spot that made her shiver with pleasure. Mary's eyes closed and she bit her lip at the rush of sensation. "You are a wicked, wicked man."

"Should I stop then?"

"No. That would be even more wicked," she confessed. "I could not bear the disappointment."

"Have I told you how much I love you?"

Her lips curved into a soft, contented smile at that. "You have. But as I will never tire of hearing it, you may certainly feel free to tell me again."

"Then I love you. More than life. More than my next breath… and I cannot wait to be done with London and return to Wolfhaven with you at my side."

Mary's smile turned into a frown. "I know you said we would be poor, but will we be so poor that we have to keep Mrs. Epson on?"

Alex laughed. "I've already sent a letter to her instructing her that she is to retire to a small cottage on the estate and will receive a small pension. I would not put either one of us through that torment. We have both suffered quite enough without having to continue eating the vile concoctions she calls food."

"Speaking of food… I'm famished. You were quite persuasive when it came to skipping breakfast," she said. "I need food, Alexander."

He rose then, tugging her up with him. Mary watched as he

donned his dressing gown. Taking her wrapper, she slipped it on and then the two of them made their way down the stairs. They were staying at a smallish house in Mayfair that was owned by Lord Ambrose. It was not his primary residence and Mary imagined that prior to his failing health, it had been used as a home for his mistresses. The servants had been given the day off as they'd wanted privacy instead. But the kitchen was well stocked as they raided the larder and amassed a feast of cold meats, cheese, bread and fruits. There were also some lovely lemon tarts that she was horribly tempted by.

"Lord Ambrose was the friend who held your mother's jewelry in safekeeping, wasn't he?"

Alex nodded as he slathered butter on a piece of bread and handed it to her. "He was. I know he's quite scandalous, but he has been a true friend."

"We should see him when we return to Wolfhaven, or here in town before we leave should he return."

Alex raised his eyebrows at her suggestion. "You do realize that entertaining Lord Ambrose, or entering his house, would make you a pariah in society? When I say he's scandalous, Mary—suffice it to say he has gleefully and with great abandon earned his reputation."

She made a face. "I'm the daughter of heaven knows what sort of people! My mother could have been a common prostitute for all I know! I'm scandalous already."

"And your father could have been Prinny himself," he pointed out.

"Or a dock worker! Would it be so terrible if I'm just a low-born, bastard child and that I don't have some exalted lineage like Benedict?" she asked.

"Not for me... but I worry about it for you," he admitted. "I think it bothers you more than you say. And I want you to have those answers. I think there is more to be learned from Harrelson's journals and those retrieved from Madame Zula. Middlethorp has set the hounds on her manservant, hoping to find him and any information he might possess."

Mary nodded. "And you are writing letters to Ambrose, finding out what he might know or who he might be able to coerce into helping you dig further?"

Alex shrugged. "He's a good friend, even if the world thinks him a bounder."

"It doesn't matter. You trust him and I trust you. And he is your friend. Society can rot for all I care."

He pulled her close and kissed her again. "In that case, perhaps we could be scandalous, too?"

"What did you have in mind?" she asked.

He lifted her onto the countertop, her knees bracketing his hard thighs. He had that look in his eyes—feral, predatory, even, and so very appealing. The bread she'd been nibbling on turned to sawdust in her mouth. The rumbling of her stomach was forgotten entirely as another need pushed to the forefront and demanded fulfillment.

"Have you ever made love in a kitchen, Lady Wolverton?"

"I have not, as well you know," she countered. "Is it very bad of me to say that I'm intrigued by the notion?"

His hands shifted on the backs of her thighs, just behind her knees and tugged her forward. Mary's arms closed about him and she felt the hard ridge of his arousal press against her belly. Yes, she thought. Their impromptu luncheon could certainly wait.

"I would be more affronted," he whispered, his breath hot against her neck, "had you said you were not."

"I admit to being somewhat puzzled by how such a thing would occur," she teased. "Perhaps a demonstration is in order?"

And he did demonstrate it. Thoroughly.

The End

Author's Note

Mary and Alex will return in the final book of the *Lost Lords Series*. I realize there are remaining questions about how Alex's property will be returned to him and the legal woes he faced, but when I tell the story of Cornelius Garrett, the heir to Lord Ambrose (whom you saw very briefly in this book) you will get to find out exactly how all of that transpired.

I hope that you all have enjoyed reading the Lost Lords Series as much as I have enjoyed writing it. I also hope that you will continue the journey with me into my next series for Dragonblade Publishing, *The Hellion Club*. If you'd like to know more, please join my reader group on Facebook or contact me via email at chasitybowlin@gmail.com.

Facebook Reader Groups:

Chasity's Book Nook:
facebook.com/groups/chasitysbooknook

The Regency Assembly Room:
facebook.com/groups/TheRegencyAssemblyRoom

You can also follow me at Amazon to stay up to date on my latest preorders, new releases and sales:
https://amzn.to/2JU7eFP

Or you can follow me via Bookbub:
http://bit.ly/2rXhMrN

About the Author

Chasity Bowlin lives in central Kentucky with her husband and their menagerie of animals. She loves writing, loves traveling and enjoys incorporating tidbits of her actual vacations into her books. She is an avid Anglophile, loving all things British, but specifically all things Regency.

Growing up in Tennessee, spending as much time as possible with her doting grandparents, soap operas were a part of her daily existence, followed by back to back episodes of Scooby Doo. Her path to becoming a romance novelist was set when, rather than simply have her Barbie dolls cruise around in a pink convertible, they time traveled, hosted lavish dinner parties and one even had an evil twin locked in the attic.

40512644R00142

Made in the USA
Middletown, DE
27 March 2019